'Funny, violent and surreal . . . *Hitman* will blow you away'

Howard Marks

HITMAN

Max Kinnings

FLAME
Hodder & Stoughton

First published in Great Britain in 2000 by Hodder and Stoughton
A division of Hodder Headline

10 9 8 7 6 5 4 3 2 1

British Library Cataloguing in Publication Data

A CIP Catalogue record for this title is available
from the British Library

ISBN 0 340 76596 8

Typeset by Palimpsest Book Production Limited,
Polmont, Stirlingshire
Printed and bound in Great Britain by
Mackays of Chatham PLC, Chatham, Kent

Hodder and Stoughton
A division of Hodder Headline
338 Euston Road
London NW1 3BH

For Ange

1

I'm doing sixty down Highgate Hill and the Laughy Woman is doing my head in. Titch is all set to ask this morning's questions on Titch's Triffic Trips but she won't let him get a word in. Fair enough, have a laughy woman by all means, most breakfast shows have one and, to be honest, when you're half brain-dead in the mornings and you've joined the legion of sad bastards on the way to work, it's quite reassuring to have some over-cheerful woman laughing her head off at the trivial inanities of the DJ.

But the trouble is that I'm not on the right wavelength this morning, mentally that is. Rather than eight hours' sleep, followed by a shower and coffee in preparation for this banal breakfast bollocks, I've been pulling on huge reefers at Luke's place in a vain attempt to calm myself down from an ill-advised acid trip in readiness for Mar Kettle. The daft bastard had told me the trips were old, that his crusty mate

1

Spanner had had them for months and they probably wouldn't even work. I wish mine hadn't. Instead of the mellow euphoria, heightened sensibility and giggling I'd hoped for, I found myself locked into a full-on serotonin knees-up, pupils like dinner plates and hallucinations when I shut my eyes that made me feel as though my brain was plugged into the Internet web of some weird cartoon planet. What's more, we trashed the place.

For starters, we decided it might be fun to have some bathtub soup and proceeded to empty the contents of Luke's fridge and cupboards into the bath. That done, Luke decided to give it a stir. Within seconds, a splatter fight had erupted between us and within what was probably no more than ten minutes but which appeared to us in our drug-addled state as about two hours, the whole of Luke's bathroom was pebble-dashed with everything from frozen peas to taramasalata. Both of us received a good ducking in the bathtub soup and managed to spread further crap all over the flat. Then it was time for Subbutteo. But instead of playing a traditional game it turned into a game of hide-and-seek using the players, the idea being to conceal one's entire team in unlikely places. This kept us amused for a while until I discovered that, in a desperate bid to win the game, Luke had glued his goalkeeper to the roof of his mouth. It was while I was trying to prise it loose that I remembered Mar Kettle and my nine a.m. appointment. Thank God Luke's got a recently acquired washer-dryer, so I was able to sort out my physical appearance if not my mental.

The latter, he assured me, would all be taken care of by his new Amsterdam-cultivated laboratory skunk. I could tell that it was strong, that it had twice the THC content of its nearest rival. But the LSD break-dancing on my synapses wasn't going to succumb to any herbal brakes, however strong, and continued its chemical trajectory unabated. To speed up the comedown, we shared a bottle of cooking sherry, probably the only foodstuff in the entire flat that hadn't made it into the bathtub soup.

I left Luke standing in the doorway of his flat, his clothes still caked in bathtub soup in varying shades of congelation, his beady rodent face stretched into a lunatic grin, a thick tress of hair curling back over his crown like a handle so I almost felt as though I could pick him up by it and carry him around like an appliance – the Portable Drug Abuser, perhaps. When the intensity of the trip began to subside of its own accord, I was left just pissed and stoned – which is not the ideal state to be in for a nine-o'clock with Mar Kettle.

Being Friday, this is the deciding round on Titch's Triffic Trips. Will it be Maureen from Orpington, some disembodied housewifey drone or Jeremy, some over-cheerful wanker from Wandsworth who will take the mystery trip of the week? Last week, a butcher from Neasden won a fortnight in the Seychelles. But with Titch thinking himself a bit of a zany bastard and the station strapped for cash, often the mystery trip is a total let-down in a hey-look-at-us-we're-bonkers local-radio kind of way. Another time, some la-di-da woman chiropodist from Surbiton won a trip to a funfair in Dundee. She was livid but, for once, my sense of humour coincided with the Laughy Woman's and together our laughter filled the interior of the Beamer. But today she's gone over the top so much so that Titch has to tell her on air to calm down and I don't know whether it's the drugs or not but this morning, more so than usual, I can detect all the inflections of her forced laughter. Mind you, what a bum job, when you think about it, having to feign amusement and fake laughter at the vapidities of some irritating little shit like Titch Allcock, my old school buddy.

He wasn't always known as Titch: that became his nickname once he took to the airwaves. When I knew him at school, his nickname was 'No Balls', on account of his surname, Allcock. He was a couple of years above me but due to his diminutive stature I could get away with calling him names. He wasn't the type to exact physical retribution. He was one of those kids who was the smallest in his class but had the largest head and the loudest, most booming voice. Always wanted to organize everything and take over. An annoying bastard, really, but perfect radio-jock material, I suppose. It was no surprise when I turned on the breakfast show one morning to hear his over-familiar morning-mate voice. Initially, he had a different laughy woman but she wasn't laughy enough so he got this one who overdoes it in the extreme.

Finally he manages to shut her up and we get Jeremy, the wanker from Wandsworth. While he's running through what he'll get up to at the weekend (rugger on Saturday morning, beers with the chaps later), I can imagine him sitting there in his pinstripes and brogues with a shit haircut and I'm willing him to lose even if it means that Maureen, this menopausal old boiler from Kent, can win. Now it's her turn for a little pre-competition chit-chat with Titch: when asked what she'll get up to at the weekend she starts on about her fucking garden and has to be cut short. At least she doesn't try to be funny, which is something. Now's the time for the jingle – 'Titch's Triffic Triiiips' – all cheesy synth-and-drum machine and we're into the game.

'OK, Maureen?'

'Yes, thank you, Titch. Bit nervous.'

'No need. Here's the first question to you. Who sang: "Like a bat out of hell I'll be gone by the morning light"?' Not content with just answering the question, Maureen decides to show off her rock 'n' roll knowledge and says, 'It's that fat man with the long hair. It's Meatloaf.'

'Correct. Now, Jeremy, your first question.' (I'm willing him to cock it up). 'Who sang: "Because the night belongs to lovers"?'

'Patti Smith.'

'Correct. But I bet you don't know who wrote it.'

'Bruce Springsteen.'

'Maureen, you're in trouble here, this guy knows his stuff. It's one all. OK, Maureen, for your second question I want you to tell me who wrote *The Singing Detective*?'

'Oh, that was Dennis Potter.'

'Congratulations, Maureen, that's two out of two.'

'Now, Jeremy. Your second question is this: who wrote the brilliant television series *Pennies From Heaven*?'

'Golly, erm, that's a trick question, isn't it?'

'It might be.'

'That's Dennis Potter as well, isn't it?'

'Correct.'

The Laughy Woman sees an opening and inserts a couple of cackles.

'OK, Jeremy and Maureen, this is your third question. You've both got two right so, from here on in, it's sudden death. Maureen, who played Hutch in the seventies American detective series *Starsky and Hutch*?'

'I can see him. Tall, blond. Lovely singing voice.'

'What was his name, Maureen?'

'Oh, I don't know.'

'Have a guess, Maureen.'

'No, it's gone.'

'You'll kick yourself.'

'I know.'

'David Soul,' he says as though counselling a potential suicide.

'Oh, no.'

'Never mind, Maureen. It's not over yet. Jeremy from Wandsworth still has to get this right to win this week's Triffic Trip. OK, Jeremy, here goes: who played Jack Regan in the seventies British detective series *The Sweeney*?'

I've reached Mar Kettle's place by now and although I'm ashamed to admit it, I have to sit in the Beamer and hear the outcome of Jeremy and Maureen going head-to-head. I'm willing Jeremy with all my might to get it wrong but I know he won't.

'John Thaw.' Shit.

'Congratulations, Jeremy, you've won this week's Triffic Trip. How do you feel?'

'I feel fab, Titch.' *Fab?* Cunt.

'That's great and it just remains for me to express my commiseration to Maureen' – they can't even be bothered to put Maureen back on air – 'and to thank everyone who's taken part on this week's Triffic Trips before passing you over to the delightful Carol' – the Laughy Woman – 'who will reveal Jeremy's Triffic Trip.'

This is the high point of the week for the Laughy Woman, the one time when she isn't just a disembodied laugh, a mere knee-jerk reaction to Titch's bullshit. And every week she hams it up, revelling in having the airwaves to herself. She knows that out there, in their kitchens, cars, offices and factories and in their hospitals and on their building sites, there are tens of thousands of Joe Publics hanging on her every word. But she doesn't give a shit about them. All she cares for are the handful of radio and television executives who might be tuned in, any one of whom might like what he hears and whisk her away so that she's no longer just Titch Allcock's laughy woman, but what? Newscaster? Weathergirl? TV prime-time laughy woman? Chat-show host? Game-show host? Anything!

'Thanks, Titch. Well, Jeremy, how're you feeling?'

'Great.'

'Well, here in this envelope I have before me are the details of your Triffic Trip but I must warn you and explain to all those of you who haven't tuned in before that—' – portentous whisper now – '—it might not be quite what you were hoping for. It might not be the fortnight in the Bahamas, it might not be the ten-day safari in Kenya but, in the words of Mick and the boys in that terrific group The Rolling Stones, "You don't always get what you want but sometimes, if you're very lucky, you might just jolly well get what you need." Laugh. 'Now, Jeremy, are you still with us?'

'Oh yes, Carol.'

'Nervous?'

'A little.' You can tell that Jeremy's busting his braces to find out where he's going and so am I as I'm now running late for Mar Kettle.

'OK, here goes.' The Laughy Woman rustles some paper to make it sound like she's opening an envelope.

'Jeremy?'

'Yes.'

'You've won a weekend for two, potholing in Dorset.'

I'm banging on the steering wheel and roaring at the windscreen. Poor old Jeremy, he's gone through a week of this. All his family and friends have tuned in, he's finally won the game and all they can give him is a weekend crawling around under Dorset. The Laughy Woman acts all concerned.

'It's not quite what you were hoping for, is it, Jeremy?'

'Not quite.' All that Jeremy wants to do at this moment in time is play football with the Laughy Woman's severed head but instead he has to put up with her glib radio-speak and noises of consolation.

'Is there a Mrs Jeremy?'

'No.'

'Girlfriend?'

'Er, yes.'

'Well, maybe she likes potholing.'

'Maybe.'

Bet she fucking doesn't. He's totally gutted but I'm made up. Jeremy's demise has done me a power of good: instead of the usual sense of foreboding I have before a visit to Mar Kettle's, I feel full of the joys of spring and jump from the Beamer, locking it with a careless over-the-shoulder flick from Frank (the zapper). There's nothing I like more than to see smug bastards done down.

A couple of grubby kids tease a Jack Russell on a patch of grass at the foot of the tower block. They throw a tennis ball to each other and the dog jumps and snaps at it. I press the button to call the lift. As it approaches, the ball is thrown too near the dog and he snaffles it up, ecstatic for a moment that he has it clamped between his jaws until the grubbier of the two kids looms over him and shouts in that robotic voice so prevalent amongst kids that age, 'Give me the ball.' As the lift doors open, I see the little dog relinquish his prize and the game begins again.

On the floor of the lift is an elaborately constructed stack of turds, each of a uniform size, texture and taper at the ends. They are angled one to another in an intricate lattice-work effect. The lovingly arranged bowel movement is offset at its peak by the flowing golden locks of a Barbie doll's head which rests in a tenderly whittled groove on the uppermost turd. The lift ascends, drawing me nearer to Mar Kettle's and, with the ever-present aroma of piss probing my nose, I muse on the intellect of the person who has constructed this faecal sculpture. I think to myself that if I were to write this all down – which I intend to one day – I could use it as a metaphor for Mar Kettle's tower block. But before I can come to any hard and fast literary conclusions, the lift doors open and there I am, right at the very top – the doll's head, if you like – and there to greet me as always is Mar Kettle's long-suffering butler, Archie. I step out of the lift and shake his hand.

'All right, Archie? You're looking well. How's things?'

'Very good, sir.' Archie's got his butler's phraseology off pat but his gruff cockney lets him down somewhat. 'Mar's been expecting you. Please come through.'

Archie has the rather bizarre distinction of being the first and probably only-ever Jewish skinhead in London. Of course, he didn't know that he was Jewish when he became a skinhead, owing to confusion on account of his adoptive parentage, but when he found out, it put paid to his aspirations within the hierarchy of the British Movement. That was the early seventies and Mar Kettle always says that it was the best thing that could have happened to him. Overnight, he went from being a mindless thug to being a sensitive fashion-conscious cross-dresser. It was as though he had to flee from his former identity as far as he could and in so doing found solace in his sister's wardrobe.

Unfortunately, Archie's family were none too supportive of his gender confusion and booted him out, leaving him to walk the streets in nothing but a cocktail dress and a pair of slingbacks. Being a skinhead was one thing, but being 'a fuckin' poofter', as they put it, was another altogether. That was when Mar Kettle took him in and appointed him as her butler. She even paid for cosmetic surgery to remove the SKINS boot-polish tattoo from his forehead that, in true skinhead style, he'd done in the mirror so that it ended up written back to front. He still has LOVE and HAT written on his knuckles. It had originally been LOVE and HATE, of course, but he'd lost his left-hand little finger in a drunken game of dare with his skinhead mates. I'd love to have seen the expression on the face of the manicurist who calls at Mar Kettle's once a week when Archie first plopped his hairy mitts down on her lap to have his nails filed.

Sadly for Archie, it's not just the tattoos that set him apart: he makes a dreadful woman all round. For starters, his appearance is somewhat less than feminine. He stands six feet four and possesses all the grace and deportment of a bulldog rearing up on its hind legs. But, despite this, you can tell that he takes a great pride in the way he looks. Today he's wearing a low-cut velvet ball gown, the hair carefully plucked from his bulging pectorals across which lies a string of pearls that match his earrings. These are only barely visible amidst the carefully teased tresses of a blond wig. He never bothered to grow his hair – in that, he's still a skinhead at heart.

Despite the fact that I've been here a hundred times before, Archie looks over his shoulder at me and, although I'm doing so already, asks me to follow him. He heaves open the two-inch-thick steel security door and I ask him, 'What's going on, Archie? Why the urgent meeting? Mar Kettle never usually wants to see me on a Friday. What's going on?'

'I have no idea, sir, but you *are* a little late. So if you'll just follow me?'

'Come on, Arch, this is me, for Christ's sake. Cut the butler crap.'

'Please, sir.'

He's having none of it and continues clicking down the corridor on his high heels.

Tasteless though it is, the opulence of Mar Kettle's home never ceases to amaze me. That and the incongruity of its position, perched on top of this high-rise hell-hole. Whereas each of the other twenty-two storeys are subdivided into eight separate flats, Mar Kettle has the whole of the top floor all to herself, apart from a spacious bedsit in the east wing that Archie calls home. The interior was designed and furnished by the Uruguayan designer Ernesto Kuroyan who achieved some prominence in the early seventies, mainly through his exorbitant fees and a style that was characterized by the extensive use of animal furs and parts. In 1972 he was commissioned by Ricky Speed, a minor pop star of the era, to decorate his Sussex mansion. Kuroyan's ensuing work on the building involved, among other excesses, the wholesale slaughter of five thousand Amazonian tree-nesting frogs whose skins he used to wallpaper the drawing room.

As you'd expect, Kuroyan's tenure in the upper echelons of the most-wanted designers league was short-lived: his career came to an abrupt halt in 1975 when, on safari in Tanzania to collect animals for a commission on a Saudi Arabian princess's town house in Belgravia, he was gored by a charging rhino whose eye sockets he'd intended to use as light fittings. Mar Kettle, who counted Kuroyan among her few close friends, joined a small group of mourners at a remembrance service held, tastelessly enough, at London Zoo. In death as in life Kuroyan had a predilection for the macabre and in his will he left strict instructions that his corpse be stuffed and seated at a table in a bar in his boyhood suburb of Montevideo where it remains to this day.

The smell of old ladies' heavily powdered cheeks alerts me to Mar Kettle's presence nearby and Archie ushers me through one of the many mysterious doorways housed within the labyrinthine corridors.

'Thank you, Archie.' And there it is, that unmistakable voice, croaky and hoarse from a lifetime's nicotine abuse yet resonant and demanding of unwavering obedience. And there *she* is, reclining on a chaise longue, her rotund form nestled in baby-panda fur. Inlaid into the arm of the chaise longue is half a lemur's skull, inverted and now the receptacle for the ash from her cigarette.

13

'Make yourself comfortable,' she says and gestures for me to sit next to her. 'If you feel cold, put another log on the fire.' The fireplace is mounted within the bleached jaws of a great white shark and, above them, a stuffed snow leopard leaps from the wall, teeth bared as though about to devour us both.

'I won't beat around the bush,' she says to me while pulling her cigarette butt from its tiger-tooth holder and grinding it out in the lemur's skull. 'I've got a problem that I need you to deal with.'

Mar Kettle never has problems. She occasionally has 'little somethings that need sorting out' so her use of the word 'problem' hints at a disaster of gargantuan proportions. I look into her face that, as the years go by, looks more and more as though it were boiled, such is the disengagement of skin from bone, and, for the first time in all the years I've known her, I can see that she's afraid. That she should succumb to fear seems almost impossible. Seeing as it'll no doubt be me who has to remove the cause of said fear, then even at this stage, when I'm none the wiser as to the nature of my assignment, I experience a pang myself.

It was five years ago, almost to the day, that I first came here. Little did I know it then but Mar Kettle was to become a sort of saviour to me as time went by. It's down to her that I have what most people would deem an easy life. I was working for an investigation agency in Soho at the time. It was the last in a string of dead-end jobs I'd had since I was booted out of college a couple of years before. The agency specialized in divorce cases and the occasional child-custody battle. It was boring work but it gave me the opportunity to get out and about instead of sitting behind a desk all day. It was also bloody good for chatting up the women, especially the young impressionable ones who thought that it was all high-speed car chases and international espionage. Little did they know that I travelled everywhere by bus and the nearest I got to international espionage was to follow dirty-weekending couples to Bognor to prove infidelity in the more sticky divorce cases.

One day, I was called into the boss's office and sent off to a Margaret Kettle, known to the very few who still remembered her as 'Mar' Kettle, an actress in a handful of forgettable B-list Ealing comedies a lifetime before. What she wanted he couldn't tell me as he didn't know. She'd asked for me personally, he said. That's always perplexed me: when I built up the courage to ask her about it a few months later, she was vague and said she'd heard my name mentioned in passing. When I pressed her to tell me who exactly had mentioned me in passing, she shrugged her shoulders and changed the subject as though it were a matter of the utmost unimportance.

In my professional capacity I did nothing more taxing than keep an eye on her accountant whom she suspected of swindling her. All this entailed was the occasional night-time visit to his office so's I could snoop around the files and see if there was anything untoward. Why she wanted me to do this God only knows as I didn't have a clue what I was looking for in the first place. What I did was go in, remove some files that appeared to be relevant, take them to my office, photocopy them and take them back before they were missed in the morning. I then gave the photocopies to Alfie, our financial man, who *did* know what he was looking for and who checked them over. There wasn't a penny going missing. If anything, Alfie said, the accountant was too honest.

When I reported our findings to Mar Kettle she was unconvinced and instructed us to continue the surveillance and broaden it to include the account-ant's private life. She paid over the odds to induce the agency to carry out highly irregular procedures involving phone taps and telephoto lenses that proved nothing more than that he enjoyed being spanked by his wife.

But even Mar Kettle's paranoid spending spree, which surely cost more than the accountant could have got away with even if he had been defrauding her, couldn't save the agency. When it went down the tubes, I was left overdrawn at the bank and at a total loss about what to do. I went to see Mar Kettle and, playing on her paranoid delusions, managed to land myself a cushy little position on retainer. I continued my surveillance of the accountant, along with the night-time prowls of the office. But without Alfie's financial nous at the agency I hadn't got a clue what I was looking for. What the hell, I thought, I was getting paid ludicrously well and if Mar Kettle didn't want to believe that he wasn't defrauding her, who was I to tell her otherwise? Gradually, the correlation between the work I told her I did and the work I actually did grew more and more disparate. She even bought me a car, the Beamer, and what a car it is too.

The bottom line is that Mar Kettle enjoys having her own private detective. And if she's prepared to pay good money for me to report back to her my increasingly fictitious investigations, then so be it. I throw in the occasional hint that perhaps there *is* some irregularity in her affairs in case she should grow tired of my inconclusive results. But as time goes by I've come to realize that my position is relatively safe. I say 'relatively' as she's old, probably about eighty, and supports a forty-a-day cigarette habit.

Today she appears more agitated than of late and asks if I've seen anything unusual on my way here.

'No,' I say, 'nothing so's you'd mention. Although there *was* something in the lift.'

'What was it?' She grabs my leg right at the top, right by my bollocks.

'Just a pile of shit. That's all.'

'Oh.' She looks disappointed. 'Was it animal or human?'

'It's difficult to say. Human, I think, but what made it curious was that it had a doll's head resting on the top of it. It was the head of a Barbie doll, I think.' This induces near-apoplexy in her. She throws her head back and gasps, 'Oh, my God.' I feel her fingers tremble through the cloth of my trousers. She rolls her eyes and for a moment I think she's about to croak.

'What's the matter?' I ask as reassuringly as possible.

'It's him. I'm sure of it,' comes the response.

17

'Who?'

'Oh, my God.'

I know little of Mar Kettle's personal history apart from what she's deigned to tell me. I should have found out more, especially with me a private investigator, but I'm a lazy bastard at the best of times and so long as I get my pay cheque at the end of the month and the Beamer's in full working order I'm not bothered. This is what I do know: she was born in 1918 in Chigwell, East London to wealthy parents. Her father was a merchant banker and her mother was a teacher. She was an only child and, from the word go, spoilt rotten. She went to all the best schools, rode her own horses, car on her sixteenth birthday, finishing school in Switzerland. A proper little madam, I shouldn't wonder.

Her first husband was a fighter pilot who died during the Battle of Britain. Despite being one of the most decorated pilots and flying literally hundreds of missions his death wasn't at the hands of the Germans but happened when he walked into the propeller of his own plane. Husband number two was a film producer and despite being fat, ugly and hung like a hamster, as she puts it, he was also extremely wealthy and allowed Mar to achieve a long-held ambition to act. After a couple of supporting roles in Ealing comedies after the war, however, it became obvious that stardom didn't beckon so she made do with the role of the fabulously wealthy producer's wife, holding lavish parties and befriending the stars and starlets of the time on both sides of the Atlantic.

One of the few photographs that Mar has dates from this time and shows her standing between Clark Gable and Montgomery Clift, both of whom she claims made passes at her – although, looking at her in the photograph, it's hard to see why. Her face was too round and plump to be called anything approaching beautiful. Not long afterwards, Hamster-dick died – on the job, as it happens. Despite her evasiveness about her past, she's not afraid to give me the full picture on occasions. When she tried to rouse him from his post-coital nap, she found that he was already succumbing to rigor mortis.

During the next twelve months, Mar inherited not only all Hamster-dick's money and estate but that of her parents as well, due to their deaths in a boating accident in the south of France. She was, by now, fabulously rich and roamed the globe with her own entourage that often included a couple of the young, good-looking bohemian types for whom she had developed a predilection.

From then until Mar moved here in the early seventies, her recollections are vague and sporadic, to say the least. She's admitted to her hopeless cocaine addiction in South America in the late fifties, her nervous break-down, incarceration in some exclusive funny farm in Sussex and her subsequent release just in time to host some of the most notorious parties of Sixties London (so she claims). But about the mid-fifties she's curiously reticent. However, by the sound of things, I'm about to learn some more about this mysterious time of her life.

'In 1954,' Mar says, cigarette smoke chugging from her nostrils like exhaust fumes, 'I moved to north Africa, to Tangier. It was what's known as an international zone at the time and for the operators, expatriates, fugitives, drug addicts, writers, spies, black marketeers, freeloaders, perverts and downright degenerates who were drawn there it became something of a boom town. It was also a playground for some of the more intense members of the international jet set, a group whose membership included myself. I had a villa on the side of the hill overlooking the Straits of Gibraltar – gardens, swimming pool, tennis court, servants – it had the lot. The lifestyle was so lavish it was obscene. My next door neighbour—' she shifts nervously in her seat '—was a man called Hassan Nazar. He was the most handsome man I have ever laid eyes on and, believe you me, I've met some handsome men in my time. Eyes that sucked you in and skin like velvet. I had met him and his wife only a handful of times on the social circuit but each time I had become aware of his eyes burning into me. His wife was a gorgon, had a face like an arse. But then, I suppose I'm biased. I could never cope with competition from other women, least of all from the wives of husbands upon whom my sights were set. You have to remember that, in the world in which I lived, marriages were at best just brief flirtations with commitment. Her family, of which she was the last surviving member, had supplied half of Europe with hashish. To look at me now you'd never know it but I was used to being the best, the richest certainly, and in Tangier I was convinced that I would be. But this woman, my neighbour, had upstaged me, or so I imagined. There was no way that I was going to play second fiddle to this old hag. With nothing to do all day but swim, play tennis or make love with one of the young writers or artists who had drifted into my circle of acquaintance, my mind became consumed with jealousy and mischief. I decided that to prove my superiority over this woman I would sleep with her husband. Petulant and childish, I know, but at least I now had a goal to strive for and something to focus on. Unfortunately, before long my addictive personality took over and I was flying in private detectives from London to maintain round-the-clock surveillance on the two of them to ascertain their exact movements, their appointments, details of overseas trips et cetera, et cetera.'

With each 'et cetera', Mar waves her hand. Then she waves it a third time and enquires, 'Tea? Or something stronger?' I'm feeling strangely vacant. I hadn't noticed in the car because of Titch Allcock and the Laughy Woman but I'm still subject to a psychic tug-of-war between the diminishing but nonetheless still potent effects of the LSD pulling one way and the laboratory skunk pulling the other. I've found Mar Kettle's story soothing. I can lean back in the baby-panda fur and let the words wash through me but being asked to contribute a response to even a question as mundane as whether I want a cup of tea or not snaps me out of my reverie.

'Er, yeah, tea would be fine.'

She calls to Archie who lumbers through. 'Two cups of tea, please, Archie, and some of those lovely biscuits you picked up last week.'

'Yes, ma'am.'

'He's a sweetie, isn't he? I don't know where I'd be without him.' I can think of many ways of describing Archie but 'sweetie' isn't one of them.

'Now, where was I? Ah yes, my seduction of Hassan Nazar. So one day I get a call from one of my private detectives who informs me that Madame is taking a trip into the mountains to some exclusive hotel to convalesce after a bad case of flu and, conveniently enough, she's not taking Hassan with her. He had some business to attend to and would follow on a couple of days later. So there was my chance. In all the time I'd had them watched, this was the first occasion they'd been apart. As soon as one of my men assured me that she was ensconced within her own private train carriage en route to the Atlas Mountains, I called Hassan and, as though in all innocence, asked if he and his wife would care to join me for dinner. He duly informed me that his wife was away so I promptly narrowed the invitation to include just himself. At first I thought that my ploy would be thwarted when he said that he was expecting an important telephone call and couldn't leave the house. So I decided that I'd really lay it on thick and told him that I was lonely and miserable having just received news of a close friend's demise in a car crash. I could sense him ruminating on the other end of the line and then my fortune changed. He said that although he couldn't come to see me, there was nothing to stop *me* coming to *him* for drinks by the pool. Perfect, I thought, and spent the next hour preparing myself. By the time I'd finished, I took one last look in the mirror and knew that he was as good as mine. I'd dressed casually, just jeans and a white shirt buttoned low but I'd gone to town on the make-up – and remember, I was somewhat of an expert in that department after my career in films. I was looking good and compared to his wife I looked a million dollars. Once poolside at his place, fizz in hand, it all went perfectly. I arrived at seven, by eight he was making goo-goo eyes at me, by nine he couldn't keep his hands off me and by ten he was humping my brains out in the master bedroom.'

When Archie reappears, Mar Kettle waits until we're sipping our Earl Grey before she continues.

'The following morning, Hassan asked me if I'd help him tidy up their room so there'd be no evidence of our indiscretions. Now, if I'd been a scheming bitch the night before, I was doubly so that morning because, you see, only half of my plan was complete. Fun though it was, there was no point sleeping with him without letting Madame know what we'd done. So, while pretending to assist him in his erasing of evidence, I sealed all our fates and left my knickers in her knicker drawer. He didn't notice me putting my jeans back on without them and I ensured he was out of the room ordering breakfast when I secreted them there. Now, just a pair of knickers on their own would not have been sufficient evidence for Madame to pin the blame on me. But I'd worn a pair that had been hand-made for me by a Parisian fashion designer I'd dated briefly a year or two before and lovingly embroidered on the gusset were the words: 'Pour MK, ma petite, l'amour toujours, Philippe.' Bingo, there was no escaping that one and thus I became the mistress of all our destinies.

'The next few days were torture. Hassan, who much to my disappointment had started to behave like a love-sick puppy towards me, eventually took to the mountains to join his wife. I was left torn between feelings of remorse for my childish seduction and fascination about the outcome. I spent hours staring out across their perfectly tended lawns and pristine flower beds towards the huge house where the occasional curtain fluttered in the breeze as a servant aired a room. Behind this façade of calmness and serenity was a time bomb planted by my own fair hand: how I longed for it to explode!'

She reaches for a biscuit and as she crunches on it she fixes me with her gaze.

'You probably think me an evil old witch for what I did, don't you?'

There's nothing she dislikes more than bullshit so I make my answer as equivocal as possible.

'I'm sure you had your reasons.' This soothes her stare.

'Yes, I had my reasons. But what pathetic reasons they were when you think about it. When you think that I was prepared to destroy the marriage of a woman I didn't even know, a woman who bore me no malice, just because she had more money than I did, because she had a beautiful husband and, more than anything, because I was just plain *bored*. There I was, prepared to go to all this bother and expense just so's I could wreak a little havoc and create some drama. God, if only I'd known. So, after a couple of weeks, they returned home and at first, much to my disappointment, nothing happened. They arrived back at lunchtime and all afternoon, nothing. They took dinner by the pool, that much I could see for myself from my attic window. By nightfall I was convinced that some servant must have found the offending knickers and removed them. Thoroughly deflated, I had a couple of drinks and went to bed. Around midnight, I was awoken by a scream emanating from their house and a couple of minutes later came the ringing of my doorbell. I dashed down to find Hassan standing there wild-eyed, covered in blood and clutching a knife in his trembling hand. The first thing he said to me was, "I have killed her." Before I even had time to register the horror of the situation, he was holding me in his arms, telling me that he loved me, that he'd done it for me, that everything would be all right, that we could run away together. I told him that I'd fetch him some tissue to wipe himself with and promptly went and called the police. There was nothing else I could do. Even if I had been in love with him there was no way I could last five minutes on the run. Then there was the matter of the private detectives I'd hired to keep surveillance on them. That was bound to come out so I thought the best thing all round was if I hired a good lawyer and told the truth. Of course, once I'd got the best lawyer in Tangier, Mohammed Yacoubi, he played fast and loose with my concept of the truth and I ended up taking the stand to claim that I had hired the detectives on Madame's behalf because she was afraid that Hassan was up to no good with her money and afraid that he might even have designs on her life. I was brilliant. It was by far the best piece of acting I'd ever done and by the time I'd finished it was all over for him. I even explained away the presence of the knickers, claiming that I'd never seen them before and that they must have been planted by Nazar in an attempt to implicate me in the murder. He never took his eyes off me through the entire trial. Those beautiful eyes, welling up with love and hurt and betrayal. It scared me half to death, I can tell you. He even refused to take the stand to plead his case. It was as though he'd given up altogether. When they sentenced him to life, he didn't even blink. He just carried on staring at me. A couple of days later, I found this in my purse.'

She pulls a yellowing scrap of paper from her handbag and passes it to me. On it is written:

My sweet traitor,

Please accept this letter as proof that I am always nearer to you than you think. Instead of a letter in your purse, next time it could be a knife in your back or a kiss in the dead of night. This will be our first and last correspondence but through a series of signs you will know that I am close at hand: be assured that our paths will cross once more. At such time I will mete out my justice to you just as you have seen fit to mete out your foul justice to me.

Till then,

Hassan

'Couldn't you have gone to the police with it?' I enquire, handing the letter back to her.

'Oh, I suppose I could have. But there's one thing about this letter that you won't have spotted. One thing that unnerved me more than the fact that he'd had it placed in my purse, even unnerved me more than his understandable desire for revenge. You see, what really got to me was that the letter was written in my handwriting.'

'But that's not possible,' I say, suddenly alert.

'You're telling me. Well, there was no way I could go to the police with a letter written in my hand but purporting to be from Nazar. My involvement in the whole sorry episode was suspect enough without that. So I just kept quiet. You see, as far as you and I are concerned, this bizarre twist is all a total impossibility. But what you've got to remember is that Morocco isn't like England. Here the vast majority of the population don't believe in witchcraft and magic but in Morocco people accept supernatural powers as you or I would accept the reality of electricity or television. Here, if someone upsets you in some way, you can take them to court. In Morocco, and especially in the Morocco of a few years ago, it's just as likely that you'd put a curse on them. And believe you me, curses if conceived properly really do work. One of my gardeners in Tangier, for example, had an altercation of some sort with his aunt who promptly struck him down with an illness of such vigour that he was reduced to a bag of bones in no time. In the end, I went to see the aunt and managed to get the curse lifted and he was as right as rain after that. So, take my word for it, curses and magic really do exist and when a man like Hassan Nazar sends you a letter written in your own handwriting telling you that he'll be the architect of your doom, no two ways about it, you take heed.'

'But that was over forty years ago,' I say as she drains her teacup. 'Maybe it's all forgotten.'

'I wish that were true,' Mar replies rolling her eyes towards the ceiling. 'But I know it isn't. You don't get a man locked up for forty years in some stinking hell-hole and he goes and forgets all about it. What's more, they released him the day before yesterday.'

As she tells me this, her eyes fill with tears. I've never seen her like this before. Unsure of quite what to do, I move closer to her and put my arm around her shoulders.

'Just because he's been released doesn't mean he's necessarily intent on revenge,' I tentatively offer. 'I mean, after forty-odd years behind bars, I'm sure he's got better things to do than dig up old grudges. I'm sure there's a hundred and one things he would rather do first than come looking for you. For all he knows, you could be dead.'

This does not have the consoling effect that I had

hoped for but, warming to my theme, I press on regardless.

'Let's face it, after the length of time he's spent inside, he's probably gone stir-crazy. He's probably as mad as a hatter. You know what they say . . .'

'Shut up!'

The ferocity and volume of her outburst startles me. She shrugs off my arm and I sidle back along the chaise longue.

'Don't treat me like a batty old woman,' she says, turning on me. 'From the moment he became a free man I had him followed. The last time he was seen he was boarding a British Airways flight to London. That was yesterday afternoon, hence my desire to see you so urgently. Despite his advancing years, he's as fit as a fiddle and totally compus mentis. I know this because my Moroccan lawyer managed to access his prison files. Unfortunately, by the time Yacoubi got word to me that Nazar was on his way he had cleared Customs – which means that he's here, wandering free in London. For all I know, he could be coming up in the lift as we speak.'

'Well, have you tried calling the police?' As soon as it comes out, I know it's the wrong thing to say.

'The police? Oh, *please*. I haven't had any dealings with the police for years. Bunch of bloody morons. I would never entrust my fate to people who don't have a vested interest. At the end of the day, what do the police care whether an old woman gets carved up by a mad Moroccan? That would be just another statistic to them. They might try and catch him once he's done me in but not beforehand. They'd think I was senile or something. No, I don't want Hassan Nazar apprehended, I don't want him locked up, I want him *dead*. Now, the police aren't going to help me kill him, are they? They're more interested in restraining orders and ineffectual rubbish like that. No, this man has haunted me for over forty years and now he's out to get me. Remember the letter: *I will mete out my justice to you just as you have seen fit to mete out your foul justice to me.* It's kill or be killed.'

Now's the time for the sixty-four-thousand-dollar question: 'What is it that you want me to do?'

'I would have thought you might have guessed that already,' she intones through gritted dentures. I think I have but I wish I hadn't, so in an attempt to forestall the harsh realization I tell her, 'I'm a little confused.'

'Come now,' she says, leaning forward and placing her hand on my thigh once again. 'This is not the time for games. This is the time to be straight with one another. Now, I know that as a private detective you're not up to much. But it's not through lack of ability, it's through laziness. It doesn't bother me unduly because I've got plenty of money and I like you.' She gives my thigh a squeeze and, lending her voice a conspiratorial tone, she says, 'All you need, my lad, is a little push, a little incentive and then you'll work your heart out for me, I'm sure. How does a hundred thousand pounds sound?'

'A hundred grand?'

'To kill him.'

'Well, I . . .'

'Shush, I don't want you to thank me, I think we understand each other well enough. This is an important job for which you will receive ample reward. Think what you could do with a hundred thousand. And all you have to do is find him and kill him before he finds me and kills me. Got it?'

'Yes.'

'Now, I'm going to stay here. I've lived here since 1974 and I haven't been outside since 1984 so I don't see why I should move now. This place is a fortress. There's only one way in from the rest of the building and that's via the lift. There's a closed-circuit camera hidden in it which switches on as soon as someone presses the button for the twenty-third floor. If we don't want that person coming up, the lift doors won't open. Even if they did manage to get out of the lift, they'd never get in through the security door which is made of reinforced steel. If they did somehow achieve the impossible and manage to get through it, the alarm system would be activated and Archie would be there to meet them with his revolver. In addition to all these precautions, to all intents and purposes this place doesn't even exist. The plans for this tower block show only twenty-two floors. I bribed the building contractor to build this one especially for me. As far as the outside world is concerned, I live at 25 Glynbourne Road, Hampstead. That's my official home, if you like, although I've never been there. Through an intricate network of subterfuge, I have maintained the pretence of living in Hampstead when, in fact, I've lived here all along. So, seeing as he'll probably go there first, perhaps that's where you should begin your quest. Maybe have it staked out or whatever you people do. Archie will give you a set of keys on the way out. Now, before you go, tell me some more about this lump of shit in the lift.'

'Oh, I'm sure it was just kids mucking around like they do. I shouldn't worry.'

'Yes, well, he'll find it difficult to cast his spells with a bullet in his guts. Now, you've got my number. Make sure you keep me posted. I'll want to see the body before you dispose of it, of course, just to be certain it's him. Strictly cash on delivery, that's how I've always done business. Archie will sort you out with the necessary equipment. And remember, a hundred thousand when he's dead.'

As if I could forget. I take my leave of the old woman, duck beneath the talons of the osprey mounted above the door and make my way to the end of the corridor where Archie presses a box and a set of keys into my hands and waits with me for the lift.

'Funny, isn't it, Arch, how things turn out,' I say, looking up into his lavishly made-up eyes. 'It's like with you: you start out as a skinhead and then, through some strange twist of fate, you find out you're a Jew, the very object of much of your – let's face it – pointless racial hatred.' He looks down at me as though he'd like to tear me limb from limb but I carry on nonetheless since the lift has another ten floors to go before it reaches us. 'And then you become a transvestite, of all things. Take me: I walked in here an hour ago, a somewhat fraudulent and you might even say inept private detective, and I walk out a hired killer, a bounty hunter, for God's sake. Ironic, isn't it?'

The lift doors open, I step in and turn to face Archie. He makes no reply. The doors close and the lift descends. I look down and notice it's gone – the Barbie doll's head and the pile of shit, that is.

2

At the foot of Muswell Hill I floor it, unleashing all two and a half litres of fuel-injected Beamer engineering: it feels as if I could actually take off at the top of the hill and sail on over the Broadway towards the North Circular. As it is, I slam the anchors on halfway up – which should scare the shit out of the guy in the souped-up Escort who's been tailgating me since Crouch End. Just as he's stamping on his low-tech brake pads and staring at the blue-and-white legend of Bavarian Motor Works only inches from his bumper, I'm gone, swung out left down a side street with a tweak of the powered steering. Lovely.

I park up and switch off the radio, scoop up the box that Archie gave me and dash over the road to Luke's front door, locking the Beamer with a backhand zap from Frank as I go. Luke buzzes me in on the intercom and I take the stairs two at time, opening the box as I do so and pulling out the Smith & Wesson. I can hear him shamble along the hallway behind the door and, as he opens it to reveal his idiot grin, I dash in and shoulder-barge him to the floor. As he tries to scramble to his feet, I catch his backside with a killer left foot that sends him careening head first into his living room where he comes to rest sprawled across his coffee table. Before he has a chance to get up, I'm on him. I grab a handful of hair, snap his head back and thrust the barrel of the revolver into his startled, gawping mouth.

'Now listen, you snivelling piece of shit,' I scream in his ear, 'this is the end. No reasons, no bullshit, no simpering goodbyes. This is where you get off the bus. Say goodnight, motherfucker.'

His lips tremble around the barrel of the gun and I watch his eyes blink frantically before I pull the trigger – which snaps them shut.

'I don't know what the fuck you think you're playing at, coming in here trying to freak me out like that,' he says after he's pulled the barrel from his mouth. 'You have absolutely no idea what drug schedule I'm working to this morning and that kind of behaviour could have pushed me well and truly over the edge. What the hell are you doing with a revolver, anyway? I know you have aspirations to be Dick Barton but don't you think you're taking things a little far?'

'Mar Kettle gave it to me,' I say, checking for traces of bathtub soup before stretching out on the sofa.

'What's the senile old bag want from you this time?'

'Get this: she wants me to snuff out an old Moroccan bloke who she thinks is trying to kill her.'

'She wants you to murder someone?'

'And if I do it, she'll give me a hundred thousand quid.'

'You're kidding.'

'Nope.'

'Then I take it she's finally lost the plot.'

'Who knows? If I can get my hands on the money, I don't give a shit.'

'So let's get this straight. You've got a real gun and real bullets, I take it?'

'Yup.'

'And you're actually going to kill this bloke?'

'If I can find him. You can help me out if you like. What are you doing tonight?'

'Not much. I was going to check out a band, The Gurning Mandibles. They're supporting Gallbladder at The Scala. They're on stage about nine, I think. After that, nothing.'

Luke is head of A&R for Wow Man Smell My Finger Records, an independent label working out of Camden. His main triumph during his five years there was his discovery of the chart-topping Manchester band, Gobshite. Ever since he signed them up after a gig in a pub in Rochdale, brought them to London, put them in the studio and their debut single 'Come And Have A Go' went top five, his position at Wow Man has been unquestioned despite his erratic and some-times non-existent work schedule. He's got almost as cushy a number as I have. Basically, he does sod all and gets paid well over the odds for it. Gobshite have been catapulted far beyond their indie band roots and, as

Luke puts it, they've crash-landed in the mainstream. Being a close friend of Baz the lead singer and of the band in general, should he never discover another band as long as he lives, he would never become dispensable to Wow Man. If he left, Gobshite would go with him. Luke's life is just one long backstage party, so being his best friend has its advantages: I get to hang around with the sunglasses-after-dark brigade and take the best drugs. This is the scallywag jet set: designer labels, floppy haircuts and mountains of charlie.

'What are they like?'

'The Gurning Mandibles? Oh, some sort of techno, hip-hop hybrid, I'm told. Apparently well worth a look. As you know, I have to keep up to date with what's on the scene.'

Gobshite are presently in the studio in Wales and with them away Luke feels he ought to turn up at the office once or twice a week, go to the odd gig or two, at least make some pretence of earning a living. So, after an afternoon spent caning the skunk, we take to the Beamer, the Smith & Wesson safely concealed in the glove compartment, and head on down to Kings Cross.

The Scala: they're about to come on. I'm completely stoned and a pint shy of pissed.

'Why are they called The Gurning Mandibles?' I ask as though I can expect a sensible reply. Just to goof things up, I get one, sort of.

'Basically, it's all about being off your face, I should imagine, and chewing like a bastard. You know, completely fucked.'

Thank you.

The music from the PA fades and the house lights dim.

'I was going to save these until later,' says Luke into my ear, pushing a Rhubarb and Custard ecstasy tab into my hand.

I'm startled by the reception the Mandibles receive. It's pandemonium down the front even before an identifiable sound has issued forth from the speakers. An elderly man in a suit walks onto the stage. Without so much as a glance at the heaving throng of bodies, he pushes a button, one single button amidst the banks of dials, switches and diodes. Crackling film screens burst into life behind what could have been a band if there was one and nosebleed techno hammers from the speakers, slashed apart by bursts of savage punk-rock guitar. The old boy exits stage left and there's not a human being in sight.

The Rhubarb and Custard comes on strong, lending a cartoon aspect to the storm of computer-generated images and spastic lasers raging on the stage. I know it's a bad move to be off my face, what with my planned surveillance of Mar Kettle's official residence but what the hell, I'm quite happy bouncing up and down and chewing like mad, my jaw a veritable Gurning Mandible if ever there was one.

Half an hour after it starts, it all comes to an abrupt halt as the old man makes a reappearance and presses another button that throws the interior of The Scala into silence and kills the projectors and light show. The punters implore him to switch it all back on but he shuffles off as though he can't hear them. I manage to dissuade Luke from trying to find him and we leave as Gallbladder take to the stage.

'That lot are gonna get signed pronto and if it's not Wow Man Smell My Finger, it'll be someone else. It was crawling with A&R in there.'

'You're supposed to be helping me out,' I say, cuffing him playfully across the head. 'Besides, you can call their manager on Monday morning.'

'All right, then.' Luke's always a pushover when he's off his face, which he is most of the time.

I'm driving along the Euston Road, Luke's playing Mr DJ with the car stereo and it occurs to me that driving while under the influence of lager, laboratory skunk and ecstasy is not one of my better ideas. I was trying to put a stop to this sort of behaviour. My main worry is a kid running into the road: with my present reaction speed, the first I'd see of it would be a flattened bloody mess in my rear-view mirror. But then again, what would a kid be doing on the streets unattended at this time of night anyway? That stuff's just scaremongering by the Safety Nazis.

Hampstead: in order to convey the impression to someone who might be watching the house (Moroccan, just off the plane, etc.) that Mar Kettle or at least *some* old woman lives there, we have decided to employ some dodgy method acting. We pull up opposite the house. I go around to the passenger door and help Luke from the car. He's wearing a headscarf and over his regular gear he's put on a shawl and an old floral dress, all courtesy of Oxfam, and he stoops and dodders and holds onto my arm just as I told him to. All's going well, despite his muttered protestations to the contrary, when some chinless wonder in a Mercedes hurtles around the corner and slams his brakes on just in time to slide to a halt only inches from us.

'Leave it, Luke,' I hiss at him but his dander is up. It would've been fine if the bloke had a chin, was in a Ford and minus the cravat but, as it is, to Luke's mind this is public enemy number one.

'What the hell are you playing at?' he screams, his bloodshot eyes searing through the windscreen at Charles/Henry who gawps back at him. 'You could have killed us.'

Charles/Henry's got the window down now and attempts conciliatory and apologetic noises. But Luke breaks from my grasp and starts kicking the door of the car. Charles/Henry closes his window, guns the engine and pulls away. A yowling scream follows him down the street, echoing and re-echoing off the houses: 'Wanker!' This is not the low-key approach to the house that I'd hoped for.

With all semblance of façade well and truly rubbished, I dig my fingers into Luke's arm, drag him across the road, unlock the door and we're in.

25 Glynbourne Road is a typical Hampstead town house: high-ceilinged rooms with long sash windows, loads of bedrooms and a garden that seemingly stretches into the middle distance. The only difference between this and all the other houses nearby is that this one is uninhabited. Nonetheless, Mar Kettle has a cleaner

come in a couple of times a week to vacuum and polish and a gardener who does his stuff out the back. The place is spotless.

'Can you *imagine* how much all this stuff is worth?' says Luke as he's taking off his old-lady disguise. 'I don't know much about furniture and paintings and all that but by the look of this lot it's gotta be worth a fortune. The best thing we could do is forget about Mar Kettle and her pathetic feud with this old Moroccan geezer, which is probably all a figment of her imagination anyway, get a van, clean the place out and flog the lot. We could hotfoot it abroad, bum around the world for a couple of years until the heat's died down and then return. She's hardly going to kick up much of a stink with you knowing all about her murderous exploits. What do you reckon?'

Luke's full of such schemes that will change his – and, usually, my – life forever. Now, as always, he stands looking at me as though I would be a fool not to pay heed to his words. 'We ride the waves of the future,' he tells me with a grin, 'our surfboards are our destinies. All we can do is point them in the direction we want to go and let the sea of life do the rest.' He's also full of irritating little sayings like this that he's picked up from pub toilets and car bumper stickers.

'Sit down and stop talking shit,' I tell him. 'Anyway, if I can tap into the hundred grand, I'll see you all right, don't you worry. Now, let's get on with the job we came here to do in the first place.'

'Which is, exactly?'

'We've got to hang around and wait for Hassan

Nazar. This is the only place where Mar Kettle's registered as living so, if he really does want to kill her, the chances are he'll come here. I've got absolutely sod all else to go on. She didn't even have a photo of him.'

Luke stretches out on the sofa while I take the armchair opposite and put the box containing the Smith & Wesson on the coffee table between us.

'So, let me get this straight: I'm talking crap when I suggest that we should empty the place and sell the lot – a mere redistribution of property that harms no one. But you think it's perfectly acceptable to kill a man. Well, I'm sorry, but I think your morality's all screwed up.'

'Do you, now?'

'Well, if you really mean business, why don't you load the gun?'

'I think I might just do that.' I take it from the box, click open the chamber and slide the six bullets in. As I close it, he says, 'Do you really think you're in a fit state to be doing that?' Bloody-minded and annoying though he is, he's got a point.

'Have you ever used a gun before?' he continues.

'Yes.' I'm lying.

'When?'

'A couple of years ago on a range. Now stop trying to piss me off, you're giving me a headache.'

We remain silent for a few minutes. A grandfather clock ticks in the corner of the room, a car races along the street outside. I stare at the gun, Luke lies on his back and contemplates the ceiling.

'You do realize,' he says, turning to look at me, 'that

by bringing me here, you're making me a potential accessory to whatever you decide to do.'

Every comment that he makes weakens my resolve, makes me ponder on what the hell I'm doing here with a loaded gun, a headful of drugs, a cantankerous bastard and the possibility that I'll kill someone.

'Listen,' I shout at him, picking up the Smith & Wesson. 'If you don't shut up I'll empty this into your fucking skull.'

'Nice of her to give you a silencer.'

'What?'

'Well, if you let that thing go off you'll probably wake up the entire neighbourhood. Come on, Wyatt Earp, why don't we forget the whole deal? If you step on it, we could maybe catch the end of Gallbladder's set.'

The doorbell rings.

All my dread and paranoia of the last few minutes is focused into a knot of terror in my stomach. My ears burn and my mouth becomes spontaneously devoid of saliva.

Luke's smug philosophizing vanishes and he's up on his feet and whispering to me, 'What do we do now? Do we answer it? What if it's him, Hassan Whatsit?'

It's time for me to take control of the situation. I put the Smith & Wesson down on the coffee table, tell Luke to sit down and shut up – which, for once, he does – and cradle my head in my hands in an attempt to cajole a reasoned, well-judged thought from the maelstrom of confusion within.

'OK – if it *is* Hassan Nazar, he's not going to be

content with just ringing the doorbell and going away. He's going to want to come in and do what he's come to do which means that when no one answers he'll try and find another way in and when he does, we pop him. On the other hand, if it isn't him, what's it matter? Whoever it is'll most likely go away and leave us alone. So my vote is we do nothing and see what happens.'

'Good idea,' says Luke. Suddenly, he's all in agreement with me. Cowardly bastard.

The doorbell rings again, a longer, more persistent ring this time. A third one follows soon afterwards but this is more desultory – a parting shot, perhaps.

'Shall I take a look out of the window and see if he's gone?' asks Luke. But before I can reply the sound of breaking glass comes from the back of the house.

'Oh, my God,' he says under his breath, looking as though he's about to burst into tears. 'What now?'

I pick up the gun, take Luke by the arm and pull him out of the room and up the stairs. In the darkness we stumble and fall over each other. There are footsteps in the kitchen below. In front of me, I can just make out a door and I head towards it. The hinges haven't been oiled in years and a loud creaking resounds around the house as I pull it open.

'Come on,' I hiss and push Luke through the open door and shut it behind us. It's the airing cupboard. There's no point hoping that the intruder hasn't heard us but I pray that perhaps he's just a burglar and might be scared off. Luke is fast approaching hysteria, pleading in whispered screams, 'Jesus, what the fuck are we going to do? I'm so strung out I could shit

45

myself. Don't ever let me get this wrecked before doing anything remotely dangerous ever again. In fact, if we get out of this OK, I'm never going to take another drug as long as I live. I'll turn myself in to the police, I'll do anything.'

'Shut up. I'm trying to listen.'

Aside from our short nervous breaths and the ticking of the grandfather clock far below, there's silence in the house.

'I knew it would end up like this,' he continues, 'I just knew it, I foresaw it somehow.'

'Shut up.'

'But I'm too young to die.'

'For God's sake.'

With no attempt to mute the sound, he starts to sob. I manage to find his head in the darkness and, suppressing the urge to club him with the Smith & Wesson, I gag him with my sleeve.

From the foot of the stairs comes a voice: 'Hello?' A deep voice, throaty and, although I'm no linguist, Moroccan. Luke's knees have given way and all that holds him up is my arm around his head.

'Hello? Hello?' Footsteps on the stairs. A light goes on. I can see the tips of my shoes by it as it shines in from under the door. The sound of door handles being tried, more lights being switched on. Footsteps down the landing towards us. The door is opened. As the light pours in, my startled eyes make a snapshot of the scene before them. He's an old man, dark-skinned and swarthy. His greying hair is swept back from his forehead and thick with lacquer as, too, are the

46

needle-sharp ends of his moustache. He's dressed in blazer and slacks and holds a cane, raised up over his shoulder. There's a momentary look of quizzical indecision on his face before he bolsters his resolve and steps forward, ready to bring down the heavy silver top of the cane upon my head. I level the Smith & Wesson with his chest and fire.

I've never shot a gun before, never felt the metallic explosion in my hand as it rears up, relinquishing its ominous payload. There's a flash of light, the expanding air punches my eardrums and there's a tearing sound as though I've ripped a hole in the fabric of time and space. I open my eyes. Through the smoke I see him lying on the carpet, a growing red stain on the white of his shirt, the cane still raised above his head. A lifetime of television, thousands of make-believe bullets pumped into thousands of make-believe people but it's no preparation for the real thing. Mingling with the smell of gunsmoke is the smell of shit: Luke has filled his pants. I remove my arm from around his head and he falls to the floor, whimpering. I tell him to shut up, the old man's trying to tell me something. I kneel down at his side.

'Tell Mar Kettle,' he wheezes, 'tell Mar Kettle Hassan Nazar, Hassan Nazar . . .' His head lolls to one side and a thin trickle of blood works its way from the corner of his mouth to drip from his chin onto the carpet. It's a classic Hollywood death. Mesmerized, I feel as though I should say something like, 'Old fella never had a chance,' or something equally crass.

But Luke starts wailing a seemingly endless mantra of 'Fuuuuck, fuuuuck,' and spoils the moment.

'Come on,' I tell him. 'Snap out of it. You've got to help me.'

'But I've shat myself.'

'Don't worry about that now, we've got to get the hell out of here and we've got to take him with us.'

'Is he dead?'

'He's dead.'

'You murdered him.'

'Don't start.'

I know that I'll have to keep my mind occupied with the mechanics of removing the body in an attempt to stave off the full realization of what I've done. With the Smith & Wesson safely holstered in my pocket, I take the bedspread from the master bedroom and roll the body in it. Luke alternates the subject matter of his whimpering between the horrors of murder and the amount of crap in his trousers. Fearful that he might slip into some sort of catatonic trance on account of the shock, I slap him around the face a couple of times, then drag the body down the stairs and leave it in the porch before dashing back upstairs to turn out all the lights. Downstairs once more, it's just a short walk to the Beamer with dear old Hassan, the soon-to-be-stiff Moroccan. But just as we're clear of the house and staggering up the pavement, Luke at one end of the corpse and me at the other, we're approached by a podgy-faced man in his early thirties, dressed à la cuboid in slacks and nylon shirt. He's walking a poodle that starts barking at us.

'What are you doing?' asks the man.

'None of your fucking business,' I reply automatically.

'What have you got there?'

'Nothing, now fuck off.'

'Listen,' he says, 'I'm an off-duty policeman. Show me what you've got there.' Blood from the bullet wound has seeped through the bedspread and the dog starts licking at it.

'Listen, mate,' I say changing my approach and coming on all chummy with him. 'It's very late, you're off duty, you've probably got to be up early in the morning, why don't we forget all about this and go our separate ways?'

'Not until I've seen what you've got there.'

'Oh bollocks—' reverting back to former tack '—you're not looking in here and that's final. And anyway, what the hell is a policeman doing living in Hampstead, eh?'

'What do you mean?' I've got him on the defensive now.

'Well, I wouldn't have thought you'd have the money.'

'I live with my parents but that's irrelevant. Show me what you've got there.'

'I think I'll need to see some ID first.'

'What?'

'Got a search warrant, have you?'

'It's quite obvious,' he says quivering with rage, 'that you've got a body there.'

'Oh, is it, now?' I enquire, imitating his tone.

'You leave me no other option but to arrest the pair of you.' His dog has switched its attention from the bloodstain and is now jumping up, trying to get a sniff at the shit in Luke's trousers.

'Sorry, mate, we're in a hurry. Perhaps we could pop down the station tomorrow and fill in a form.' I pick up my end of the body and Luke picks up his but our new-found friend has other ideas and stamps his foot down on Hassan's midriff.

'Excuse me, officer, but this is a gross infringement of our civil liberties.' It takes a moment for it to register that this is Luke speaking. He's come to his senses and sounds more reasonable and sane than ever.

'This is indicative,' he continues, 'of the heavy-handed interventionist approach of the police in this country. Unless the continued extension of police powers is curtailed and the erosion of our personal freedom is reversed, our so-called custodians of law and order will begin to resemble nothing more than a bunch of gung-ho fascists.'

Even the dog has calmed down under Luke's withering tirade.

'So I suggest you allow two honest, upright, law-abiding citizens to go about their business unheeded. After all, your job should be to protect us, not persecute us.'

'Yeah, so piss off,' I add, just for good measure. We pick up the body and make for the car, leaving the podgy git standing bemused on the pavement.

Due to Luke's bowel problems it's almost preferable to have the stiff in the car with me and Luke in the boot. But we manage to fashion a sort of nappy out of a plastic bag which he wears over his jeans.

I call Archie on the car phone and tell him to prepare for our arrival. Such is Mar Kettle's excitement at being finally rid of her tormentor that, despite the late hour, she actually meets us at the lift with Archie. They make a bizarre couple. There's Archie in a pink nightie, his thick legs shaven to an even stubble and his feet wedged into pink fluffy slippers. Despite his clearly having been roused from his bed, his make-up is impeccable and his wig brushed. Mar Kettle, standing a good foot and a half shorter than him, has squeezed her corpulent frame into a kimono and on her head is what appears to be a jewel-encrusted shower cap. It's the first time I've ever seen her standing up and outside the confines of her living room.

'Who the bloody hell is that?' she croaks, nodding at Luke.

'This is my friend Luke. He's been helping me out,' I tell her.

'Can he be trusted?'

'Oh yes, implicitly.'

'What the bloody hell's he wearing?' she asks. But, thankfully, before I can think up some spurious reason as to why Luke should be wearing a plastic supermarket bag as a nappy, she turns her attention to the body lying at our feet.

'Come on, then,' she says. 'Let's take a look at the bastard.'

I fumble with the bedspread. But just as I pull it apart to reveal the face within, all the lights go out.

There's something wrong and I don't just mean with the immediate situation – although, God knows, that's bad enough. It's as though the sudden darkness has tripped a switch in my head. In the past twenty-four hours or so I've ingested a pretty impressive amount and variety of drugs, seen one of the best bands of my life – although I suppose that's not all that important, considering – and lastly, I've killed a man. I've killed a man I've never met before just because a mad old woman asked me to. And none of it really fazed me, not until now, that is. My bowels feel as though they could be heading the same way as Luke's.

In the impenetrable darkness, Mar Kettle screams at Archie, Luke screams at me and there's another voice amidst the incoherent cacophony – mine, mumbling, my lips and tongue bouncing around, reeling off non-sensical syllables of their own accord. I grind my jaws together and clamp my lips tight shut. Somewhere there's a light, dim and moving. It's the digits counting down above the lift doors. They go to zero and stop. The others cease their hysterical bickerings and watch the illuminated numbers as the lift approaches.

'Archie?' asks Mar Kettle.

'Yes, ma'am,' he replies, deadpan, as though awaiting orders for a cup of tea.

'Have you got the gun?'

'No, ma'am.'

The lift's at the tenth floor and rising.

'Let's all get inside and lock the door.' She struggles to get the words out as fear rattles in her throat.

'I wish it was that easy,' says Archie. 'But, you see,

with the power cut and all, the door will be automatically locked already. That's how you wanted it.'

'Yes, yes, all right. Jesus Christ, what the hell is going on? Why is the lift working and nothing else? I don't like the look of this. There's something wrong.'

As the lift reaches the fourteenth floor, I remember the revolver in my jacket pocket and pull it out, relishing the reassurance of its cold steel in my hands.

'It's OK, everybody, just relax, I'll handle this.' I speak with such calm assurance that I almost convince myself. But then, my mouth seems to be achieving an increasing autonomy from my frightened rabbit of a brain. I step over the body and position myself in front of the doors as the lift continues its inexorable ascent.

'I don't care who it is,' Mar sounds more herself now, as though my B-movie heroics have bolstered her confidence. 'I don't give a damn if it's the devil himself or the bloody archangel Gabriel, if it comes to that. Whoever it is, if they come up here you shoot and you keep shooting until they're halfway to kingdom come.'

The whirring and clanking of the wheels and cables in the lift shaft grind to a halt and a metallic click announces the opening of the doors. As they slide back, I steady myself and point the gun into the band of light that opens up before me. I want to dive in shooting, spitting death and bullets. I want to rub it all out, erase the fear, make it all go away. Every vestige of narcosis has left me, it's just me and the interior of this wire-strung cage. It's so simple, so screamingly straightforward. I can squeeze my finger and it's bye-bye. But bye-bye what? Bye-bye dog? For standing there, poised trembling on its stubby little legs, is the Jack Russell I saw this morning being teased by the kids outside the tower block.

Mar Kettle's shouting at me to shoot.

Bang. All the lights go out. Again. Only this time, they're mine.

3

I feel like Bugs Bunny when he's being chased and he runs off the reel of cartoon film and ends up suspended in mid-air. The thing is, he always manages to run back into the cartoon. I'm not sure I can do that. The base of my skull is swollen and feels like it could burst. The action of lifting my head off the carpet upsets the delicate equilibrium in the swelling, sending shock waves of pain around my head. As I prepare myself for re-entry into consciousness, an object suspended above me switches into and out of focus. It's a chandelier, that much I can make out. But it's only when my vision clears that I can see it's a huge nest of bones glued together to create a spherical lattice-work of ribs, limbs, jawbones, teeth and spinal columns, all purloined from the sorry carcasses of beasts whose untimely deaths have served no purpose other than to provide a bizarre skeletal adornment for Mar Kettle's ceiling.

I sit up and look around the room. Before me, there are three armchairs placed in a semicircle, their three occupants fast asleep. First, there's Luke who's curled up in a foetal position, dribbling strings of phlegm onto his plastic nappy. Next along is Mar Kettle, her slumbering face an imploded mass of collapsed skin, and finally there's Archie who sits resolute and stiff-backed with the 'L' of LOVE on his index finger curled around the trigger of the revolver in his lap. Sleep doesn't soften his brutal features. His wig's slipped, which lends him a comical air, but I'm not laughing.

I stand up and allow myself a couple of seconds to adjust to the high altitude I seem to have achieved by so doing. This is the calm before the storm. One sound and they'll fall upon me like a pack of wolves. I consider trying to creep out without waking them but I'd never make it. Oh well, here goes.

'Morning.'

They jump to their feet as one and Luke and Mar Kettle gabble away at me while Archie looks on, the gun clenched tight in his fist. Mar Kettle's words are rendered incoherent by her attempts to install her dentures while speaking, so I concentrate on Luke.

'Jesus, man, I thought I'd killed you. You went out like a light. I didn't mean to hit you that hard, I was just worried that you'd shoot the dog. You know what I'm like about animals. It was the weight of the fire extinguisher that did it, I must have overbalanced. Much good it did the poor little bastard.'

Mar Kettle's teeth are in situ by now and her voice

comes through loud and clear: 'What the hell did you think you were playing at, you murdering bastard? That wasn't Hassan Nazar that you put a bullet into last night. That was my lawyer Mohammed Yacoubi, the finest legal brain in North Africa.'

She stares at me, awaiting a response. Out of a fog of narcosis and concussion, the events of yesterday emerge to confront me. All I can manage is, 'Are you sure?'

'Of course I'm bloody sure. I've known him for over forty years.'

'What was he doing snooping around your house?'

'He was on business in London, I spoke to him only yesterday about Nazar. He must have been try-ing to warn me about something. Besides me, of course, there's only you and Archie and now this moron,' she motions at Luke, 'who know where I really live.'

'How was I supposed to know it was him and not Nazar?'

'Well, you might have checked.'

This is all too much for me. I've got to go home.

'Come on, Luke, let's go.'

'That's right,' she barks, 'you just walk away from this like it never happened.'

Despite the sarcasm it sounds like a good idea. I make towards the door. Archie's gone through ahead and Mar Kettle and Luke follow on behind.

'All I would ask you to remember,' she continues, 'is who it is that pays your wages, and who it is that pays for the car you're about to drive off in.'

Archie struggles with a large object at the end of the hall.

'And another thing.' She pokes me in the back. 'Don't leave without it.' I don't know what she means so I just keep walking. But then I see what it is that Archie is holding. The bloodstain has grown to the size of a dinner plate and turned brown at the edges where it's dried. Archie's wrapped parcel tape around the bedspread, which accentuates the outline of the body.

'We can't take that outside in broad daylight,' Luke complains. 'Why don't you have him stuffed and mounted like all the rest?'

Archie tips the body towards me and I have to steady myself against the wall to prevent it from knocking me over.

'Come on, Luke, grab his feet.'

'But what are we going to do with him?'

'I'll think of something.'

No one notices, or if they do it doesn't register, but the lift arrives even though no one has pressed the call button.

'You've fucked up once,' says Mar Kettle, her slippered foot preventing the lift door from closing. 'Don't let me have cause to doubt your abilities in the future. And if, through some misguided notion, you decide to try and terminate our business arrangements, then God help you when Archie catches hold of you. You might think of him as slightly less than macho but be assured, when it comes to acts of extreme physical violence, he's all man.'

The lift is devoid of its usual smell of urine and in its place is an exotic aroma that I can't place.

'What the fuck is that smell?' I ask Luke.

'Just piss,' he says, which worries me.

'Can't you smell it? It smells as though someone's been frying spices or something.'

'You've had a bang on the head. You've got to take things easy,' I hear him say. But after that his voice is drowned out by the sound of drums that seems to grow out of the rattling of the lift within the shaft. Weaving through the rhythm comes the sound of stringed instruments and voices strained in pitch, wailing some bastardized call to prayer. The lift has lost its downwards trajectory and starts to spin around us. The metallic angles and planes that form its interior shoot into and out of focus, ricochet off the walls and fragment into infinite reflections of each other. I try to focus on Luke but there are thousands of him, millions, all chewing their lips and staring at me. Then I hear a man's voice that is at the same time both reassuring and demonic and imbues me with a paradoxical wave of love and loathing, excitement and disgust. It's just a whisper but amplified to an ear-splitting volume. I can't make out what it's saying, although the words register on some hidden level of consciousness and portend a malevolence of such acute intensity and unimaginable horror that I feel the life force of my body cowering in the pit of my stomach.

The lift stops and with it the hallucination – if that's what it was.

'Are you all right?' asks Luke. 'You look a little peeky.'

'I'm fine,' I lie.

'Should I check the coast's clear?'

'No, come on, take his feet, let's go.'

'But what if anyone sees us?'

'At this moment in time, Luke, I don't give a shit. If you want to go home, that's fine. I'll drag the stiff to the car and do what needs to be done myself. I got you into all this and if you decide to bugger off and leave me, I'll understand.'

I'm trying to wear an expression of sincerity while inside I'm hoping to hell that he won't take my half-baked get-out option. I look at him standing there in his makeshift nappy, every fibre of his skinny frame racked with indecision. He's not cut out for a life of crime. He's not cut out for anything much beyond recreational drugs and knowing a good band when he sees one. Life for Luke is just a medium for getting from one party to the next, just something that happens while he gets stoned. Murder's not his scene at all.

'Seriously, Luke, why don't you go home, pretend last night never happened. I'll sort this out. I shouldn't have got you involved.'

'Well, what'll you do?' he asks.

'I'll think of something. Don't worry. I got myself into this, I'll get myself out.' I can't believe what I'm saying but, thankfully, just as I think I've blown it and he will leave me, he looks up, gives me one of his Disney-on-acid smiles and says, 'Nah, come on, you're bloody useless on your own, I'll give you a hand but you've got to promise to drop me home afterwards.'

I could kiss him.

'And then,' he continues, his smile fading, 'I want to hear no more of Mar Kettle and your rather pitiful impersonation of a hit man.'

'OK, you're on.' We both know I'm lying.

We cross the patch of grass to the car with our heads bowed and our shoulders hunched as though this might make us and the body we're carrying less conspicuous.

The confidence-boosting properties of the Beamer never cease to amaze me. Once safely ensconced within the leather upholstery, steering wheel sliding through my hands and the pedal to the floor, my headache eases off and, for the first time since I regained consciousness, I can think straight.

Now, what to do with the stiff? There's cremation, I suppose, but then neither of us have a garden or anywhere to do it. The easiest thing we decide, would be to take the traditional route and bury him so Luke grabs the A-to-Z and suggests we snowstorm some ideas. Snowstorming is to the employees of Wow Man Smell My Finger Records what brainstorming is to the rest of us. The only difference being the 'snow' they hoover to assist them. He pulls a wrap from his shirt pocket, opens it on the dashboard and we dab it up with our fingers. It's strong. But then, Luke's drugs always are.

'So, where to lay the poor bastard to rest, then, eh?' Luke says, proceeding to whistle as he flicks through the A-to-Z. He answers his own question: 'The most convenient place for me, seeing as you're going to run me back to Muswell Hill, is Alexandra Park. We could pick up a spade at the garden centre there and then look for a suitable plot. It'll be less crowded than Hampstead Heath. Less chance of being spotted. If you step on it, we could do the business, go back to my place, get cleaned up and, if all goes well, we could be sofa-surfing just in time for *Football Focus*.'

Ten minutes later we turn into the garden-centre car park. The intensity of the initial coke rush is wearing off but I'm still wired and an unfortunate side effect is that it's aggravated the wound on the back of my head. The swelling feels as though it's developed a set of lungs all of its own that keep in sync with mine. I dodge into a space in front of a fat middle-aged bloke in a Jaguar who glares at me but, even through two windscreens and across twenty feet of car park, he can see that I'm on the edge and does nothing.

'Tell you what, man, you go and get the spade and I'll skin up a number to round the edges off the charlie. How about that?'

'Nice one, Luke.'

Taking drugs is, to Luke, an act of creation. Like an artist, he is constantly aware of detail, texture and the vast difference that can be brought about through the most minute modification. He is forever on the lookout for the perfect high for each and every occasion. I can tell that he's trying to do something special for me today. Whether it's embarrassment about his crapping himself last night or whether he's worried about me and this is his way of showing it I don't know, but, for once, he can't do enough.

'What sort of spade are you looking for, sir?' asks the assistant. He's one of those surly youths, a student on his weekend job, I'll bet, and he uses the 'sir' not as a mark of respect but as an insult. What he's really saying is, 'What sort of spade are you looking for, shithead? Though you think of me as some servile shop assistant, I can in fact look down on this facile salesman–client relationship from the viewpoint of someone who's your intellectual superior and, although I can play along with the situational niceties, I am in truth laughing at you, yes, laughing at you and all you stand for.'

I narrow my eyes, pause just long enough to let him know that I'm onto him and whisper, 'Just an ordinary spade so's I can bury the man I murdered last night. And, if you don't hurry up, I'll take out the gun I shot him with, shove it up your arse and blow your guts out of your ears.' I feel like adding 'Capice?' like some Hollywood Mafioso but I check myself and opt for 'Got it?' He nods and fetches a spade. I kind of enjoy the power that my psychosis has lent me. If I can turn into some hard-edged latter-day Raymond Chandler type, wisecracking all over town, I might just drag myself out of this godawful mess.

Unfortunately, the sack of pain bobbing against my collar has other ideas and behaves like a physical extension of my conscience. As I swagger through the car park, the spade slung over my shoulder, feeling momentarily cocksure after my exchange with the sales assistant, it sends a double-barrelled pulse of pain and dread through my head with such ferocity that it feels as though my skull might crack in two. To hell with Philip Marlowe: I feel like crying.

'Here you go,' says Luke, waving the joint at me from the midst of his smoky cocoon. 'Have a pull on this little number. It'll sort you right out.'

It's still early and there're only a few people out and about in the park, just some joggers and dog walkers. I park up at the side of Alexandra Palace and cautiously step from the car, fearful of upsetting the wound on my head. Luke joins me and stares at the city below us stretching to the horizon beneath a grey sky. He sucks on the joint and smiles to himself.

'What is it with you?' I ask, finding his good humour irksome. 'Last night you were so scared you crapped yourself and blubbered on about not wanting to die and how you'd mend your ways if you survived. Now look at you: it's like you don't give a shit.'

'Listen, man, there's no one more upset about what happened last night than I am, believe me. A man died, for God's sake, and it doesn't get any heavier than that, I know. But hey, just when you think things can't get any worse, everything changes and it's a new day, the world keeps on spinning and we move on.'

He passes the joint to me and stands there, staring into the middle distance, hands on hips, head held high, taking big exaggerated breaths as though savouring the clean air of an alpine mountaintop rather than the halitosis of the city below.

'Come on, laughing boy,' I tell him. 'Let's plant the

stiff.' We hoist the body from the boot and, with the spade resting on top of it, carry it across the road and down the steep grass bank. A public park on a Saturday morning in broad daylight is not ideal for the disposal of a body but I'm hoping that our suicidal lack of subtlety will evoke only disbelief in the minds of potential onlookers.

We head for a cluster of shrubs and bushes down the hill from the Palace. An elderly man sits on a bench, watching us as he fills his pipe. Luke, with his shit-filled nappy and newly found beatitude, his fingers curled around the ankles of a murder victim, grins at him and shouts, 'Don't worry, it's rag week.' The man gives us a cheerful wave and turns his attention back to his pipe. We reach the bushes and, for once, we're lucky: they're planted in a horseshoe shape, allowing us protection from prying eyes on three sides.

'God has truly smiled on us today,' Luke tells me.

We lay the body down. I take the spade and start digging. Within ten minutes I've cleared an area of turf that's roughly body-sized. We need to go just a little deeper and then we can lay Mohammed Yacoubi, brilliant lawyer and all-round dead bloke, to rest.

Luke takes over the digging and some minutes later says, 'Come on, man, this must be deep enough.' It is – just – but we have to lay Yacoubi on his side as it's a bit narrow. I pick up the spade, ready to fill in the hole.

'Don't you think we should say something?' asks Luke.

'Like what?'

'Well, maybe we should say sorry or something.'
'But he's dead.'
'Well, as a mark of respect we should at least say a few words, perhaps express our regret for what happened and wish him well for whatever lies ahead.'
'Go on, then, if you must.'

Luke wears a pious expression but it's not the piety of the cleric so much as that of the mentally ill. With the spade poised ready over the mound of earth we've created, I wait for him to blurt out whatever his drug-addled brain has decided he should.

'I feel that it is important to remember that this is not just a body we are burying here but a person. Here lies someone's father, someone's brother, someone's lover, someone's husband—' he slows down for emotional effect now '—someone's son—' big dramatic pause, then '—someone's friend.'

My hands flinch with anticipation of their grave-filling and dislodge some soil that tumbles into the hole. Luke takes his gaze off the clouds and looks down at the body wrapped in the bloody bedspread and parcel tape. I'm about to start shovelling when he starts up again.

'Let us consider for a moment the positive aspects of this man's life. His, erm, childhood and his, er,' Luke's taken the wrong turn with his dreadful tribute speech but he's determined to guts it through, 'his law degree and his job and family and all that, so let's not allow this man's death to cast a tragic shadow across his life.'

'Luke, for God's sake, just say what you've got to say and let's go.'

'Hello.'

So shocked am I by this unexpected greeting from behind us that I drop the spade, which slides down the mound of earth and comes to rest against the body. I turn around to see a rotund man dressed in blazer and slacks and with a golfing jumper pulled over his pot belly. His thinning hair frames an eager face all chubby and flushed. I recognize him. He's on TV or he used to be.

'What's going on here?' he asks.

He's been in loads of things but never starred in anything. He's one of that legion of nameless British TV actors who've been in your living room so many times that when you see them in the flesh you feel you know them personally, as though you share some common history. Now, what is his name? This'll really annoy me. I suppose I should be afraid that we've been caught in the act of burying the stiff but I'm more shocked by the fact that it's what's-his-name off the box. Now what the hell *is* his name?

Luke approaches him, stands almost face to face with him and says, 'You're the stationmaster off *Dewdrop Junction*, aren't you?'

'I worked on that show for many years, yes.'

'What's your name? No, hold on, don't tell me, you're—' he screws up his brow with concentration and slowly enunciates the words as though he's incanting the meaning of life '—you're Geoffrey Lobshaw.'

'Yes, I am.'

Luke is ecstatic and starts jumping up and down as though he's scored a goal. But I'm not satisfied. There's still one more question that I need answering. I step forward and ask it. 'What was your name in *Dewdrop Junction*?'

'You're evading the issue,' says Geoffrey Lobshaw. 'I'm going to have to call the police.'

My entire flow of being has reached a bottleneck. It feels as though, unless I find out Geoffrey Lobshaw's name in *Dewdrop Junction*, I will be forever trapped in this moment in time. 'Come on, tell me, what was your name?' I ask him. 'I can explain everything afterwards.'

'This is ridiculous.'

'Come on, please. I'm a big fan.'

'It was Stationmaster Simpkins.'

A jolt of pleasure shudders through my body, almost sexual in its intensity. I feel faint. Luke stands there with his arm flung around Geoffrey Lobshaw's shoulders, laughing uncontrollably and repeating 'Stationmaster Simpkins' over and over as though this were the funniest joke in all the world.

Geoffrey himself has begun to look afraid. The gravity of his situation has sunk in: namely, that on his Saturday-morning walk he's stumbled upon two crazed murderers in the act of burying a victim. He takes Luke's arm from around his shoulders and makes a couple of steps backwards.

'Oh, you can't go, Geoffrey,' says Luke and panic flashes across Geoffrey's face. He clearly sees this as proof that we can't afford to let him live to tell the tale.

'You don't mind me calling you Geoffrey, do you?

I mean, I've never met you before but, hey, fuck it, it feels as though I've known you all my life. You don't want to worry about all this.' Luke gestures at the grave. 'You see, we're filming a play for television and this is the scene where we bury the bloke we've murdered. Realistic, eh? Trouble is, the film crew and director haven't turned up yet. Saturday morning, that's the problem, probably sleeping off a hangover or up to their bollocks in someone they shouldn't be.'

Luke's attempts at placation fall on deaf ears. Geoffrey Lobshaw turns around and runs at full pelt down the hill.

'Nippy little fella, isn't he?' says Luke watching him go. His sudden exit bursts my bubble of TV nostalgia and it's back to the job in hand.

'Listen, Luke, let's get the hell out of here. He may be part of our TV heritage but that doesn't mean that he's not going straight to the pigs.'

I start shovelling the soil on top of the body while Luke paces around me, his demeanour radically altered by my urgent tone.

'We will get away with all this, won't we?' he asks as I pat down the mound of soil with the spade. I don't want to give him even a hint of reassurance, in case he reverts back to his holy-man impersonation, so I tell him that I have no idea and fling the spade into a flower bed. He follows me up the bank towards the car.

'What happens if Geoffrey Lobshaw does go to the police?' he asks as we drive off.

'We just have to make sure that we stay one step

ahead of them the whole time.' I enjoy saying this – I almost slip into an American accent as I speak. If I have to find a way of dealing with all this by mining a seam of dodgy American TV dialogue, then so be it. It won't make the events of the past few hours any easier, far from it, but it just might help me build some personality armour around my bewildered psyche. OK, so the personality's not mine, it's the cobbled-together product of a thousand scriptwriters' minds, but let's not quibble: I need all the help I can get.

I unlock the car with a zap from Frank, open the door and climb in. Luke takes his seat and lets out a terrified scream. A Jack Russell terrier has darted out from underneath the seat and sunk its teeth into his leg, just below the knee. I make a grab for the dog and manage to get my hands around its neck and drag it off. It barks and snarls and runs away.

'What the fuck,' gasps Luke.

'It's the dog from Mar Kettle's place, the Jack Russell. It must have followed us out this morning and hidden under the seat.'

'It can't have.'

'Jesus, we ought to get you to a hospital. It looks bad.'

'It can't be the same dog.'

'What's it matter? You're bleeding like a bastard.'

Luke grabs me around the neck, pulls my face to within inches of his and hisses, 'That dog is fucking dead.'

'There's no point threatening the bloody thing.'

'I don't mean I'll kill the dog, I mean it's already dead.'

'Listen, Luke, you've gone into shock. This is a bad end to a bad night. We're both freaked out. Now, let's get you home and get you bandaged up. The longer we stay out here the more dangerous it's going to become.'

'Just shut up for one minute,' he shouts. 'I know the fucking dog's dead because I killed it.'

'Luke, what the hell are you talking about? I thought you clubbed me with the fire extinguisher to stop me from shooting the dog?'

'I *did* hit you with the fire extinguisher. But it wasn't so much a hit as a throw and the fire extinguisher bounced off your head and landed on the dog. I killed it stone dead.'

'So what?'

'What do you mean, so what?'

'Well, obviously you only stunned it and this morning it revived and decided to get its revenge by hiding in the car and waiting for the right moment to get its own back.'

'You don't get it. I *killed* the dog. And even if I didn't, even if I did only stun it, it most definitely wound up dead because Mar Kettle's butler, that daft bastard in the wig, threw it out of the window. So unless they've started making bouncing Jack Russells, that's one fucking dead dog that just bit me.'

'So what you're telling me, Luke, is that, to add to all our other troubles, we're now being stalked by a zombie. But no ordinary zombie, oh no, we're now being stalked by the zombie of a fucking Jack Russell.'

'Yup.'

We set off, but even the silky-smooth transmission of the Beamer can't reassure me now. My head throbs, my hands sweat on the steering wheel and my foot trembles on the accelerator pedal. What makes Luke's words so scary is that I think he might be right. Nothing would surprise me now.

'OK,' I say at the bottom of Muswell Hill, 'so you've just been bitten by a dead dog. Fair enough. Well, I can match that.' I don't know whether it's wise to tell him this, as though saying it out loud will lend some authenticity to it and make it true, but I'm going to tell him anyway. 'I think I might have been cursed.'

'Cursed?'

'Yeah, by this Hassan Nazar bloke.'

'And you think *I've* lost the plot.'

'This morning, in the lift, I had a visitation of some sort. Someone or something spoke to me.'

'You've been watching too much television.'

I shouldn't have mentioned it. Not even a man who believes he's just been bitten by a dead dog will believe me.

We pull up outside his flat and he steps out. Luke doesn't ask me in, just hobbles across the pavement and in through the door. I'm about to drive off feeling paranoid and dejected – not even my best friend can offer me some reason for all this – when he puts his head back around the door, shoots me a grin and says, 'Watch the skies.' I'm grateful for this brief sniff of bonhomie but although it makes me feel better momentarily, by the time I'm in second gear I've got the fear again. Only one thing for it, I'll go see my father. This usually has the effect of messing with my head but, in the state I'm in at the moment, it may be an interesting diversion, take my mind off things.

I head for the old Locarno on Blackstock Road. I'm probably one of the few people in London who still refer to it as that. It's not the Locarno any more and hasn't been for years. It became a bingo hall in the late seventies and subsequently it's been converted into Nu War Meltdown, one of those futuristic warfare games in which people are given laser guns and run around shooting at each other. But to my father it will forever be the Locarno. The passers-by who see my father standing outside it don't realize that he's waiting for someone, someone who's about ten years too late for the appointment. They just see him as a strange old man in a shabby suit who's lost his marbles and is locked into some fixation that makes him wander the same few yards of pavement day in, day out.

Opposite the old Locarno is my dad's local, the Hope & Glory. It's there I look first after I've checked outside and can't see him. Sure enough, he's sitting in the corner, hunched over a pint.

'Hi, Dad.'
'All right, son.'
'Any sign?'
'Not yet.'

Not long after my mother's death, an event which was a catalyst in all this, I'm sure, my father went with a party of work colleagues to the Locarno to *An Evening With Bernie Mann*. Bernie was a self-styled showbiz impresario and talent-spotter whose career peak came when he appeared on the panel of judges on *New Faces*. He ran his own agency, called Mann's People, and booked acts into working men's clubs and town halls up and down the country. After his appearance on *New Faces*, he briefly took to the stage himself to compere a cabaret show he'd developed, at the end of which he would invite a member of the audience onto the stage to perform a song or stand-up routine. My dad always fancied himself as a bit of a singer so, on the night in question, he volunteered and as fate decreed was chosen to take the stage to sing 'My Way' with the Mann Band. It was clearly more than a passable rendition because when Bernie Mann came to give his verdict (à la *New Faces*), he announced that he would make Dad a star. A couple of years previously, he'd managed to pluck someone from the crowd at a show, an impressionist, who went on to appear on a *Sunday Night at the London Palladium*. This was evidence enough, he believed, of his abilities to spot a potential name in lights. But as his fleeting celebrity status nosedived along with attendances at his shows, he lost interest in making anyone a star, himself included, and became more interested in hitting the bottle.

The show at the Locarno was one of the last shows that Bernie Mann ever did. Within months, his career was in ruins, Mann's People had gone down the tubes and there were debt collectors coming out of the woodwork. The last thing that would have bothered him in his drunken stupor was a handful of wannabes who might be bitter that he'd given them cheques for stardom which they couldn't cash. But then, the majority of them were no doubt playing with a full deck, mentally that is, and recognized Bernie Mann's I'm-going-to-make-you-a-star routine for the horseshit it quite clearly was. What could they do, sue him? My father, on the other hand, by now playing with half a deck and a couple of jokers, took it all in his stride. He wasn't concerned one iota about Bernie Mann's fall from grace, so convinced was he that it was only a minor hiccup in the trajectory of his inevitable celebrity supernova.

Dad kept in touch with Bernie, sent him letters of support, even offered to do a benefit gig for him, but the flow of communication was one-way only. Bernie didn't give a shit. He was forging a career as a full-time drunk, replacing his former image of perpetual suntan, cheesy grin and plastic hairdo with one of three-day benders and pissed-in trousers.

I get the beers in and take a seat opposite Dad.

'Seen much of Ken?' I ask. Ken is Dad's best mate, a man who knows all about the Bernie Mann situation but chooses to overlook it, probably as part of a non-spoken pact in which Dad overlooks Ken's fixation on Shirley Bassey. There are fans, there are obsessive fans and there's Ken. Every single, album, compilation album, video, bootleg, magazine article,

T-shirt, ticket stub (all gigs in a thirty-mile radius of London from '71 to the present day), every poster, biography, scarf, pendant and badge that ever bore Shirley's name is catalogued and displayed lovingly in his house – along with three pairs of her knickers and a pair of shoes that are kept in his bedroom for those special moments. Short of becoming Shirley Bassey's gynaecologist, he couldn't know more about her. The official Shirley Bassey fan club, the SBFC, drummed Ken out after it was discovered that he'd hatched a plot in which he would purloin one of her turds fresh from the toilet of the Dorchester where she happened to be residing – he's a plumber by trade – bake it hard and mount it on a plinth in his sitting room. That was much too hard-core for the SBFC.

'Saw him last week. Went to the pictures.'

'Anything good?'

'French film with subtitles.'

'Any sex?'

'Yeah, some,' he chuckles. He likes it when the conversation becomes blokeish: it reminds him of his days in the merchant navy. They were the best days of his life, so he tells me.

He's itching to hit the streets to watch out for Bernie Mann, so we finish our beers and go for a walk. Youths are pouring out of Nu War Meltdown. He looks at them all individually, as though one of them might mutate spontaneously from a pimply technoteen into an alcoholic ex-celebrity clutching a recording contract.

'I nearly forgot,' he says after his identity parade has proved fruitless. 'I met someone in the pub before you arrived. Name of Hassan something, sort of Arabic-looking. Charming fellow. Said he knew you.'

4

Mum was killed during a police reconstruction. She was knocked down by a car. The others, the camera crew and the drama students, got out of the way. But Mum, even though she could walk and was only acting the part of the cripple, tried to wheel herself away in a wheelchair. Whatever made her do this when she could have run for it like all the rest, I'll never know.

She was obsessed by violent crime and the exploits of the dangerous and the homicidal. Whether it was a book by an eminent professor of criminal psychology or a true-life crime rag, she devoured the lot. Our house became a shrine to violent death. My dad indulged her for many years but when she started discussing with him one day, rationally and composed as always, whether he'd mind if she removed the Constable prints from either side of the fireplace to replace them with scene-of-crime photographs, he decided that enough was enough. Always a mild-mannered man, he issued no ultimatums, just steered her towards college where she studied criminology. She subsequently found employment as a researcher for Crimewatch UK. Not long after it first went on air, a sixty-five-year-old woman suffered a brutal beating at the hands of a gang of youths. What made this crime all the more shocking and therefore ripe for lurid coverage by the Crimewatch team was that the victim was confined to a wheelchair. She had no legs. They didn't explain that the reason for her shortage of legs was due almost entirely to her sixty-a-day cigarette habit. This would have sullied her image in the eyes of the Crimewatch viewers.

It was a hastily devised reconstruction, made all the more so by the fact that the BBC camera crew and director took the wrong turn on the way there which meant that they turned up forty-five minutes late. The police press officer and a group of drama students from the local college who had been enlisted to act out their parts as brutal muggers were left shivering on the pavement. Finally, along came the Crimewatch boys with Mum and set up for the shoot. To make matters worse, the actress who was due to play Mrs Sixty-a-day had been taken ill so, in the absence of a suitable understudy, Mum offered to help out. Just as they made a start, a Mr Ed Norris, an ex-World War Two fighter pilot, was climbing into his Vauxhall Viva to make his weekly trip to the Three Lions bowling club. He turned out of his garage, pulled along the road, saw what he thought was Mrs Sixty-a-day being savagely beaten by muggers for the second time that week and, appalled by this brutality, kamikaze'd the Viva straight at them. Bye-bye, Mum.

After the funeral, I went to see Mrs Sixty-a-day in the vain hope that this might offer me some solace in my grief. Sadly, it didn't. All I found was a sack of fucked-up blood vessels struggling for breath. It was depressing.

As the saying goes, you don't know what you've got till it's gone and despite my mother being an obsessive crime addict and all-round odd bird, she was still my mum and I loved her, just as I love my dad. Perhaps I love them more because of their quirks and eccentricities. Anyway, I'm not going to let some loopy Moroccan with a grudge take away the only parent I have left.

Heading up Camden Road, I reach for the car phone. There's something vaguely repugnant about the way Mar Kettle answers the phone. She takes a deep wheezing breath that mutates into the most malevolent, untrusting 'Hello' you ever heard. The conversation goes like this:

Me: He's on to us.

MK: I told you not to call here. Someone might be listening in.

Me: There's no doubt about that. But then, the man we're dealing with knows what we're up to anyway.

MK: Look, if you need to speak to me, you'll have to come here.

Me: I've had enough.

MK: Enough of what?

Me: I quit.

MK: You can't quit.

Me: He's on to me. He knows everything I do, everywhere I go. He went to see my father today.

MK: You cannot quit.

Me: I can't go on like this. This is way too weird for me and what's more, I don't want to involve my father in murder and black magic.

MK: What do you mean, black magic?

Me: He's put a curse on me. I'm convinced of it.

MK: How do you work that out?

Me: Well, this morning in the lift leaving your place, I don't know how to put this, but I had, shall we say, a visitation.

MK: A what?

Me: A visitation. I blacked out and heard all this Moroccan chanting and then later, when we buried your lawyer, Luke was bitten by a Jack Russell. He's convinced that it's the one that Archie threw out of the window last night.

MK: For goodness' sake, man, pull yourself together, you're talking like a madman. There are perfectly rational explanations for all of this. That moron friend of yours crowned you with a fire extinguisher. The reason you felt so strange in the lift was concussion and as for the dog, well, there are thousands of Jack Russells in London, all almost identical and all most definitely alive. You're just shaken up.

Me: You know that isn't true. How do you explain my Dad's visit this morning? What about all the supernatural stuff you told me yesterday that Nazar was capable of? The magic letter in your handbag, remember? Can't you see that I'm way out of my depth here? A hundred grand is a hell of a pay-off but can't you see that there's no way I'll ever collect? This guy's some kind of ghoul. I don't know what I'm dealing with. I get the feeling that he's just playing with us all and when he gets bored it'll all come to an end.

There's silence on the other end of the line. I've never spoken to Mar Kettle like this before. I've never dared.

MK: OK, so you quit, then what? I'll tell you what: the next call I make is to the police to report the murder of a certain Mohammed Yacoubi. I'll deny all knowledge of our meeting yesterday. You'll go down for twenty years.

Me: If I do, then I'll take you with me.

MK: It'll be your word against mine. It wouldn't be the first time I'd convinced a jury of my total innocence, *remember*? Now listen to me for a minute. This is stupid. You can't quit, he'll kill us both. I'll tell you what, I'll increase your money, how does that sound?

Me: What is this, some sort of murder game show? What good is money going to do me when I'm six feet under? You don't seem to realize, I'm no hit man, least of all when it comes to doing a hit on something out of *The X Files*. Why don't you get someone more heavy-duty, someone from the East End, one of your old cronies from way back?

MK: Because *(she's spluttering and gasping and scrabbling*

around for words – I almost feel sorry for her) I don't know them any more. *(She's wailing now.)* I haven't seen them in years, they wouldn't know me.

This, I must concede, is true. All of her so-called underworld friends are, depending on how well they did their jobs, either dead, poverty-stricken or living it up wearing lizard-skin suntans on the Costa Del Criminal. Señor and Señora Big couldn't give a flying one for Mar Kettle and her problems with Morocco's very own Paul Daniels. It'd be a case of 'I-know-you-not-old-hag.' Besides, what could they do even if they did want to help? They're probably about as well connected with the criminal underworld of present-day London as I am, which is to say not at all.

Me: Why don't you get Archie to sort him out for you?

MK: No, I need him here to look after me. Besides, he's no hit man either.

Me: In that case, *(I feel a rush of B-movie dialogue coming on)* my only advice to you is, get yourself a priest.

I know that Mar Kettle is Church of England but 'Get yourself a vicar' is not a good line. Before she can say anything else, I hang up.

I can go weeks on end without shouting anything out of the car and then the urge just creeps up on me unawares. Down comes the window, out goes my head and there I am, casting my pearls of wisdom before an unsuspecting public. I like to think of it as part of an ancient tradition of street preaching, updated for modern times and made available to a wider listenership through the use of the motor car. Psychologically, I suppose, it's nothing more than a classic case of letting off steam.

I'm doing thirty along Camden High Street which is highly dangerous, this being a Saturday and there being crowds of people about, and I'm shrieking out of the window at the top of my lungs: 'You're all going to die, every last one of you, you're all going to die! Worm-food, compost, die, die, die!' I feel it needs to be said and repeat it a few times in various word permutations, finishing off with a 'You're all going to die, motherfuckers!' for extra pith and gravity. It charges me up and clears my head. I love a Camden Market crowd as well, all students and serious haircuts.

I park in a lock-up just off Chalk Farm Road. I used to refer to it as the Bat Cave but I don't any more. No reason, really, except maybe it's a bit naff and I can't think of anything better to call it. But it makes me sleep better at nights knowing that the Beamer's safe under lock and key. It also gives me the opportunity to switch number plates away from prying eyes should the need arise.

I push my way through the crowds to the canal and take the towpath towards Regents Park. A couple of hundred yards and there she is, the *Griffin*, thirty-two-and-a-half feet of glorious green canal boat. You can keep your bricks and mortar, keep your back yards and your gardens, I like to wake up to the sound of water slapping against a wooden hull six inches from my head. Get bored of my surroundings and I can move on, although if truth be told I haven't moved much in the past couple of years. I like it round here.

The *Griffin* was an acquisition I made during my days at the detective agency. It was a high-profile divorce case. The wayward husband was Gary Budmore, the soccer pundit and commentator who was maintaining a clandestine relationship with a Soho lapdancer named Marlene. His wife had hired me to gather sufficient evidence for her to take him to the cleaners in court. Such was her anger at his indiscretions, she also decided to sell her story to the national press so as to publicly humiliate him.

It was one of the easiest jobs I ever had to do. Mrs Budmore, Cheryl, gave me the exact location of the *Griffin* and the exact time to be there. The curtains were even left sufficiently open for me to take a perfect shot of Gary Budmore, ankles up by his ears, his young mistress kitted out dominatrix-style and thrusting a greased riding crop up his arse while holding a bottle of amyl nitrate to his nose. It was not a flattering portrait and definitely not one that he would want splashed all over the *News of the Screws*. As I had the photographs, I called the shots and rang Budmore to let him know of my scoop. Understandably, he didn't seem to care much about the proof of adultery: it was the riding crop and the amyl nitrate that bothered him. It all fell into place perfectly. Budmore agreed to give me ten grand and the *Griffin* in exchange for the photographs. As part of my obligation to his wife, I also made him agree to pose for some straightforward snogging shots with his lapdancer. In the end, everyone was happy – the *Screws* had its story (albeit a watered-down one), Cheryl Budmore had her proof of adultery and the newspaper exposé, Gary Budmore managed to keep the full extent of his sexual proclivities out of the public eye and I had the ten grand and the *Griffin*. A job well done.

I climb aboard the fruits of my conniving mind and, first things first, I need pain relief. I swig down three Nurofen with some week-old red wine and stick my head under the cold tap. Assuming the role of the invalid, it's off with my clothes and straight into bed where I make a soft plinth for my head with the pillows, lie back into it and shut my eyes.

There's something wrong but I can't work out what it is. I'd intended to sleep for hours, days if possible, but all of a sudden I'm wide awake in the middle of the night with the unsettling feeling that something's just woken me. But what that something is I haven't a clue. I used to have a recurring nightmare in which I had murdered someone. The actual murder was not in the dream, just the horror of what I'd done. It made waking up the most wonderful feeling, a sudden lifting of an unbearably guilty weight. For a moment back there, it was the same. I felt wonderful, like it had all been a dream, until I realized that it hadn't.

The wind's picked up and sends ripples across the surface of the canal to beat against the *Griffin*'s hull but it's not that that's woken me. I've lived on the canal long enough to recognize the origin of all its sounds. I can, for instance, just from the sound of a boat's engine in the distance tell whether it's a canal boat or a cruiser. But what I'm hearing now is neither. It's not mechanical and yet there's a constant quality to it that suggests an engine of some sort. Whatever it is, it's getting closer and I'm afraid.

I jump out of bed, pull on jeans and T-shirt and venture out through the hatch. The sound is much clearer out here. It's coming from the canal itself rather than the towpath or surroundings. It's an animal, an animal growling. There's a dark, flat object, I think it's a door, floating towards me through a triangle of light thrown onto the surface by a nearby street lamp. There's something on it. It's a small dog and as it approaches I can see that it's the Jack Russell staring right at me. So this is a joke, OK, like some cheesy TV personality's going to step out of the bushes and present me with an award for playing the fall guy and how we'll laugh about it with the studio audience in a couple of weeks time when it goes on air and I'll be thanked for being such a good sport. Come on, for Christ's sake, let it be a joke, let the past two days be a joke, I swear I'll be the best fucking sport of them all.

The gun's in my jacket which is below deck. But then, shooting at the dog might not be a great idea as it's dead already and if it isn't dead then I've really lost my marbles. Or maybe that should be the other way around. Whatever, the gun stays where it is. Now that the dog has eye contact with me, its growl intensifies and when it draws level it starts barking, going crazy. Though I'm none too conversant with the physical capabilities of dead Jack Russells I derive some consolation from the fact that if it were alive, it'd never make it across the gap between us.

The wind blows the dog past me and I watch it go. Even when I can see it no longer and I've gone below, I can still hear it barking and, as I throw myself on to the bed, the barking breaks into a howl. This is horror-movie territory and I don't like it. It's just not credible, for starters: as a messenger of doom, a Jack Russell is not the dog of choice. I can't see how he got the gig. For this sort of work you need something big and menacing like a Dobermann, not an ankle-biter. But the little bugger's putting his heart and soul into it, that's for sure, and I for one am scared.

Sleep comes easily, too easily as though I'm sucked into it: although it bears all the characteristics of sleep, I'm conscious of it being a medium for something else. When I awake some eight hours later, I feel anything but rested. Fucked-up and paranoid would be more like it. There's only one thing for it, I'll go see Joyce. If she can't calm me down then no one can.

She has the best houseboat on the canal, well, the best I've ever been aboard. Although I'm a relative newcomer to the canals of London, I can't believe that there's many better. It's like a haven from the outside world, like a warm red womb. It's everything I need right now. What have I got to do today, anyway? I might as well spend the day with Joyce.

Joyce was born on VE Night and reckons she absorbed the atmosphere of the celebration. Certainly no one enjoys a party more than she does. She grew up in the

East End. Her father counted Ronnie and Reggie as close personal friends. She worshipped her father and often reminisces of the excitement she felt at getting up in the middle of the night to accompany him in his van to the Kent coast to collect contraband from where it was dropped on the beach. She was never happier, she tells me, than sitting next to him in his van as they motored along the early-morning roads. His business was 'exotic literature', a fifties euphemism for soft porn, which usually came in the form of what were known as dirty books. Joyce was an avid reader and, despite her father's attempts to dissuade her, she read literally hundreds of these books that, as she grew older, became more and more graphic in their descriptions of the sexual act. By the mid-sixties the books had given way to magazines in which people humped each other in glossy colour. Her father supplied Soho with its best under-the-counter titles. In the early seventies, he moved into films but, this being the era just pre-video, these were tricky to distribute and he hit hard times. What made him decide to give up the porn industry altogether was that one day, while checking through a batch of recently acquired Dutch movies on his home projector, he came across Joyce, his little princess, slurping on a big dick.

Some years before, Joyce had joined a troupe of dancers. It was not a conscious decision to break into show business: she was having an affair with the choreographer of the troupe who, in an attempt to avoid the suspicion of his wife and colleagues, claimed that he was nurturing her dancing talents. Joyce decided to go along with the subterfuge and, being an OK dancer, joined him on a European tour. Within a couple of months, the relationship had soured and when the show reached Amsterdam she left him but decided to stay on in the city. She found herself a job dancing in a club. Before long she was stripping and from stripping, for Joyce at least, it was only a short ideological step to performing in a live sex show. Her chosen partner in the imaginatively entitled Real Fucking Show was one Maurice Benson, a merchant seaman who had recently gone AWOL in Marseilles and resurfaced in Amsterdam. At her suggestion they decided to take advantage of the burgeoning market in live sex. Maurice was somewhat reticent at first but the extra money and minor celebrity he accrued soon changed all that. They did three shows a night with Sundays off and gained the reputation for putting on the best live sex show in town.

Despite the gruelling schedule, Joyce's and Maurice's romance flourished and they got married. It was a quickie ceremony with no honeymoon as they couldn't get the time off work. They had to rush straight from the reception at their favourite coffe shop back to the RF Show where they consummated their marriage in front of a hundred-strong audience, many of them friends who had watched them exchange their vows earlier in the day. Joyce said that it was the best show they ever did and at the end of the extended set they received a standing ovation. Were it not for the risk of encroachment upon the performance time of the next act, Bangkok Betty's Ping Pong Party, they would have done an encore. It wasn't long, however, before they separated.

It was an important night for Joyce and Maurice because there was to be a well-known pornographic film director attending the Real Fucking Show, specifically to catch the three a.m. performance. They were excited, Joyce in particular, at the thought of perhaps being spotted and whisked away from the live sex industry into the movies which, although not Hollywood by any means, was a long way from grinding away night after night in front of a roomful of fumbling old men and pissed-up beer boys.

Unfortunately, during their midnight show Maurice slipped over and pulled a muscle, thereby putting himself out of action for what they'd convinced themselves was nothing short of an audition. To his horror, Joyce told him that, in the best showbiz traditions, the show must go on. He pleaded, he ranted and raved, he called her every name under the sun but it did no good. At three a.m. Joyce took to the stage with Marcel, the barman, who had long fancied himself a sex performer and was finally being given his shot at fame. Maurice sat in the audience and watched the whole thing. At the end, he stood up, limped out and Joyce never saw him again. The show, however, was a resounding success and she was indeed offered a part in the director's next movie.

Within a couple of years, Joyce had built a reputation for professionalism and enthusiasm within the industry, which meant that she was much in demand.

She worked with all the best leading men of the time and travelled extensively throughout northern Europe plying her trade. Many of the films she made during these years found their way across the Channel into the back of her father's van and it was with much regret that she discovered that he'd watched the opening scenes of one of her most notorious movies, *Penile Dementia* (1974), and had realized that the young woman bestowing her fellating skills on Hosepipe Eric was none other than his daughter.

In the late seventies, Joyce's position as one of the leading ladies in Europe was slipping as younger women, enticed with the promise of wealth and glamour, joined the 'circus', as she calls it. Rather than feeling jealousy towards them, as many would have in such a competitive world, she became a mentor to them, dishing out advice to the naive and comforting the distressed. To one girl in particular she became a saviour.

It was during the making of the movie *Beyond The Elbow* (1978) that Joyce became close to Natasha Bloch, her co-star. They were due to shoot a scene together with Thierry Blaupunkt, one of a new breed of actor/directors who were notorious for brutalizing their crew and cast and paying them as little as they could possibly get away with. Blaupunkt prided himself on never writing anything down, which meant that the screenplays for his movies were all in his head. Ideas for scenes and what dialogue was required were all off the cuff. He changed his mind constantly and often worked himself into violent tantrums when fellow actors could not follow his direction. He had a reputation throughout the industry for going beyond the bounds of common decency even by the standards of hard-core pornography and he made it clear at the start of shooting *Beyond The Elbow* that this was to be his most no-holds-barred movie to date.

With the money he'd made from his previous movies, Blaupunkt had shunned the trappings usually associated with successful porn-film directors and had opted for a lonely existence on a farm outside Cologne where he bred German Shepherd dogs. It was one of these that he brought along to the first day's filming. No one thought much of this as he was rarely seen without one by his side and Joyce thought nothing of his request that Natasha apply a specially prepared body lotion, which she did before awaiting further instructions. The dog became increasingly agitated by the smell of the lotion and when Thierry let it off its lead it went berserk, threw itself at Natasha and tried to mount her. It was clear from the reaction of the crew and from Blaupunkt himself – who urged on the animal – that this was the lotion's desired effect. It was left to Joyce to save the poor girl. She pulled the dog off Natasha by his bollocks, took the girl by the hand and, amidst the howls of the frustrated dog and Blaupunkt's furious rantings, led her away.

After this, Joyce's heart was no longer in the job and a couple of movies later she retired, returning to London for a tearful reunion with her father who was by now running a second-hand-furniture business in

Stepney. She lived with him until his death three years later and then bought the *Porcupine* where she's lived to this day, working on her memoirs entitled *Up The Boulevard*. Whether this tome will ever see the light of day remains to be seen: twelve years into the project, she still hasn't finished the first draft. Nonetheless, she gets up every morning and works at her laptop until lunchtime. The only occasion when Joyce is anything other than her usual charming self is when her precious writing time is interrupted. Fortunately, today being a Sunday I am assured of a warm welcome as she doesn't write at weekends.

'How's your life?' she asks me as I take a seat opposite her in the cabin. I run through the usual trivia, avoiding the events of the last couple of days, of course. She knows that I work for Mar Kettle and although I've never been reticent in telling her about any aspect of my life, such is her skill as a listener, I feel that now is not the time to confess to my murderous escapades. Tea is served, as it always is at Joyce's place at any time of the day or night.

'So what about you, Joyce, what you been up to?'

'Nothing much, working on the book as always, watching lots of television, reading, looking after the little horrors.' These are her cats, Pauline and Roger. 'Had some friends around last night for dinner. I called for you but you were doing your detective number, I shouldn't wonder.' I nod. 'You could have saved me from Frank. That man's an octopus.'

Frank Molloy is a fellow canal-dweller who, being a pornography aficionado, immediately recognized

Joyce when he first met her. They subsequently became friends but Frank is obsessed with her past.

'I keep telling him that my sex life is a closed book, that I haven't been interested from well before I even finished making the films but it just doesn't seem to sink in. He sees me as this nymphomaniac who wants to jump on every dick in sight. He doesn't seem to realize that these days I'm more interested in putting my feet up with a good book than getting laid. He doesn't seem to realize that I'm an old woman.' This is Joyce's one concession to vanity: she refers to herself as an old woman even though she's only in her early fifties and looks ten years younger.

'You're not old, you're young and beautiful and you know it.' This is a standard exchange between us and she loves it.

'Oh, you.' She flicks a tea towel at me.

'Joyce, nothing strange has happened here in the past couple of days, has it? No unexpected visits or anything?'

'No, why?'

'Oh, nothing, really.'

'"Oh, nothing, really"? You might as well say there's a mad axe-wielding maniac on the loose and he's heading this way. Honestly, you watch too much television. Now spit it out, what's wrong?'

Fuck it, I've got to tell someone and it might as well be Joyce, my mother-confessor. I've never been able to bottle things up.

'Something's happened, Joyce, and I really don't

know how to cope with it. You know what I do for a living?'

'Yeah, you think you're Columbo or something.'

'I'm being serious.'

'God, you are, aren't you? Sorry, love. You work for that old bird, don't you?'

'I do, well, I used to, until yesterday, that is.'

'What happened?'

'I quit.'

'What made you want to do that?'

'It wasn't the work, that was easy as you know. It's just she asked me to kill someone.'

'That's as good a reason as any, I suppose.'

'The thing is, I did.' Her smile freezes. 'But, unfortunately, I killed the wrong man.'

Now's the time, I suppose, that I should break down, rant, sob, tear my hair out. But I can't, not even with Joyce who is perhaps the one person with whom I should. I should let it all out and she'd listen. But it's as though by so doing, by accepting it and allowing emotion and grief to enter in, I wouldn't be achieving some sort of catharsis so much as casting myself into the abyss. There'd be no coming back.

'You're a right one, you are. Killed somebody! Next you'll be telling me that your mad mate Luke is standing for parliament.'

'I'm not joking, Joyce. On Friday night I killed a man. It was a case of mistaken identity.'

'You *are* joking.'

'God, I wish I was.'

She laughs nervously, waiting for me to break the

façade, to join in, to admit that I'm faking. I maintain a deadpan expression and her laughter stops. She puts her head to one side and looks at me. In her gaze I can see a complete reappraisal of my character, like she's looking at me for the first time.

'I'm as shocked about it as you are. It hasn't sunk in yet,' I go on.

'Are you going to tell me about it?'

'Do you want me to?'

'I think you'd better.'

My brain's on autopilot and I tell the story right from the start. I listen to myself as I'm talking and it doesn't even sound like me. I try to modify my voice but that just makes it worse.

'. . . And then he opened the door. I just presumed it was him. After all, he was the right age and the right nationality. I wasn't expecting anyone else, least of all an elderly Moroccan who wasn't Hassan Nazar, and seeing as he was about to club me with his cane I shot him.'

She listens to me intently and it occurs to me that perhaps I shouldn't be telling her all this, that I might be putting her in danger by doing so. But the urge to confess is too powerful to contain.

'. . . So the Jack Russell bit him in the leg . . .'

'This is the *dead* Jack Russell, I presume?'

'Yeah, that's right.'

I can't believe what I'm saying but I press on anyway, bringing her right up to date, right up to the moment when I stepped aboard the *Porcupine*.

'And that's it,' I finish.

Against all the odds, she chuckles and shakes her head.

'You know what your problem is, young man? You've been working too hard. I've seen this before, you keep pushing yourself on and on and before you know it you're losing your grasp on reality. What you need to do is take some time off and take stock of what you want to do with your life. You don't want to be working for some mad old woman. She's making you ill. All this business about bumping people off, it's not healthy.'

'Joyce, it's the truth, believe me.'

'Look, I wasn't going to mention this but I know you're no stranger to drugs.' I try to butt in but she raises her hand and continues, 'I'm not saying that it's wrong. God, you don't think that me of all people would be puritanical about these things. I didn't live in Amsterdam for all those years without partaking of mind-altering substances. I've probably smoked enough grass to turn me into a bush. But tell me, what have *you* taken in the past few days?'

'Acid, ecstasy, cocaine and grass but . . .'

'There you go! What more proof do you need that it's all in the mind?'

'Joyce, it's not the drugs, this is real.'

She moves closer, puts her hand on my shoulder and says, 'Just listen to yourself for a moment. All this business about ghost dogs and curses, it doesn't make sense, it's all fantasy.' She kisses me on the cheek with such motherly warmth and reassurance that I want to believe her. 'It's all in the mind.'

'I hope you're right, Joyce. Nothing would make me happier.'

'You've quit your job, or at least you think you have, so take the week off, lie around, do nothing, watch television, listen to music, do whatever you want. I'll be here to look after you. Trust me, everything'll be fine.'

Sounds good to me. In the face of adversity, do nothing. A great principle to live by. I know my story doesn't make sense. I know I'm wrapped up in something way too freaky for me to try to mentally digest it so I might as well switch off. There's no point proving to Joyce that what I've told her is true. She's dealing with my account of events within her own frames of reference, those of a sane rational person.

'Maybe you're right, maybe I should kick back for a few days and recuperate.'

'Of course you should.'

It feels good to resign responsibility for my actions. I settle back into the rich red velvet of the seat and finish my tea. Joyce asks me if I would like to stay for Sunday lunch and the thought of her roast chicken with roast potatoes, parsnips, peas, carrots and gravy is impossible to resist. She does a great Sunday lunch.

In the distance, a dog barks.

5

The Laughy Woman starts to choke. For the past five minutes, her laughter's been out of control but now it's seemingly taken on a life of its own and sounds as though it could kill her. Now that *would* be funny. I can just see the headlines: *RADIO LAUGHY WOMAN CAROL BOLLOCKS* – or whatever her name is – *LAUGHS HERSELF TO DEATH LIVE ON AIR.* Ever the consummate professional, Titch takes control of the situation, makes a big deal out of slapping her on the back and goes straight into the jingle for Titch's Triffic Trips. I've been holding the receiver to my ear for so long now that it's slippy with perspiration.

'OK, Carol, it's time for you to choose who will take part in the first round of this week's Titch's Triffic Trips in association with the Grape Escape, for swift relief from the pain of haemorrhoids.' I always wondered when Titch and his producers would prostrate themselves before the gods of corporate sponsorship and I'm glad that they've attracted a company that so aptly embodies their broadcasting profile. 'We have ten callers on the line, Carol, and, as always, it's up to you to pick the lucky two – if you've quite finished choking to death, that is.'

'Ha ha haaaa! Thanks, Titch, well now, let me see' – the Laughy Woman likes to milk this bit for all she's worth – 'all these lovely listeners, it's just so hard, Titch.'

'That's what they all say, Carol.' Great, now we have to endure thirty seconds more of the Laughy Woman laughing her fucking head off. I consider hanging up but I've never got this far before so I might as well see it through.

'Oh Titch, you're terrible, you really are, you've made me blush.'

'Come along, Carol, we can't keep them waiting.'

'OK then, I think I'll go for number seven and number one.' I'm number one. My fingers tighten around the receiver. This is it.

'Number Seven,' says Titch, 'tell us all about yourself.'

'Well, Titch,' says Number Seven, 'my name's Graham, I'm from Braintree in Essex and I'm a warehouse manager.'

'Hi, Graham, and welcome to Titch's Triffic Trips.'
'Thanks, Titch.'

'And now, number one, tell us who you are, where you're from and what you do.'

I've got to lie. I can't let Titch know who I am: he's

bound to remember me from school and that won't do my chances any good at all. Memories of being called 'No Balls' for seven years will come flooding back to him and I'll end up answering questions on astrophysics.

'Hi, Titch, I'm Derek from Camden and I'm a magician.'

'A magician?'

'Yes, kids' parties and so on.'

'Excellent, Derek. Well, welcome to the show and good luck.'

'Before you go on, Titch, I'd just like to say that I'm your number one fan.'

'Good on you, Derek.'

'Thanks, Titch.'

He smarms his way through the rules and we're into the first question: 'Graham, who hosted *University Challenge* before Jeremy Paxman?'

Piece of piss.

'Erm, I suppose I should know this but I don't watch much television.' Graham is one of those radio quiz show contestants who constantly excuse themselves for their ignorance. By the time he's explained that he prefers board games to television, I'm pretty sure that I'm on to a winner. But then, as if from nowhere, he blurts out 'Bamber Gascoigne' and I realize that Graham could be one of that even rarer breed of radio quiz show contestants who appear to be dullards, 'um' and 'ah' and gibber away and then get everything fucking right.

'Derek from Camden, tell me who was married to

the actress Sharon Tate who was brutally murdered by the Manson Family?'

Now I know this. I once read *Helter Skelter* but for the life of me I can't remember the name. I can picture the guy. He's a small Polish film director who was subsequently banned from the US for sleeping with an under-age girl. This is typical. I've come so far. I've got through on the phone, I've managed to be chosen, I'm on the show and now I'm all set to fall at the first.

'I'm going to have to hurry you. You'll kick yourself, you know.'

He's wrong: I'd much rather kick him.

'It was Roman Polanski. Bad luck, Derek.'

I swallow the expletives hurling themselves up my throat and say, 'Of course.'

'OK, Graham, you're one up. Next question, who played the Boston Strangler in the film of the same name?'

He'll never get this, not a chance. He sounds like the sort of guy who maybe goes to the cinema once a year with his kids to watch the latest Disney but, just as I'm looking forward to erasing the Roman Polanski nightmare, he blurts out, 'Tony Curtis.'

I'm two-nil down and gutted.

'Derek, there's all to play for now.' Titch acts serious, trying to instil a sense of tension in the minds of his listeners.

'Who wrote the classic spy thriller, *The Day of the Jackal*?'

'Frederick Forsyth.'

'Correct.'

Two-one.

'OK, Graham, this is your third question. Get this right and you're through to tomorrow's game. Here goes: name the leading man and the leading woman in the film *Gone With the Wind*.'

I'm done for. Only a resident of another planet or the terminally stupid would get this wrong.

'Vivienne Leigh and Cary Grant.'

'You're sure about that, are you, Graham?'

'I should be, it's one of my favourite films of all time.'

'Well, Graham, I'm afraid you've got it wrong. It was Clark Gable, not Cary Grant.'

I can't believe it. A totally cinch question and he's blown it. I ready myself for my third question which will pull me level when Graham goes through an on-air character change, growls 'Fucking wanker,' and slams the phone down.

Titch is fazed by this, I can tell. He puts on a record. Tina Turner. Things are bad. As the final bars of 'Steamy Windows' fade out, he says, 'I'd like to apologize to all our listeners for that outburst from our previous contestant and I'd like to congratulate Derek the magician from Camden for winning this morning's first round on Titch's Triffic Trips in association with the Grape Escape for swift relief from the pain of haem-orrhoids. Same time, same place tomorrow, Derek?'

For a moment, just for the hell of it, I'm tempted to go down the same route as our man Graham, sacrifice my chance of winning the competition and call him a cunt just to really upset him. But I don't. Instead I say, 'Cheers, mate,' like the usual sort of cretin who phones in to radio quizzes.

'That was Derek, a magician, of all things. Hey, Carol, it must be handy to be a magician, don't you think?'

'Why's that, Titch?'

'You can make people disappear, like your mother-in-law.'

The Laughy Woman's forced cackle belts out from a million radio speakers. Titch, you fucking kill me. A woman comes on the line, takes my number and tells me that I'll be called at 8.55 in the morning for the next round. I thank her and replace the receiver. After seven years of listening to Titch Allcock, I've finally made the grade. Luke will be delighted as Titch's Triffic Trips holds a special place in his it's-so-bad-it's-good hall of fame. I give him a call to tell him the news. But all I get is his answer-machine message which informs me that he's been involved in an appalling industrial accident and has thereby been rendered incapable of coming to the phone or indeed lifting the receiver and that should he pull through after extensive corrective surgery he will try to return the call. I'm surrounded by comedians. I try him at work but I know it's pointless as he hasn't graced the offices of Wow Man Smell My Finger Records before noon for years. No reply. I try his mobile but most of his mobiles just ring wherever he happens to have left them the night before. This time, however, I'm in luck. He answers.

'Luke, it's me.'

'Hi, man.'

'Guess what?'

'What?'

'I've just made it through to the second round of Titch's Triffic Trips.'

'Oh.' There's something wrong. He should find this hilarious.

'Cool, huh?'

'Yeah.'

'What's wrong?'

'I dunno.'

'Where are you?'

'I'm in Alexandra Park.'

'Have they found the body?'

'That's not why I'm here.'

'What are you doing?'

'I'm not sure.'

'Luke, go home and I'll meet you there as soon as I can.' He sounds strange, sort of distant. I get dressed and make for the Beamer.

Twenty minutes later I park up outside his flat. He opens the door like an automaton. His face is pale and glazed with sweat.

'You look as sick as a dog,' I tell him once we're seated.

'Funny,' he blurts out in response.

'Luke, what's the matter?'

'I wish I knew. Look.' He pulls up the right leg of his jeans to reveal the bite wound inflicted on him by the Jack Russell.

'Healing nicely,' I say.

'Yeah, too nicely.'

'What do you mean?'

'I was only bitten two days ago and already it's almost completely healed. Now, listen to me for a minute and don't interrupt. Last night, I started to feel totally fucking weird, like I'd never felt before. At first I thought maybe it was the flu or a fever of some kind so I went to bed. But when I got to sleep, all I kept dreaming about was dogs. It drove me up the wall, so this morning I got up and thought it might do me some good to go for a walk in the park. I was still dizzy and feeling weak so I didn't go far. I ended up sitting on a bench. There were people around, some of them with dogs and I found the dogs totally mesmerizing, like my entire being was reaching out to them. One of them ran up to the bench where I was sitting. It was a black Labrador, I think, and before I knew what I was doing, I was on my hands and knees, with this intense desire to sniff its arse. Man, I think I'm turning into a dog.'

I think I should find this funny but Luke looks far too distraught for me to laugh at him.

'I presume this dog you're turning into is a Jack Russell, is it? Sort of like a werewolf, only a Jack Russell instead?'

'I suppose so.' He stares at me, checking for any signs of laughter in my face like he knows I can't take this seriously. It takes a gargantuan effort to maintain a deadpan expression but what saves me is the memory of the Jack Russell floating past me on the door the night before last.

'You realise how totally off the deep end this sounds, don't you?'

'Tell me about it.'

'Don't you think maybe you're in shock or something? Look, the other night, you witnessed a killing and, accident though it was, you were very frightened as well as being totally whacked out of your nut. Don't you think this dog business is all just a figment of your imagination? OK, so you were bitten by a Jack Russell. But it was a living, breathing, leg-cocking, arse-sniffing Jack Russell. It's upset you, it's set you off on a weird train of thought but you've got to get a grip.'

'Listen, man.' He's getting angry now but, behind the anger, I can tell that he's shit-scared. 'I've taken a few drugs in my time, I know what it's like to get seriously out there but what's happening now is *real*. Something seriously weird is happening. You've got to find this Hassan Nazar bloke and make him stop.'

'It's not that easy.'

'Why not?'

'I've quit the job.'

'Fuck the job, do it for me.'

'And if he won't stop?'

'Well, kill him. You're the fucking hit man.'

'I'm not killing anyone else. I am not a murderer. Now I've told Mar Kettle to shove her job and I'm leaving well alone. If all this is to do with Hassan Nazar, as you're so sure it is, then it's just illusion and you've got to fight it.'

'Oh, so that makes everything all right, does it?

Well, just excuse me for a moment while I cock my leg against the sofa and give my bollocks a good lick. I don't care who he is or what he is, you got me into all this shit and I suggest you get me out. Now, kill the bastard.'

'Sardinia,' says Gavin from Chertsey.

'I'm sorry,' says Titch, 'it was Sicily. Which means that Derek, the magician from Camden, is today's winner on Titch's Triffic Trips. How do you feel, Del boy?'

'Great, Titch.'

Tuesday morning and I'm through to the next round.

First call of the day done. Next one: Mar Kettle. Well, if I am going to snuff out Nazar, I might as well get the money. The phone rings. I've rehearsed my speech and it goes like this: 'Hello, it's me,' – no pause, no chance for a tirade of abuse – 'I'm back on the case. I was scared back there, I'll admit, but now I'm OK and I'll finish what I've started. The deal's the same, a hundred grand cash on delivery.' A brief discussion will ensue and I plan on finishing off with something like, 'Rest assured, he ain't gonna make it.' But there's no reply. This is a first. It could be that she's so paranoid by now that she's given up answering the phone. But I'd better investigate anyway, especially if I want my job back.

I dress and take a look in on Luke who's fast asleep in his bed. I stayed over at his place last night. He was afraid of being left on his own.

Ten minutes later, I'm winding my way down

110

Highgate West Hill in the Beam Machine, doing about forty, when a Morris Minor driven by some retired schoolmaster by the looks of him pulls out of a side road straight in front of me. Now, I don't like being a miserable bastard when I'm driving, I'm not one of these road-rage types, especially when confronted with a classic machine like the Morris Minor. But he's in my way and I'm in a hurry so, despite being on a blind bend, I drop down into third and floor it which sends me roaring past him. I'm level with the old boy now and I momentarily glance over to see him hunched forward, his knuckles white on the steering wheel.

I turn my attention back to the road just in time to see an old Rover two-litre bearing down on me, desperately trying to decelerate amidst screeching brakes and plumes of burning rubber. I'm about one and a half seconds away from certain death. Unless I take drastic action, I'll be smashed to pieces against the imploding interior of the Beamer as the two cars consummate their high-speed marriage in an orgy of twisted metal. The driver of the Rover, a middle-aged guy in peaked cap and driving gloves, stares at me aghast. We're so close now I can see not just the whites of his eyes but the blood vessels within the whites of his eyes. Only a combination of engineering excellence and supreme driving ability can save us now. I've got us into this mess and I'll get us out. He should be thankful it's me and no one else.

I swing the on-side wheels onto the pavement and as he disappears between me and Mr Chips, wondering what strange god is watching over him, problem number two presents itself, namely a lamp-post. This is solved with an expert tweak of the powered steering which flips me back into the line of oncoming traffic where I'm staring down the barrel of problem number three, namely an *Evening Standard* delivery van. I can tell immediately that the driver's one of those kids who rates himself a bit tasty behind the wheel and won't give an inch to another driver, especially a lairy bastard in the wrong lane.

There's no taking to the pavement this time. Two teenage girls are coming through a garden gate unaware of the potentially catastrophic scenario unfolding only feet away. Seemingly oblivious to all this, Mr Chips trundles along to my left going just fast enough to prevent me braking and cutting in behind him. I'm boxed in like a turtle's pecker. Taking what at first glance appears to be the most reckless course of action, I accelerate, thereby fazing Mansell in the *Standard* van into slamming his brakes on, giving me just enough time to cut back in. This goes beyond driving: this is physics, this is psychology.

One minute you're cooking in your own juice and the next you're cruising along in the sunshine, elbow resting in the door frame, pedal to the floor, with Titch Allcock telling you to 'Keep it tidy till tomorrow' and handing over to Micky Miller on the mid-morning show.

All is quiet outside Mar Kettle's place. I wait for the lift and check the concrete around it for interesting graffiti. *FUCK YOU YOU FUCKING FUCK* is written in red spray paint above the lift doors, and to the left of the lift call button *GOREFEST*, in metallic green. Nothing else of note, just the usual shits, fucks, cunts, bollox and homeboy crew names. The doors open just as my eyes catch some scribbled lettering on the plastic button for the top floor. I have to go right up close to read it. It says *Tangier 1956.*

'Somit the matter?' enquires a voice from behind me.

'Sorry,' I say and step into the lift where I'm joined by a fat bloke with a square bulldog head and tattoos up his arms that disappear beneath an oily T-shirt.

'What floor d'ya want?' he asks.

'Top one, please.'

He presses twenty-three and then twenty-two.

'Live here, then, do ya?' he asks.

'No, I'm just visiting.'

'Thought so. Never seen you before. Know her, do you?'

'Who?'

'The old bird on the twenty-third.'

Mar Kettle has always told me that her presence in the building is a closely guarded secret and that no one, least of all the other residents here, know of her tenancy on the twenty-third floor. I decide to play it cagey and tell him, 'I'm here on business.'

'What line of business you in, then?'

'Insurance.'

'Really?' He looks me up and down. 'Let you wear jeans these days, do they?'

'Yeah, it's a new policy. What line of work are you in?' I ask.

'I'm an artist.' He grins and nods as though daring me for the punchline.

'A piss artist?' The grin twists into a grimace.

'What you saying?'

'You know, I'm an artist, a piss artist. It's a joke.'

'You having a go at me?'

'No, I thought you were joking.'

'You're all the fucking same.'

He moves towards me. He's a big bastard. I pull out the Smith & Wesson and point it at him. The balance of power shifts. He's watched enough movies to know what to do. He backs away and raises his hands. I need to say something, though. You don't just point a gun at someone and keep your mouth shut. I need some dialogue. The doors open on the twenty-second floor.

'If you don't get out of the lift, I'll shoot you dead. Once I've done that I'll find out where your family lives and shoot them as well and although you're ninety-nine per cent certain I'm bluffing, it's that one per cent that is too unbearable to contemplate, that one per cent that'll make you get the fuck out of this lift.' He's frightened, I can tell, but his fear is mixed with aggression and I can see he's weighing up his options, working out whether he can make a lunge, cover the six or so feet between us, wrestle the gun from me and beat my brains out. Thankfully, he decides against it and steps out.

One floor up, the doors open but no Archie. Now this *is* strange. Archie always meets me at the lift door and, seeing as I'm probably not flavour of the month around here at the moment and I'm holding a gun that will have been picked up on the secret camera in the lift, he should be standing here pointing his gun at me. I try the door and, considering it belongs to a security-obsessed control freak, the unthinkable happens: it opens. It's dark inside and warm like someone's breath. The urge to run away is enormous but if I am to be in Mar Kettle's employ, which I suppose I must be, then I'd better face up to this problem. If she's still alive, that is. After a couple of nights' rest and abstinence from alcohol and drugs my paranoia has subsided and, all things considered, I might as well try and kill Nazar. I see the reasons for this as follows:

1. He's a murderer, so it's an eye for an eye, sort of.
2. I've already killed one man, so what's another?
3. I'm out of work, with somewhat less than excellent employment prospects. If I kill him and by so doing save Mar Kettle, at least I still have a job.
4. There's always the possibility that he'll get bored and just bugger off.
5. I could do with the money, not because I'm poor or anything: it's just I could do with it.

With the gun pointed into the darkness, I take a couple of steps down the corridor. The silence is intense. I run my fingers along the wallpaper and, a few steps further on, they find a light switch and flick it down. Nothing happens. The only sounds I can hear are the faint sounds my shoes make on the cheetah-skin carpets and the tom-tom beats of my heart.

It makes no sense. A reclusive old woman like Mar Kettle doesn't just up and leave. She hasn't even been outside for over fifteen years. Where would she go? This business with Nazar has got her scared, I know, but not enough to run away. This place is her fortress, her safe haven. So, if she hasn't left, she must have been abducted. But why would her abductor turn off all the electricity at the mains? Perhaps she hasn't been abducted at all but just murdered: any moment I'll stumble over her body and probably Archie's as well. But again, why the lights? There's only one other explanation. It's a trap.

This newly realized possibility stops me dead in my tracks. If it *is* a trap, there's only one course of action that makes any sense and that is, get the hell out of here, like fucking now. Before I can even turn around to begin my sprint back down the corridor, the lights go on. Think fast: if someone is aiming at me my best bet is to make myself as difficult a target to hit as I possibly can.

I drop to the ground and, as I do so, there's a shot. I'm showered in plaster as a bullet thuds into the wall just above my head. I can see him at the end of the corridor. He's stocky with a GI haircut and a grey suit. He lowers his aim and fires again. But his second shot hits the floor as he's already crumpling up from the bullet I've put in his stomach. My second bullet hits him in the chest and flips him over onto his back. By the time I've stood up and walked over to him, he's staring at the ceiling with dead eyes.

He's a good-looking guy, looks like a film star, but I haven't got time to study his appearance as I'm not out of danger yet. Behind me, a revolver is cocked and I spin around to see Archie standing in a doorway pointing his Smith & Wesson at me. Not to be outdone, I point mine at him and we stand there, not ten feet apart.

'Neither of us is going to miss from here, Arch, so who goes first? I reckon if you shot me I could get one off before I died so there's not much point playing this game, is there? Besides, I'm not here to kill you, I'm here to talk to Mar Kettle.'

'She doesn't want to talk to you.'

'She doesn't even know why I'm here.'

'For Christ's sake,' shouts Mar Kettle, appearing behind Archie in the doorway. 'Both of you put your guns down.'

'Before I put my gun down,' I say, pointing at the body on the carpet, 'I'd like to know who the fuck that is.'

'Who that *was*, you mean. Well, I'll tell you who that was: that was your replacement.'

'Why was he trying to kill me?'

'He was doing his job. Just think about your recent behaviour. First of all you murder one of my lawyers, then you have an attack of paranoia and tell me to stick my job, leaving me at the mercy of Hassan Nazar. Then you come up here uninvited, waving your gun around. Marcus said we should turn the lights out and ambush you and, to be honest, I agreed with him.'

'But I called earlier and there was no reply.'

'You must have got the wrong number.'

'Don't you think it more likely that Nazar engineered the whole thing? Like he did with your lawyer? Making him come to your house in Hampstead at the exact moment that we arrived. Like he's using me to carry out his dirty work?'

'I think it's more likely that you're using him as an excuse for your own ineptitude. Stop and think for a moment. That's the second person you've killed in the past few days. Before last Friday, you'd never even held a gun.'

'I watch a lot of television. Listen, I want my job back.'

'Why the sudden change of mind?'

'I need the money.'

'And you think it's still on offer?'

'Well, you want him dead, don't you? And there does appear to be a vacancy all of a sudden.'

'I suppose you're right.'

'Hundred grand?'

'OK. But you take this body with you and come back with Nazar's.'

'It's a deal.'

I put the gun back in my pocket but Archie, probably to prove a point if nothing else, keeps his trained on me for a couple of seconds more.

'Come on, Archie, pop it in your handbag and help me with the stiff before he bleeds all over the carpet.'

Hitman

I grab the arms and, for the second time in three days, I'm carrying the body of a man I've shot dead.

'You're looking good today, Arch,' I tell him as we put the body down outside the lift doors. And he does, like he really made an effort. His hair, or rather his wig hair is arranged in ringlets and his make-up is more delicately administered than usual, looking as though it hasn't been applied by the nine brutal fingers of a six-foot-three ex-skinhead.

'Knew him, then, did you?'

'Who's that, then?'

'Well, who do you think? Laughing boy here.'

'Yeah, I knew him.'

'What was he like, then?'

'He was all right.'

This stings me. In the parlance of two men talking, even if one of them's wearing a body stocking and high heels, 'all right' means that he was, well, all right, as in 'an OK guy'. We load him into the lift.

'And her Moroccan lawyer, did you know him?'

'Yes.'

'What was he like?'

'He was a cunt.' The lift stops. The doors open and standing there is the fat bloke from the twenty-second floor, a man whose family – himself included – I threatened to shoot not ten minutes ago. He's holding a shotgun and, by the looks of him, he's going to use it. I reach for the Smith & Wesson but the hammer snags on the lining of my pocket. The shotgun barrel is less than three feet away and pointed right at me. There's no time to be afraid. The mechanics of my death are set

119

in motion. The fat bastard pulls the trigger and there's a deafening explosion. I'm thrown back against the wall of the lift. Every nerve in my body trembles in preparation for the feeling of the lead from the shotgun cartridge tearing me in half.

Nothing happens. Perhaps this is what is feels like to die. Perhaps one of the strange anomalies of death is that you don't feel the actual wound that kills you. As the smoke clears, I can see that Archie has pulled the barrel of the shotgun down so that Marcus's body at our feet has taken the force of the blast. Another shot follows as Archie fires his revolver into the fat bloke's face which collapses in on itself as he tumbles over backwards. Within seconds, the floor inside and outside the lift is awash with blood. If it weren't for Archie, most of that blood would be mine.

'Archie, you big beautiful bastard, you saved my fucking life.'

'Don't bother about that now, grab a leg.'

We pull the fat bloke into the lift and place him on top of Marcus before descending once more. My ears are ringing and my entire head feels as though it's been pumped full of smoke but fuck it, I'm alive. Archie stares grim-faced at the two bloody corpses at our feet.

'You'd better get rid of them both,' he says.

'Don't suppose you could help me?'

'I'll help you to the car but then you're on your own.'

I'm so freaked by the events of the past few minutes that I wouldn't care if he told me that the best means of disposal for the bodies would be to eat them. The lift reaches the ground floor, the doors open and thankfully there's no one there.

'We'd better hurry up and get them into the car,' says Archie. 'I'll need to get back inside to clean up the mess before anyone sees it.'

'Can I keep the shotgun?'

'Do what you like.'

I lay it across Marcus's chest and drag him to the car. Archie drags the fat bloke. Both bodies are bleeding heavily and we leave trails of blood across the grass and along the pavement.

Now there's one thing I hate and that's mess in my car. But it's broad daylight, there's people around and I've no other option but to put both stiffs in the boot. I can clean up later. We have to position them so's they're embracing in order to get the boot lid shut. I sling the shotgun onto the back seat and jump behind the wheel. Archie is walking back across the grass towards the tower block. I lower the window and shout after him, 'Oi, Arch.' He turns to face me. 'Ironic, isn't it, not ten minutes ago you were about to kill me and just now you saved my bacon.'

He rolls his eyes and walks off. I watch him go, tottering across the grass in his high heels, and notice there's a lump of something bloody, most probably flesh or bone, stuck to the side of his blond wig.

With a stamp on the accelerator, I'm off. Almost immediately I want to shout out of the window, such is the nervous tension I feel. I love an adrenalin rush, especially one brought on by a near-death experience, but I've never come so close before and the rush is proportionately massive. I need a big crowd. I head for Oxford Street, probably the biggest crowd I can muster at this time of day.

It's beautiful, man and Beamer as one. What others might consider risks, situations where the odds on survival narrow, are for me just moments for increased concentration so as to ensure that, should there be an area of potential danger, I am obeying my own intricate laws of momentum to move away from it rather than towards it. I turn up the radio, lower the window and let my arm hang out, the Smith & Wesson dangling from my fingers in the onrush of air.

Baker Street and up ahead there's some traffic lights at a crossroads. I'm going to jump a red light just for the hell of it. I'm not even in a hurry to get anywhere. A silver Porsche is moving off to my right. Unless one of us drastically alters our trajectory, it's certain collision. Well, it ain't going to be me. I take a shot at his wheel and, although I miss, the bullet hits the bodywork with a metallic pop that lets the driver know in no uncertain terms that I'm using his car for target practice. He slams on the brakes, allowing me to cruise by through the red light, inches from his bumper.

I take a left onto Oxford Street. I've never been involved in a police chase before and this is bad timing, with bodies in the boot, an overdose of adrenalin in my head and blood all over me. I can hear the sirens wailing in the distance and I know they're coming for me. To make matters worse, I stand out like a sore thumb. Up and down Oxford Street there are black

London taxis, red London buses – and me in a silver Beamer. I point the gun at the sky and fire off a couple of shots. People cower in shop doorways, others just stare. But most continue on their way either ignoring me, thinking that it's all pretend, which I suppose it is, or not registering what's going on at all.

'Hi there, folks. Just thought I'd take time out from my busy schedule to let you know that you're all gonna die. You're all on your way out. All about to shuffle off this mortal coil. There you are, going about your sad little lives, spending your money, bolstering your fragile existence with worthless tat. Well, I'm here to tell you that you might as well give up now and prepare for the big dirt bath. Cry, wail, gnash your teeth, do anything, but don't wander around buying crap that you never even wanted in the first place. You're all going to die you worthless motherfuckers!'

Past Oxford Circus, towards CentrePoint, and I get caught up in a line of traffic. Swinging out from behind a bus, I lunge forward into the oncoming line of cars, then cut right a couple of feet in front of a police car barrelling towards me in a strobe of blue light. I throw the Smith & Wesson on the passenger seat. Let the chase begin.

The streets are busy, full of tourists and Soho darlings. I floor it and the Beamer reaches thirty within seconds, way too fast for the narrow streets. Up ahead, I can see a police car turn off Old Compton Street and make towards me. I hang a left into Soho Square and nearly run down a young guy who's wheeling around some film cans on a porter's trolley. I spin the Beamer around the gardens, tyres screaming, and point her down Greek Street. My pursuers are just normal traffic police, handy with a Ford Sierra but not the heavy boys. Those guys will no doubt be on standby by now. You can't go around shooting at cars in central London and not expect the cavalry.

I make a lucky couple of turns, then hang a left on Shaftesbury Avenue. I've shaken off the patrol car. But this is no time for complacency and all the way up Charing Cross Road I'm on the look out for tell-tale blue lights. Nothing. Tottenham Court Road, nothing. Over the Euston Road and up Hampstead Road and the lack of police is beginning to worry me. Where are they?

Then I hear the whirring of rotor blades, so I open the sun roof – and there's the helicopter, tracking me from above. I'm in the shit right up to my eyeballs. What the fuck was I thinking? The Beamer may be a supreme machine but it's no match for a helicopter. Just as my self-belief starts to take a pounding and I think I'm done for, an idea comes to me. I pull over to the kerb just before Mornington Crescent Tube station, snatch the shotgun from the back seat, push it through the sun roof and, just as the helicopter swoops low to hover above me, I fire off a shot at its exposed underbelly. Whether I hit it or not is anyone's guess but it moves off sharpish, leaving me to slam the Beamer into gear and floor it up Camden High Street.

I can hear sirens in the distance but if I can just make it to the lock-up in time, then no one will be any the wiser. I execute a near-perfect entry beneath the still-elevating door and with it closed behind me and the engine killed, I sit in the dark, blood hammering in my ears as I frantically run through a mental checklist to work out the implications of my ill-fated excursion through the West End. All they have on me is the registration number of the car, which will lead them not to my door but to the door of one Raymond Burgess who drives an identical silver Beamer with this registration. I did some work for him when I was at the detective agency. His daughter had run off with a New Age traveller who went by the name of Chunder. Burgess, a cockney wanker dripping in gold jewellery – his Beamer was his most tasteful possession – was beside himself that his little princess had got wrapped up with a 'wrong 'un' who spent most of his time holed up in makeshift tunnels at proposed runway extensions or ring roads. He lent me his car a couple of times to visit his daughter at the various protest camps in which she was residing with Chunder and I fell in love with it, so much so that a year later, when Mar Kettle offered me a car, I knew what I had to have and bought the Beamer.

On a hunch, however, that one day I might need some cover from the law I decided to alter the number plate – and what better number plate to use than that of Mr Burgess? Change the plates and I'm in the clear. Even when they realize that Burgess hasn't been shooting at other cars in Baker Street, that in fact he wasn't even in the area at the time, and then they trace the owners of all other similar silver Beamers and come up with me, I'll just deny everything. Fuck 'em.

*   *   *

125

'Derek from Camden, you're through to tomorrow's round of Titch's Triffic Trips. How do you feel?'

'Carol, I feel marvellous.' I know we've got plenty of time left as I got every question right first time without a second thought: who played the sergeant major in *It Ain't' Arf Hot, Mum*? Windsor Davies; who was the female presenter of *Tiswas*? Sally James; and why did Stationmaster Simpkins leave *Dewdrop Junction*? He was hit by a train. There's plenty of time for her to carry out a bit of self-promotion, engage me in a bit of mindless banter (so she thinks) and plenty of time for me to take the piss (without her realizing). Glenda, the hospital porter from Esher, has said her goodbyes, having got not one question right, and the Laughy Woman and I have the airwaves to ourselves while Titch goes for a piss or something.

'So you're a magician, aren't you, Derek?'

'That's right, Carol.'

'Do you enjoy it?'

'I love it, Carol, I really do. It may not be the best-paid job in the world – I'm no David Copperfield – but the looks on the faces of those kids when I pull a rabbit from a hat, well, it's pure magic, it really is.'

'Ah, that's lovely.' She's dying to laugh at something, I can tell. She's itching for me to throw her a line she can sink her laughy teeth into. I feel it's my moral obligation to screw it up for her good and proper.

I lower my voice, as though welling up with emotion, and say, 'The thing is Carol, I do a lot of kids' parties in hospitals and it really hurts when kids I've got to know and started to care for—' I throw in a little sob here, as though I've broken down, '—don't pull through.'

She doesn't know what to say, she's totally stuffed. There's not a laugh to be had for a million miles. I've handed her a ton of lead and now she's got to run with it. There's dead air for a moment while she composes herself and then she tries to summon up compassion with the same zeal that she does laughs.

'Well, Derek, that's a tough one, that really is, but then at least you can think that, while those children were alive, you brought some joy into their otherwise tragic lives.' Fuck it, that's not a bad reply from the queen of the banal and before I can think of a worthy response, we're straight into 'Hello' by Lionel the singing horse.

Two days left and, if all goes well, it'll be a Triffic Trip for me.

Now, what to do with the stiffs in the boot of the Beamer? I call Luke. There's no reply. I try his mobile. Nothing. I call Mar Kettle's. Archie answers.

'Hi, Arch, it's me.'

'What do you want?'

'Whatever happened to all the butler stuff, all the "Good morning, sir" and all that?'

'Get on with it.'

'I was wondering if you had any suggestions regarding those bodies.'

'Didn't you get rid of them yesterday?'

'I had a little run-in with the police, nothing serious, but I had to lay low for the rest of the day.'

'Why don't you just tie some weights to 'em and chuck 'em in the river?'

'Someone's bound to see me if I throw them off a bridge.'

'Well, don't do it off a bridge, then. Go somewhere quiet, like Docklands. There's plenty of places there where you could chuck 'em in without being seen.'

'Right you are, Arch.'

I make for the Beamer.

At the garage, I quickly change the number plates, then head east. Somehow the Beamer isn't handling right. I didn't notice it yesterday, I was so charged up, but now it's preying on my mind. For starters, it's the weight. Two fully grown men and one of them a real fat bastard pushing down on the rear axle makes a noticeable difference to the Beamer's handling. Now, your average driver may not notice it – but then, I'm not your average driver and this is no average car. Maybe a few extra pounds per square inch in the rear tyres would help. But then, it's probably not worth it, seeing as my cargo's only making a one-way trip across town. I could put them in the back seat, distribute the weight better, but that would be none too subtle. And besides, there's the upholstery to consider.

By the time I make Docklands, my train of thought switches to questions of morality regarding the dumping of stiffs in old father Thames. Don't get me wrong, I'm not one of these green activist types who wouldn't drop a sweet-wrapper on the pavement, but two stiffs, biodegradable though they may be, represent something of a health hazard. It's a conscience thing but

I mustn't let it spoil my day. After all, what's a spot of river pollution compared to cold-blooded murder?

I turn off the main road at East India Dock and head between rusting warehouses to a promontory that juts out into a mooring basin. There's no one about. Archie was right.

I throw open the boot and, as I'd expected, there's plenty of blood but thankfully it's dried. Nothing that a good vacuum-and-valet won't put right. Now, I need something to weigh the stiffs down when I put them in the water and, luckily, by the side of one of the warehouses there's a pile of housebricks. I fetch some. The fat bloke weighs a ton. I manage to pull him into a sitting position in the boot and hoist him over my shoulder in a fireman's lift. My back's never been in great shape and now it feels as though it might crumble under the weight. I totter over to the water on jelly legs and lay him down on the concrete by a low wall. I stuff bricks into his pockets and stick a couple down the front of his trousers. Thankfully, Marcus is much lighter. I stuff some bricks down his shirt to make sure he sinks.

Just as I'm pondering whether I've used enough bricks, I hear voices approaching from around the corner of one of the warehouses. I have to move fast. I start by rolling the fat bloke onto the low wall so's I can just let him drop into the water. Looking over my shoulder I see two figures moving towards me backwards from around the warehouse. One of them is holding a film camera and the other, obviously the sound man, is holding the microphone boom. A couple of yards behind them is a young woman who's sobbing violently. I push the fat bloke off the wall and he hits the water with a splash. Thankfully, they're so intent on their filming that none of them look my way. I reach for Marcus and, as I do so, I hear one of the men say in an American accent, 'OK, cut, that'll do for now.' I pull Marcus onto the wall and roll him over backwards into the water. He breaks the surface with barely a plop. When I look round, I see the cameraman put his camera down and walk towards me. I shut the boot and reach for a cigarette as a prop for my hastily constructed act of nonchalance.

'Hi there,' he calls to me.

'Hi.'

He holds out his hand. 'My name's Howard Martin.' We shake hands. 'As you can see, we're making a movie here. It's a little low-budget thing that we've been putting together for a couple of months now. We're from Columbia University in New York.'

He's so fucking American. I've never had much to do with Americans before, not in the flesh. I've lived with them on the television all my life but it feels kind of weird to be talking to one. Only I'm not talking to him really, as my ears are tuned in to the sound of bubbles breaking the surface of the water behind me. If only I could talk, then perhaps I could mask the sound.

'So what sort of film are you making, then?' I begin as an uprush of air blurts out of the river. He doesn't notice or doesn't appear to.

'It's kind of experimental. What we're trying to do

is create a mood within the film that will draw the audience into a state of complete desensitization to the sort of violence we're subjected to every time we switch on the television or visit the movies.' Another huge fart erupts from the water and he pauses, leans to one side and tries to take a look over my shoulder. I lean with him so that my face blocks his view. He continues, 'Once this is done we then totally disorientate the audience by introducing a scene that is in direct contradiction both thematically and emotionally to the rest of the piece, a scene shot through with the grief and sadness of a young woman whose lover has been gruesomely slain. So what we're doing is drawing the audience into a state of mind where they're revelling in dehumanized Hollywood violence and then we turn on them with a scene of such poignant human tragedy that they'll come away from the experience questioning the very fabric of modern cinema itself. Well, that's the idea, anyway.'

'Hey, what's that in the water?' The actress has joined us and is pointing over my shoulder. Panic-stricken, I turn around. Thankfully, both bodies have sunk under the weight of the bricks but there are strings of bubbles rising from them.

'Well,' I start with an air of authority, 'there are a number of explanations as to the source of the bubbles. The most likely is that there's a shoal of fish down there. Despite years of appalling pollution, fish are flourishing here once more. Then again, the bubbles could be caused by any number of chemical reactions going on on the river bed.'

I've got the pair of them nodding at me. But just as I'm about to think up another spurious explanation the cameraman approaches and, in a deadpan drawl that sends a chill down my spine, says, 'Of course, they could be coming from a corpse that's been dumped in the river.'

I turn to face him and he stares at me, expressionless. I freeze, fearful that any movement or statement will give me away. Then, just as I feel myself blushing, his blank expression breaks into a grin and he says, 'Hi, my name's Alex. You must excuse me, I always look for the sinister in everything. I'm a compulsive conspiracy theorist.' We shake hands. He introduces me to the actress. 'This is Darcy, she's more likely to think that the bubbles come from some monster of the deep.'

'Yeah,' says Darcy, her tombstone teeth chewing bubblegum, 'I love all that shit, ya know, Loch Ness and all.'

I can't think of anything to say. She's beautiful, I'll give her that, but it's a sort of plastic beauty, like you could stick your finger into her cheek and pull away a hunk of synthetic skin to reveal wires and circuit boards beneath. She finds me interesting for some reason and, as the other two busy themselves with their equipment, she smiles and asks, 'So, what are you doing here?'

'I just decided to go for a drive. It seemed like a nice day for it.'

'So what do you do when you're not driving around London all day daydreaming?' She smiles as she says 'daydreaming' and I smile back. 'I'm a hired killer,' I tell her. She throws her head back and laughs.

'Seriously, now.'

'OK, I act a little.'

'Oh, really?'

'Yeah, I haven't had much regular work recently but I did a TV commercial a couple of months back.'

'That's great. What was it for?'

'A new quality dog food.'

She's laughing again.

'Hey, do you work for the company or something? Like, not just a dog food but a new *quality* dog food. That's great.' She puts on a bad American English accent as she impersonates me.

'How long have you been here?' I ask her.

'Coupla days. I'm not really an actress, I'm studying to become a film editor. I'm putting this thing together with the guys and we can't exactly afford to pay professional actresses, especially on location.'

'How come you're on location?'

'Howard's dad works for the government, the US government, that is, in London. It's the CIA, if you ask me. He gets us cheap flights and an apartment to stay in so we thought that, seeing as everyone else was doing their thing in New York, we'd do something different and come here. Hey, Howard,' she calls over, 'don't you love this guy's voice? Maybe he could introduce the next scene. You see,' she says, turning back to me, 'each scene is introduced by a different person. It can be anybody we meet, like the janitor of our apartment block or maybe the maître d' of the restaurant we're in or even a bum on the streets. But the thing is that at the start of the movie the introductions are honest, like what the person says is going to happen actually happens. But later on, when we start turning on the audience and throwing it all back in their faces, what's contained in the introduction to the scene and what actually happens in the scene can sometimes bear no relation to one another, thereby disorientating the audience still further.'

I can tell by the way she looks at me that I'm meant to be impressed by this, so I shake my head and make a 'Wow' face.

'So waddaya reckon, Howard?'

'Reckon to what?'

'To – sorry, what was your name?'

'Erm, it's Derek.'

'To Derek here introducing the next scene.'

'That's cool with me.'

'Alex?'

'Fine.'

'So waddaya think? Wanna go at the part? As a favour to us?'

'Yeah, why not?'

They set up their equipment while I smoke another cigarette.

'What sort of character am I supposed to be for this?' I ask, just for something to say.

'You can be who the hell you want to be,' says Darcy. 'It's kind of free-form, you know what I mean?' She takes a sheet of paper out of her file and passes it to me.

'OK, let's go.'

'Don't I even get a chance to read it first?'

'No, that's all part of the fun. If we let you read it first, you'd read it differently than if we just got you to read it straight off. We live and die for spontaneity.'

'OK, action,' says Howard.

I begin: '"Her lover dead, she drags herself through the streets of Old London Town. She's wept so much that her entire being is numb. She's reached the bottom of the pit. There's nowhere further to fall but hope is futile nonetheless. There is no light at the end of the tunnel, just more of the same, more horror, more bullets, more death. It has to be this way because she's made her decision, made her choice and there's no turning back. The killers will be killed. She will kill them."'

'OK, cut. That was great, Derek. Bravo.'

'You don't you think I could have put more feeling into it?'

'No, it was fine, it had just the right balance of realism and melodrama.'

'So what happens?'

'To the woman?'

'Yeah.'

'Well, first of all we wrote it that she tracks the killers down, finds out where they live, arms herself to the teeth with every weapon she can lay her hands on and then gets run over on the way there, thus turning on its head the typical Hollywood denouement of good triumphing over evil. But then we changed it so that she arms herself to the teeth, finds the killers and then falls in love with one of them, forgives him for killing her lover and ends up marrying him. Which ending do you prefer?'

'The first one.'

'Oh well, you win some, you lose some.'

'What's it called?'

'We don't have a definite title at the moment. Its working title is *Kiss It Worse*.'

'Nice.'

'Sure is.'

'Well, I'd better be on my way. Plenty of daydreaming to do in my car. Thanks for my first film role. I'll be in touch when you're the toast of Hollywood.'

'More like the scourge.'

'Whatever. Bye.'

'So long.'

I wave to Howard and Alex but they have their heads buried in their equipment and don't notice. I make my way back to the Beamer and drive off, two bodies lighter. I'm glad to be out of here, I've never liked it around here. It's a cliché to say it, I know, but there's no soul to this place.

'Now there's no extra points for this but I want to see whether you're a film anorak or not. Can you tell me what the film that documents the making of *Apocalypse Now* is called?'

'That'd be the one made by his wife.'

'That's the one.'

'*Hearts of Darkness*.'

'Correct. Derek, you really do know your stuff.'

'Thanks, Titch.'

'OK, it's one-all with all to play for. Now, Stephen from Camberwell, who starred alongside Richard E. Grant in the film *Withnail & I*?'

'It was one of the McGann brothers. I'll go for Paul.'

'Well, you'd be right to. Now, Derek from Camden, a television question for you and a tricky one, if you ask me. What sort of car did Roger Moore drive in the *The Saint*?'

'Volvo.'

'Correct. That's two-all. OK, Stephen, how did the lead singer of T Rex, Marc Bolan, die?'

'Was it choking on his own vomit?'

'It's an easy mistake to make, Stephen, and one that unfortunately means that, should Derek get this next question right, he automatically goes through to the next round. Marc Bolan died when he crashed his Mini into a tree. You're not telling me that you've never heard the one about Marc Bolan's last hit?'

'No.'

'Well, that's what it was.'

'What?'

'A tree.'

'Oh.'

The Laughy Woman belts out a couple of hoarse cackles in appreciation of the joke.

'OK, Derek, here goes. You realize that, if you get this question right, you'll go through into the final round of Titch's Triffic Trips and get your chance to win this week's Triffic Trip.'

'I do, Titch, I do.'

'OK, staying in the same vein as the last question, can you tell me how Sid Vicious died?'

'Thanks for the clue, Titch. Sid Vicious died from a heroin overdose.'

'Correct, Derek, you're through.'

Sadly I don't get a chance to chat with Titch or the Laughy Woman as they're running late and it's straight into the news. Last night, Joyce and I polished off three bottles of wine between the two of us and I'm feeling a little jaded. I know I should track down Nazar but I haven't got a clue where to start. He seems to have taken enough of an interest in me that one day very soon our paths must surely cross and, when they do, hopefully I'll be ready for him. Not perhaps the ideal way to carry out my job but it's the best I can do at the moment.

I'm about to nod off when something collides with the hull, sending a shudder through the *Griffin*. I jump out of bed and climb through the hatch to take a look. At first, I can't see anything. But as my eyes become accustomed to the harsh glare of daylight I can see that floating in the canal is a wooden door like the one the Jack Russell skippered the other night: it's resting against the stern. On top of it is a small wooden box that is intricately designed and, of this I have no doubt, Moroccan. I reach down and pick it up. Inside, there's a letter that I open. It reads as follows:

Greetings from North Africa. Despite our lack of formal introduction I feel I know you already. As you are no doubt aware, I visited your father some days ago. He is a charming old man and, if you don't mind me saying so, a little eccentric. We are of the same age and it was good to discover that we share similar outlooks on life despite the differences in our parent cultures. Men of a certain age share a belief structure that is underpinned by distrust of the young and nostalgia for the past. Your father and I fall into this category. We look back on times gone by when we were young men and through rose-tinted spectacles we see only the happy times. I don't know what knowledge you have of my personal history: I presume that your employer has divulged some basic if somewhat prejudiced views about me but I have spent the vast majority of my adult life within a correctional institute in Morocco. Thankfully, for much of that time I was in what you would term an open prison in the Atlas Mountains and, despite a certain lack of freedom of movement, I was able to enjoy the benefits of that most beautiful part of the world. Due to contacts within the government, I was allowed access to literature and the media. This was certainly not the arrangement for the average Moroccan prisoner. I was very lucky.

Again, forgive me if I am relating to you subject matter with which you are already familiar. But I have always been fascinated by the unseen forces of nature, what you might call sorcery or black magic, and, due to my enforced vacation from society for such a large portion of my life, I decided to make a thorough study and practice of the ancient Moroccan arts connected with it. Whilst there are people in Morocco who are far more adept at the ancient rituals than I am, I have become somewhat of an expert in certain areas.

I break off from reading the letter. Something's just occurred to me. The handwriting: it's mine. Not just a bit like mine, but mine, totally, down to the most minute detail that only I could identify. This scares me. Forget the fact that it's been sent to me floating down the river on an old door. That's just a cheap trick compared to this which is downright fucking weird. The old bastard is spooking me more than I thought possible. I mean, how's he done it? Where's he got a sample of my handwriting from, for God's sake? I take the letter below deck and continue reading it on the bed.

While for a number of years my intense desire for knowledge within this area was driven by a craving for revenge against my persecutor, namely your employer, this desire soon waned to nothing more than what you might term a grudge. My incarnation as a wealthy socialite in the hedonistic whirl of fifties Tangier had become so far removed from my life within the prison as to make it seem nothing more than a dream. Therefore I channelled my energies into making my time in jail as pleasant as possible. This would often entail dealing with problem elements within the prison such as fellow prisoners who had become aware of my former wealth and tried to extort money from me. Most of my persecutors were struck down with nothing more than a mysterious illness that would debilitate them for a few days. But others, who were more vociferous in their attempts at extortion, would find themselves struck down with more serious ailments. As I became more practised in my art, I could deal out curses like insults, quite often to terrible effect. I had to be careful, though, as curses have a curious way of rebounding and wreaking their mysterious havoc on their perpetrator. Likewise, they may find their way to a person altogether unrelated to the desired target. They're a gamble: you win some and you lose some. Personally, I have been relatively lucky or, forgive me if this smacks of conceit, skilful. But curses are only one of many tools at the disposal of a man who has mastered the art of altering events by the use of what you might term supernatural methods. Gradually, I found I could mould situations so that they developed in ways that were beneficial to myself. Indeed, I would have extricated myself from my confinement in the Atlas Mountains years before had it not been for the arrival of a man called Ali Shabbaz. Although a rough mountain-dweller who could not read or write, Ali Shabbaz was a man who was enormously in tune with the powers of the supernatural. He was what is known in Morocco as a Djeemadjalloon which means, literally, a mind demon. In return for me teaching him how to read and write, he taught me powers that I could never have believed before were possible. These were more often than not parts of ancient rituals practised over the centuries and handed down through a remote tribe of Berbers from which he came. He showed me that all life is illusion and that it is possible to control the flow and content of illusion. With Ali Shabbaz's help I began to master the techniques with which it is possible to project illusion into the consciousness of others. In time, I too became a djeemadjalloon. Allow me to give you a very crude demonstration of my powers.

I've reached the bottom of the page. I turn over. It's

blank. And then a word appears, rolling itself out in my careless handwriting:

Through what is nothing more than a cheap trick, you are now witnessing what I like to call the self-writing letter.

I look away, finding the sensation altogether too peculiar. There's a sudden stench of spices in the cabin, intoxicating, making my head swim. My eyes are drawn back to the line from which they'd fled moments before:

And, as you can see, you feel compelled to read on. I am unable to judge your point of view regarding such matters but this is what I call power. However, I am playing games. You must be wondering why I have written to you. I have two reasons. Firstly, I wanted to introduce myself to you and secondly I wanted to request that you desist from your misguided attempt to collect the bounty that your employer has placed upon my head. Although you pose no real threat to me, I find it unpleasant that one man should want to kill another for money. Your employer is, as I am sure you are aware by now, a very sad old woman locked away in her tower. It was she who was – and still is – the prisoner, not I.
I hope that you will receive this correspondence in the spirit that it is sent, namely as a gesture of friendship. And though it must also act as a warning, I bear no ill will towards you, despite your mercenary intentions towards me. Therefore, I bid you adieu and hope that we might meet at some time in the future under more cordial circumstances.

In anticipation of your compliance in this matter, I am,
Yours,
Hassan Nazar

For a finale, the letter bursts into flames in my hands and wisps of charred paper float away to settle on the carpet. As a warning salvo, it's pretty impressive.

I call Luke. His phone rings. It's picked up.

'Luke?'

There's someone there, I can tell.

'Hello?'

Nothing, then a strange gurgling sound. I dress and make for the Beamer.

From Camden to Muswell Hill in under ten minutes, something of a personal best. But this is no time for self-congratulation. I press the buzzer on the intercom and the door clicks open. I take the stairs two at a time. Luke's door is ajar. In the flat, all is quiet. I check the rooms one by one. Everything's in the usual state of disarray, crockery strewn across the furniture, ashtrays overflowing and, on the coffee table, a selection of drugs and drug detritus including a huge polythene bag of grass, a smaller bag of coke and various pills scattered among the cigarette papers, rolled-up tenners and pieces of torn cardboard. In the bedroom, the last room I try, there are more ashtrays and a half-finished bottle of Jack Daniels. Luke's nothing if not loyal to the staple diet of the rock 'n' roll wastrel. There's a half-smoked joint butt in an ashtray on the bedside table. I sit on the bed, spark it up and blow lungfuls around the room.

Aside from the traffic gunning its engines on Muswell
Hill outside, all is quiet. I wander around the rooms
as though I might have missed some clue as to Luke's
whereabouts. There's nothing. But *someone* let me in.
He's got to be here. There's only one place that he could
possibly be. I take the hook from behind the kitchen
door, open the trapdoor in the landing ceiling and
pull down the aluminium steps. All is dark in the attic
and remains so after I flick the switch. The bulb must
have blown but I don't have to worry about stepping
between the ceiling joists as Luke had floorboards put
down a couple of years ago in preparation for a subsequently aborted attempt to grow his own marijuana.
He was very serious about it all, had the lamps and
seeds sent over from Amsterdam, got everything insu-
lated, installed a hydroponic system, germinated the
seeds, loved and nurtured and worried over his seed-
lings – only to lose his entire crop one night, thanks to
a combination of power cut and loose roof tiles which
meant that his flourishing young plants fell prey to a
particularly virulent frost and died en masse.

He was so gutted he never bothered again and in the
light cast through the hatch through which I've stuck
my head I can make out all the equipment, still lying
around gathering dust. I'm about to return the way I
came, content that he's not up here either, when I hear
a shuffling and what sounds like a cough from the far
end of the attic.

'Luke?'

No reply. The noise must have come from next door.
I've got my foot on the top step of the ladder when I

hear a sound altogether more sinister and emanating – this time I have no doubt at all – from within the attic. It's a growl. Now, I'm no expert on the vocal inflections of predators but this sounds as though the perpetrator of the growl means business. I reach for the gun and have to check myself. I've only had the thing for a little under a week and already I make a grab for it at the first sign of danger. Besides, this is Luke, my best friend, and whatever's happened to him, there's no way I'd ever start shooting at him. Cursing myself for leaving the matches downstairs, I take another couple of paces down the attic.

'Luke?'

Another growl that rises in tone to an anguished howl. Enough of this softly-softly approach. I stride manfully to the end of the attic but before I can con-gratulate myself on my bravery Luke throws himself on me, teeth bared, roaring at the top of his lungs. Despite my anticipation of danger, his speed catches me unprepared and before I can even think of what to do, he's thrown me to the floor. I raise my hands but he's too fast for me. He pushes his face towards mine and I can do nothing to stop him. His breath is warm on my cheeks and reeks of alcohol. I make one last-ditch effort to push him off but it's useless: my trembling hands are no match for his mad canine strength and he turns his head to one side and presses his teeth against my neck.

So, this is it and in a way I suppose it's appropriate, all things considered, me being savaged to death by my best friend who thinks he's a Jack Russell. There's no point even reaching for the gun as it's in my jacket pocket and Luke's kneeling on it. But then, just when I'm resigned to my fate and preparing for the hereafter, nothing happens: no teeth crunching through flesh and cartilage, no warm blood swimming beneath my chin. Maybe I'm really dead this time. Then I hear crying, only it isn't crying, it's giggling. Then Luke lifts his head up and laughs in my face.

'That'll fucking teach you,' he says between breaths. 'You fell for it like a good 'un. It was Baz's idea and you took it hook, line and sinker.' From around the water tank comes a face I know only too well, a face that's stared out from countless record covers, magazines, billboards and scandalized tabloid articles, a face I've watched receiving the adulation of thousands of screaming fans, a face I've seen buried in a mound of cocaine, a face that's laughing at me now.

Baz is so famous, he is such a part of the pop fabric of the country that if he didn't exist it'd be necessary to invent him. He's a subculture in his own right. He's got the lot: the look, the voice, the hair, the clothes, the supermodel girlfriend, the epoch-defining off-the-cuff turn of phrase, the songs, the working-class Jack-the-lad drug-taking notoriety that sends the moral majority into paroxysms of envy and hatred and all of it synchronized at just the right moment in pop history. In the music business, he's every marketing chump's wet dream. And here he is, in an untidy north London sitting room on a weekday morning, cutting up lines of coke on the coffee table. That's the thing about the wealthy and famous, they can

146

get caned whenever they want. They don't work to anyone else's schedule.

'We used to live near this gypsy encampment,' he tells me, 'only these weren't your typical scrap-dealing gyppos, well, they were, they did deal scrap but what made them different was that they were totally sussed out when it came to all the traditions and rituals. They'd brought it over with them from some part of Eastern Europe or wherever they came from. They were into curses and all that, really knew their stuff and what they believed was that the only way to deal with having a curse put on you is to mess with your head, systematically derange your senses.' He bows his head over the coffee table and snorts up a line of coke, all in one fluid practised sweep. 'And this will, erm,' – sniff – 'neutralize the effects of the curse. So, my old mate Luke here who for whatever strange reason believes that this Moroccan guy is messing with his head has been following my advice and taking his medicine.'

'That's right,' says Luke, taking the rolled-up tenner from Baz, 'and already my cure is apparent. You ought to try it, man, you said yourself you thought you'd been cursed and the wonderful thing about all this is that even if he's wrong, even if the drugs make no difference at all, who gives a fuck 'cos it's fun to take them anyway. Hey, guess what?'

'What?' I enquire as Luke hoovers a line and passes the tenner to me, 'Gobshite are playing Brixton Academy tomorrow night. It's going to get announced tomorrow morning on Titch Allcock's breakfast show.'

'It's a warm-up for the tour,' says Baz, 'and a chance to try out some new material.'

'And what's more,' adds Luke, bouncing up and down on the sofa in excitement, 'we've booked the Gurning Mandibles as support. You know, that weird techno outfit that we saw last week. It'll be a top gig.'

No sooner have I snorted up my line of coke than Luke passes me a joint and I know for sure that it's going to be one of those days. And it is.

I was paranoid that I'd oversleep and miss the final round of Titch's Triffic Trips and I nearly did despite the bizarre carryings-on of Luke's alarm clock. A word about Luke's alarm clock. He bought it in Hong Kong and the alarm on it is a series of famous lines from Hollywood movies over the ages. So, for example, you might get woken by Clark Gable's 'Frankly, my dear, I don't give a damn,' over and over, or it might be Sean Connery repeating 'The name's Bond, James Bond.' Just now it was Jack Nicholson growling 'Daddy's home,' from *The Shining*. I pick up the phone, dial the number and I'm straight through to the Laughy Woman who isn't laughy at all when she's not on air and this morning has a cold who-the-fuck-do-you-think-you-are edge to her voice when I try to make pleasantries with her.

'It's been chaos,' she tells me. 'All the lines have been red-hot since we announced the Gobshite gig half an hour ago.'

'Oh, really.'

'The tickets sold out within two minutes of going on

sale and all the unlucky people who didn't manage to get one have been phoning up to complain.'

'They must be very popular,' I suggest.

'Derek, they're the biggest and hippest of them all,' she tells me in a condescending tone as though how could a square-bear magician whose nearest link to showbiz is a kiddies' party on a Saturday afternoon know about a phenomenon like Gobshite? The urge to tell her that I'm lying on a sofa not five feet away from the slumbering form of their lead singer is difficult to suppress.

'Now, Derek, I'm going to put you through live to Titch, OK?'

'Sure thing, Carol.'

'And now on line one we have Derek, the magician who has fought off contenders throughout the week to make it through to today's final. How goes it in the world of magic, Derek?'

'It's all tickety-boo, Titch.'

'Good stuff, Derek. Now, on line two we have the only man who can possibly stop you magicking away this week's Triffic Trip. OK, caller number two, what's your name and where're you from?'

'Good morning. My name's Hassan and I'm from Tangier.'

6

I'm driving like a lunatic. My usual brilliance of coordination is sorely lacking and I'm angry – which always makes dangerous driving that bit more dangerous, I find. What the hell is Nazar playing at? One minute I've taken him for a higher being, someone untouchable who I'd be mad to challenge, let alone try and kill; the next, he comes on the radio like some fucking Moroccan game show buff and snatches the victory that is morally mine from right under my nose. I just can't cope with it. He sent me the self-writing letter and I was impressed, I was prepared to back off and leave him to it. I was content that both family and friends were no longer in danger and accepted that if he wanted to wreak his revenge on Mar Kettle there was nothing I could do about it anyway. He convinced me that he was a reasonable guy, a man of honour and that I had nothing to worry about so long as I left him alone. So there I am, starting my new incarnation as an ex-hit man, indulging my passion for Titch Allcock and his crappy game show, and what does he do but steal my moment of glory. Well, that's it, I'll fucking kill him.

Even when I knew that it was Nazar I was up against, I still thought I could win. After all, bizarre psychic magician or not, he's spent the past forty years behind bars so he's hardly going to be up to speed on his pop culture. I was wrong. First question to him: who played JR in *Dallas*? Larry Hagman. Second question to me: who played Richard Burton's second-in-command in *Where Eagles Dare*? Clint Eastwood. One-all. Third question to Nazar: name the manager of the Sex Pistols. Malcolm McLaren. Easy fucking question but how does a man who's spent the best part of his adult life behind bars in Morocco know that? Fourth question to me: name the lead singer of The Stone Roses. Ian Brown. The fifth question was difficult: which sixties group starred in the movie *Head*? Now, I only know this because I watched it a couple of weeks ago with Luke but without hesitation Nazar says The Monkees and I know for sure that it's not personal knowledge that he's drawing on but some sort of mind-reading. Even so, I can't believe that he's going to snatch my prize away from me. We've declared a truce, or at least I thought we had. This could be just another show of strength to frighten me off but when it comes to the crunch, he won't actually steal what's rightfully mine. That would be a transgression of everything that he claims to hold dear. I'll just have to hang in there, I thought to myself and everything will turn out right. Then the horror really set in as Titch, who was brimming over with feigned excitement, asked me, 'Who wrote *Catch 22*?' Now this is a book I've read, a book I've loved but all I want to say is William Golding. I know it isn't William Golding, it's no more William Golding than it's Enid fucking Blyton but I've got a blockage in my Joseph Heller synapse and it just won't come.

'Derek, I'm sorry but I'm going to have to put you out of your misery.' Titch lowers his voice to a whisper as though this will make it easier to bear and says, 'It was Joseph Heller.' The Laughy Woman interjects with an 'Oh no, Derek,' and Titch decides to give me a damned good proverbial kicking now I'm down.

'That's the thing about Titch's Triffic Trips, Derek, you can go all week getting every question right and just at the last moment, just when you think you're there, when you're happy in the knowledge that you're going to pack your bags in readiness for your Triffic Trip, another contender comes along and on his first day steals it from you.'

I was so close to telling him the truth, that I wasn't called Derek, that I wasn't a magician from Camden that I was in fact the kid from school who called him Allcock-and-No-Balls and took the piss out of him mercilessly. But all I could do was mutter 'Cheers' when he told me that he was going to send me a Titch Allcock breakfast show T-shirt as a consolation prize. Jesus, that galls me, that I thanked him for his fucking T-shirt when I should have told him to shove it up his arse where it belongs. And that was it. I was unceremoniously dumped off air and some gum-chewing kid took my name and address and asked me what size T-shirt I wanted. Stunned, I put the phone down and turned up the volume on Luke's tuner until I could hear the Laughy Woman congratulating Nazar.

'Well done, Hassan, that was one of the most tense finals we've ever had. Do you get to listen to the show much?'

'No, this is my first time in London but I have enjoyed your show so much this week that I felt that I had to enter the competition today. I must say that Derek was a great competitor and I am sorry that he had to lose so that I could win. I hope that he does not bear me too much malice.'

'Oh, I'm sure he doesn't. After all, someone's got to win.'

'Yes, that is the nature of life.'

'And now, the moment we've all been waiting for, the moment when I can reveal to you your Triffic Trip, and let me tell you, Hassan, I don't know if you're a great fan of pop music but this is a cracker, it really is. Are you excited?'

'I am.'

'Well, as you are no doubt aware if you tuned in earlier on, there's a very special event taking place tonight and you're going to be a part of it because, Hassan from Tangier, tonight, as a special guest of the Titch Allcock breakfast show, a limousine will pick you up from your hotel and take you south of the river, down into deepest darkest south London to

154

the world-famous Brixton Academy where you will see Gobshite, the world's coolest rock 'n' roll band live in concert at a very special one-off warm-up to their forthcoming world tour. But that's not all, because after the show, you're coming to the backstage party with myself and Titch where you can meet Baz and the boys. How do you feel about that?'

'I am very happy.'

'Isn't it fabulous?'

'It certainly is.'

In the ten minutes since I left Luke's, I've wrestled with the following explanations for Nazar's behaviour:

1. He's an evil bastard, knows how dear the competition is to me and wants to upset me any way he can.
2. He's completely mental and doesn't know what he's doing.
3. He knows I'm going to the Gobshite gig anyway and he feels that this would be a good place for us to meet and cement the friendship that he tried to instigate with his letter.
4. He entered the competition in good faith not realizing that Derek the magician from Camden was me and just happened to win.
5. It's not the same Hassan Nazar.

At present, I'm wavering between numbers 1 and 3 and will most likely plump for a combination of the two. Either way, at least he's supplied me with a time and a place for the hit.

But as of a moment ago, I've now got more pressing matters to attend to, namely the blue lights flashing in my rear-view mirror. I'm in the mood for a serious tear-up through the streets of north London but it would only mean that I'd have to change the number plates again once I'd shaken them off, *if* I could shake them off, that is. I'm not feeling particularly lucky today and besides, I might just see what they want first. It could be that they saw me take a late red at the last set of lights. It could be they just want to give me a bollocking and leave it at that. It doesn't feel like a tense situation, just a Metro trailing me for a couple of hundred yards, a few silent turns of the blue lights and a single flash of the heads.

I pull over but realize I've cocked up when I catch a glimpse of my face in the rear-view mirror. Not only are my eyes shot to pieces, displaying the excesses of the day before in their livid blood vessels but my two-day beard and bone-white pallor give me a shifty look. I quickly check the interior of the Beamer for incriminating objects and there, resting against the front passenger seat, is the shotgun with which I carried out my helicopter target practice the other day. This is not good. A policewoman steps out of the Metro and walks towards me. I give the shotgun a shove and it falls between the seat and the door.

'In a hurry?' she asks as I lower the window. She looks like a gym mistress, all rosy cheeks and broad shoulders.

'Yeah, I'm late for a meeting, I'm sorry.' I try a

reassuring grin but I suspect that it just makes me look more guilty.

'Could you step out of the car, please?'

We stand facing each other. She looks as though she could have me cuffed and in the back of the Metro in a couple of seconds if I give her the slightest provocation.

'Is this your car?' she asks.

'Yes, it is.'

'Who's your meeting with?' Now this I hadn't expected. Who is my meeting with? Certainly not a mad old woman who's paying me to kill a problem Moroccan.

'My solicitor,' I say.

'That's handy,' she says. I let out a chuckle in the hope that she's joking. But she's not and the grin withers on my face.

'May I take a look in the boot?'

Instead of turning around and legging it, which is what I feel would be the appropriate course of action to take under the circumstances, I nod, take the keys from the ignition, walk to the rear of the Beamer and open the boot. It's caked in dried blood from which a musty, metallic smell rises. The Smith & Wesson's in my jacket pocket and could be out and pointed at her in half a second if needs be. She looks inside. Her partner steps from the car and peers over at her but doesn't seem to care much, like this is the last in a long line of cars that he's stopped this morning and he can't muster any enthusiasm for the job in hand.

'What's all this?' she asks gesturing at the dried blood. My hand moves towards my jacket pocket.

'It's mud.'

'Mud?'

'Well, compost, to be exact. I had a sack of it in there and it burst. It's a bugger to clean.'

Against all the odds, this satisfies her curiosity and she starts admonishing me about the speed I was going, giving me the usual number about being dangerous in a built-up area. As she's doing this, matey boy comes to stand next to her and peers into the boot as well.

'What's this?' he asks.

I'm about to give him the compost bullshit in case he missed it first time around when I see that he's holding up a set of false teeth that are smeared with what is quite obviously dried blood. I think fast but nothing comes. My brain's just too addled after yesterday's twelve-hour binge. There's nothing else for it. I pull the revolver from my pocket and point it at them.

'Get in.'

'Put the gun down,' she says.

'Get in the boot of the car or I'll shoot you both.'

The policeman hesitates, perhaps hoping that there might be someone around who might raise the alarm.

'Come on, Sherlock, get in the boot.'

'There isn't room for both of us.'

'Yes, there is, if you both hug each other.' They climb in and lie together in an awkward embrace. I take their radios, slam the boot, get back in the car and drive off. Worried that they might be able to trace me because of the radios I throw them out of the window and watch them in the rear-view mirror as they shatter on the road. The Beamer's handling is affected by the extra weight, as it was with the stiffs, but there's no time to worry about that now.

The burning question is, what do I do with them? The easiest solution would be to kill the pair of them and dump their bodies. Up until a few days ago, the thought of stuffing two policemen in the boot of the Beamer and disposing of them would never have crossed my mind. But now, it's almost viable. Almost, but not quite, thank God. Filth or not, I could never kill them. I'm a hit man, for Christ's sake, not a murderer. I'll just have to let them go and cover my tracks as best I can. It'll mean another set of number plates and, if I want to be really safe, I'd better consider the unthinkable and lose the Beamer, at least for a while. I can sort things out once I've got my hands on the hundred grand which, since this morning's revelations on the radio, seems somewhat more feasible.

For the first time during this whole saga, I know the exact time and place of my hit, namely this evening at Brixton Academy. In theory, nothing could be simpler. I go there, find Nazar and shoot him. I won't worry about the exact details now: as always, I'll just see how events develop and act accordingly. It'll be easier then. I can go abroad for a while and lie low until the heat dies down.

I phone Luke to ask his advice about my cargo. What with his Jack Russell delusion and all, I haven't confided in him much recently. I figured it'd be too much for his addled mind to cope with.

'Luke, it's me. I've got a question for you. What would you do if you ended up with a policeman and a policewoman in the boot of your car and you had to get rid of them?'

'They're alive, yeah?'

'Of course they're alive.'

'Well, since you turned into Dirty Harry, for all I know they could be riddled with bullets.'

'Well, they're not.'

'How the fuck did they end up in the boot of the car? Or shouldn't I ask?'

'Don't.'

'Well, why don't you have them strip naked and leave them somewhere?'

'What good will that do?'

'Well, it'll slow them down for starters and it'll teach them a lesson for becoming rozzers in the first place. Take them to a multi-storey car park, drive them to the top level and leave them there. By the time they get down in the buff, you'll be long gone.'

Sounds like a good idea.

I turn into a multi-storey carpark off the Marylebone Road and drive up to the top level. There's no one around, just a couple of Fords and an old Merc. I throw the boot open, point the gun at them and tell them to get out and strip.

'What do you mean?' asks the policeman.

'Just do it.'

'Me as well?' asks the policewoman.

160

'You as well.' They start to unbutton their jackets. 'Come on,' I tell them, 'I haven't got all day.'

'You realise there are security cameras in all multi-storey car parks these days,' the policeman tells me. I nod, pretending to be totally unfazed by this information while inside I curse myself for listening to Luke.

'You might as well give yourself up,' says the police-woman.

'Shut up.'

'We can make a deal with you,' says the policeman.

'I said shut up.'

Once down to their underwear, they stop and stand looking at me.

'And the rest,' I tell them.

When they're both naked I tell them to throw their clothes over the concrete parapet. They bend down to pick them up and it must be because I'm not concentrating but the next thing I know the policewoman has pulled the truncheon from her pile of clothes and cracked it across my hand. I drop the gun. The policeman makes a lunge for it but I kick it away just as the policewoman cracks me on the side of the head.

The pain is so intense I want to curl up in a ball but I have to move fast or else I'm done for. The policeman tries to rugby tackle me but I manage to step out from his grasp and I'm about to reach the gun when the truncheon comes down once more on the back of my head. The pain is such that I feel sure I'll black out but my fingers reach the handle of the gun. As my legs crumple and I fall to the ground I manage to twist

161

around and point the gun at the policewoman who stands over me, the truncheon raised above her head. My vision's fucked, everything's gone fuzzy but I've regained the advantage. She backs away. I push myself up onto my knees. There's shouting nearby. The policeman's leaning over the parapet, yelling to someone in the street below, probably another policeman.

'Mur way tom air.' Fuck it, I can't even speak. Get a grip, concentrate. 'Moof ayway from tear.' He's still shouting. I let off a shot at the wall next to him and it does the trick. Not only does the policewoman drop the truncheon and back away but her colleague stops shouting and turns around with his hands in the air. I try to stand but end up slumped forward on the concrete. There's nothing else for it, I'll just have to crawl to the car.

They look ludicrous, standing there naked. She's got a fine body, toned and muscular, but he doesn't look like he's taken any exercise in the last ten years. The fat hangs off him like a rubber boiler suit.

'Yer luck soo foonay,' I tell them but they don't share my amusement. Can't they see the funny side, for Christ's sake? I pull myself up against the Beamer and become consumed by a fit of giggles that makes the tears roll down my cheeks.

I know I'm concussed, I know I've probably got no more than about two minutes to get the hell out of here but I just can't help myself. Once I've got the door open I slump into the driver's seat and open the passenger window just so's I can tell them, 'Ya maka ma laf, ya rally da,' and my screwed-up speech sets me off laughing, so much more so that now I'm howling.

The sound of police sirens brings me to my senses and, though still giggling, I wave bye-bye to my two naked chums, start the engine, slam the Beamer into reverse, execute the most reckless but nonetheless brilliant reverse 180-degree handbrake turn and floor it, which sends me hurtling down the exit ramp. It's way too fast and when I reach the bottom and spin the wheel, the car skids across the concrete and slams into a pillar. This brings me to my senses like I've been thrown into an ice-cold bath.

I've been driving the Beamer for two years now. In that time, I've tested the bounds of human driving ability and mechanical engineering to the limit. I've broken every law of the road, often with reckless, some might even say suicidal abandon. But such is my confidence in my own driving and the supreme capabilities of the Beamer that I've never once had a crash. Sure, it's been close. It's been so close sometimes that the grim reaper's been riding shotgun but not once have I actually hit anything. It's unthinkable. I've always been invincible behind the wheel. Nothing could touch me.

In one split second, that's all changed. The door's caved in and I'm covered in shattered glass. I reverse away from the pillar, grind her into first and floor it so that in a second I'm accelerating down another ramp. At the bottom of it I'm about to swing a sharp right to take the next level when a police car screeches to a halt in front of me. I slam on the brakes and reverse up the ramp I've just come down.

There's only one thing for it. I'll have to take the ramps that service the incoming cars and hope to God there's nothing coming the other way. It looks as though I'm going to make it but, with just one level left, I see her on her way up, blue rinse and headscarf, lips pursed tight in concentration around her dentures. It's a small car, a Fiat Panda or something, and there's nothing else to do but slow down and push her back down the ramp out of the way. Apart from the size and weight advantage I've also got the advantage of gravity and, despite her panicking and putting the handbrake on, I shove her out of the way with ease. Just beyond the barrier I can see another police car. With my confidence bolstered after my grandma-bullying, I decide to stick with the same course of action and I put my foot down.

Now, in the movies, barriers like this are made of balsa wood and splinter a treat on impact. But this ain't the movies, not quite. The barrier strikes the windscreen with a smack and for a moment I think it might break the glass but then it snaps off in one piece and clatters to the ground. Just the Ford Sierra now and I'm free. I reckon I can make it if I veer off to the right, mount the pavement and hit its rear end with a glancing blow of enough force to push it out of the way.

I stamp on the accelerator and, as I hit the Sierra and rock back in my seat, I see him crouched down on the other side of the road. He's got all the kit: the black flak jacket, the black helmet, the black combat trousers and boots – and I'm staring down the barrel of his rifle. I duck down beneath the dashboard as a bullet takes out the windscreen in a shower of glass. I'd have thought that for a first-time offender they might have tried some tear gas or at least aimed at the wheels. But, oh no, fuck me if they don't just shoot to kill. As Luke'd say, it's a gross infringement of my civil liberties.

My continued forward momentum means that I've made it past the Sierra but what shape the Beamer's in after the collision is anyone's guess. Police sniper or not, I'm going to have to chance a look over the dashboard. Holding the Smith & Wesson by the barrel, I smash a hole in the frosted sheet of shattered windscreen. Through the hole I can see a clear road ahead. There's too many people around for the police marksman to chance another shot but I keep my head low anyway and floor it. I hang a right, then a left onto Marylebone High Street. It's busy and immediately I'm into a line of cars. People are staring at the car and at me through the hole in the glass. I take a look at myself in the rear-view mirror. Blood is streaming from a gash on the side of my head. To make matters worse, the sound of sirens almost deafens me. They're determined I won't get away this time.

There's only one thing for it, I'm going to have to ditch the Beamer. It's a horrible thing to have to do. It'll be like hacking off my leg while I'm running but these are hard times. What I need before I do it, though, is a little more distance between me and the police. I swing out around the line of cars, hang a left on New Cavendish Street and put my foot down. It's clear two blocks ahead. There's a Jaguar pulling out of a side road but I should be able to overtake him without too much trouble and then it's Portland Place. I reckon I'll ditch the Beamer around there and continue on foot over Oxford Street and lose myself in Soho.

The Jag's picking up speed, looking as though he'll try to make the lights before they turn red. Against the odds, he slams on the brakes and it must be the knock on the head that's robbed me of my coordination but I nearly ram into the back of him as I swing out and take off through the red light. A police car barrels in from the left. Change of plan. I turn left, figuring that I can buy myself some time while it turns around.

At the top of Portland Place, I take a right around the crescent and hit a line of traffic backed up to Euston Road.

So this is where it ends. No time for tearful good-byes. I open the door and hit the ground running. On the pavement, I turn around, aim the gun at the petrol cap and fire off a shot. Nothing happens. I fire off another – and the explosion lifts the Beamer off its wheels. The boot lid flies up and a sheet of flame tears through the interior. I take off for Great Portland Street Tube station amidst the howls of approaching sirens. The ticket hall is crammed with people, all listening to the crackling voice of the announcer on the tannoy: 'I repeat, due to a signal failure at Farringdon Road, there is no service either eastbound or westbound from this station. Passengers are advised to make alternative travel arrangements.' Fucking typical. I head back up the steps.

There're two policemen running towards me. It's not looking good. But then, like a beacon in the darkness, I see the orange FOR HIRE light of a taxi. The cabby, your typical middle-aged, overweight pie-and-chips type sees me coming with my gun in my hand and blood pouring down my head, sees the two policemen hotfooting it after me and winds up his window, knocks off his light and locks the doors. I've dreamt of being able to do this. 'Open the fucking door or I'll kill you,' I scream, pointing the Smith & Wesson at him. He does as he's told.

'Now drive.'

'It's a red light.'

'Fuck the red light.' I throw back the sliding glass partition, push the Smith & Wesson hard against the base of his skull and hiss, 'You've got three seconds to get moving before I plaster your fucking brains across the dashboard.' He pulls out into the mayhem of Euston Road and, amidst a symphony of screeching brakes and blaring horns, we turn into the westbound lanes.

'Where to, mate?' he asks. His London accent is rich with that Union Jack, East-End-during-the-Blitz British stoicism in the face of adversity.

'Shut up and drive.'

'I've got a wife and kids.'

'Like I'm supposed to give a shit.'

'I just thought you ought to know.'

'Well, if you get me out of here, I might let you live.'

I don't like taxi drivers, never have. They're a miserable bunch of bastards. Always chatting to you when you don't want to be chatted to, always over-familiar and over-friendly unless you're stranded in the middle of a freezing cold night and then it's 'Sorry, mate, I'm not going that way,' or just a curt shake of the head. And as a fellow road user, they drive as though they've got a God-given right to cut you up and fuck you over in any way they see fit.

'What's your name?'

'Bob. What's yours?'

'Never you mind what my name is. Just think how nice it'll be for you, Bob, if you get out of this alive. You can tell all your friends in the pub tonight that you had a mad gun-wielding maniac in the back of your cab today, and how you'll laugh. You'll be the local hero, you might even make the *Evening Standard*. What do you think of that, Bob?'

'I don't know, I just want you to let me go, that's all.'

'Well, Bob, you can start off by taking a right here and heading for Marylebone station. Now tell me, Bob, what do you like to do with yourself? What are you into, Bob? Any hobbies? What's your bag, Bob?'

'I like to fish.'

'Fishing, huh?'

'Yeah, I go with my son.'

'Like it, Bob. Keep reminding me of your family and I'm less likely to kill you, right?'

'No, I was just talking.'

'Well, good on you, Bob.'

There's a siren behind me and I take a look out of the rear window to see a Vauxhall Astra police car trying to weave its way through the traffic towards me. As it pulls level with us, I stick the Smith & Wesson out of the window, ready to take a shot at him. But, instead of trying to pull us over, he accelerates past without a glance.

'How about that, then, Bob? Here I was, like the conceited bastard that I am, thinking that he was after me when all along he was after someone else. Makes you think, doesn't it, Bob?'

'Yeah.'

'You can drop me here if you like.'

'Yeah?'

'Yes, Bob, this is your lucky day. Not only have I let you live but I'm even going to pay you.' I pass a tenner to him through the partition, climb out and walk into the station.

I figure they'll be looking for a man in his late twenties with a black leather jacket and a bloody head wound so I go to the Gents, take the jacket off, leave it in a cubicle and wash the blood from my head with some damp tissue. The wound is open and dribbling but I reckon I can get it patched up at Mar Kettle's which is only up the road. Looks like I shook them off again but it's too early for celebrations.

Feels odd, walking up to the tower block. Every other time I've ever been here I've pulled up in the Beamer and worried that the local kids'll scratch the paintwork or nick the radio. It's a choker that it's gone but I've got to look to the future and the hundred grand. Maybe I'll get an even better car. Now *that* would be something.

169

In the middle of the floor in the lift there's a piece of shit that's been rolled into a ball like a miniature brown snowman, with twigs for arms and a row of pebbles for buttons down the front. It's got an Action Man's head from one of the old ones: pre-realistic hair and gripping hands. It's tilted backwards so that it stares up at me or indeed anyone who goes in the lift, although I don't think it's intended for just anyone. I've got a sneaking feeling that it's been put here just for my benefit.

Archie meets me at the lift, resplendent in a slinky black number.

'Looking good, Arch.'

'It's Chanel. What happened to your head?'

'Spot of bother with the police. Nothing too heavy.'

'You'd better come in.'

I follow him through the security door and into the dark interior. Mar Kettle is sprawled on the chaise longue, looking like a distended bladder in a purple evening gown.

'At last, my private detective comes to visit me. What happened to your head?'

'I walked into a wall.'

'Spare me the lies.'

I wish she'd offer me a seat. My old place next to her is clearly no longer on offer but any old chair would do.

'Do you mind if I take a pew? I'm not feeling so good.'

'I'm not surprised. Let's just hope whoever it was knocked some sense into you. Archie, go and fetch a needle and thread, we'll have to stitch him up. Sit down there and don't bleed on it.' She gestures to her Chesterfield sofa with polar-bear upholstery. Once I'm seated, she leans forward, fixes me with a malicious glare and says, 'Well, is he dead yet?'

'No.'

'Well, don't you think it's about time you did something about it?' I can tell that she's putting all she's got into this façade of anger but, beneath it, she's shitting herself. She knows I'm her last chance and it doesn't fill her with much confidence.

'He dies tonight.'

'You'll have to do it, Archie, my dear,' she says as he returns with the sewing box and the first-aid kit. 'My hands aren't as steady as they used to be.'

'Right you are, ma'am.'

'I don't suppose you've got any local anaesthetic?' I enquire.

'Nope.'

I can't say for certain, never having had this done to me before, but it feels as though he's using a blunt needle.

'You *do* know what you're doing, don't you, Arch?'

'Not really.'

'There's a first time for everything, ain't there, Archie? Besides, you're got little choice, seeing as if you don't you're going to end up running on empty, if you get my drift.'

Archie finishes off the operation by giving the thread a yank and snapping it off between his teeth.

'So it's still cash on delivery, yeah?' I enquire while

running my fingers along the ridge of stitches on the side of my head.

'Once I can see him lying dead at my feet and see that it's definitely him and not some other poor bastard that you've killed by accident. Then, and only then, you can have the money.'

'Straight away?'

'I said you can have the money.'

'So you keep that sort of money here, do you?'

'Never you mind about that.'

'You see, once the job's done, I'll need to lie low for a while, maybe get out of the country, so I'll need the money straight away.'

'What makes you so sure that you can outwit him all of a sudden?'

'He's upset me personally, and I suppose that's what's given me the edge.'

This interests her. She leans forward and asks, 'What did he do to you to upset you so much?'

'It's not worth mentioning, just rest assured that he's going to meet his maker tonight.'

'You'd better be right.'

'Also, I could do with some more firepower if you've got it.'

'What happened to the revolver we gave you?'

'I've still got it, it's just I'd feel more confident if I had something a little more heavyweight.'

'I don't think we've got anything apart from the elephant gun.' She points to the far wall between two stuffed elephant heads where there's a short rifle with a thick brass barrel about two inches in diameter. 'It belonged to my second husband, Gordon, the film producer. We used to hunt elephants in India in the early fifties. They were happy times, when hunting was still allowed, before the simpering liberals got involved and spoilt everything. You can have it if you really think it'll help. It's got no sentimental value and it's not registered anywhere so it can't be traced back to me. The only trouble is, I can't think for the life of me where the bullets are. I know we had some at one time.'

'There's a bullet in it, ma'am,' chips in Archie. 'I saw it a couple of months back when I was cleaning it. I think that's the only one.'

'Well, there you go. If you want it, it's yours. I'll warn you, though, it makes a hell of a mess if it hits anyone. I remember one time in Himachal Pradesh when Gordon had a large bull in his sights and a local boy got in the way. The bullet left a hole the size of a football in his chest and the funny thing was, instead of dying there and then, the boy peered down into the hole, stuck his hand in it as though he'd lost something and then keeled over. It was tragic for his parents, obviously, but Gordon and I found it really quite comical.'

I'd like to take the elephant gun down and blow a hole the size of a football in *her* chest but instead I thank her as Archie fetches it off the wall and hands it to me. It weighs a ton.

'I'd better get going.' I tell her. 'I've got a lot to do before tonight.'

'I look forward to coming face to face with my

old adversary later. Just make sure he's dead, that's all.'

I stand up and follow Archie to the door.

'Oh, and one more thing,' she calls after me. 'No more mistakes, you hear me?'

'Are you a gambling man, Arch?' I ask him as we wait for the lift.

'What?'

'Sorry, that was insensitive of me. Are you a gambling *woman*, Arch?'

'Don't take the piss. Yes, I used to be, a while back. I don't get to the bookie's much these days.'

'Well, what do you reckon my chances are, then?'

'Of killing him? Well, I reckon they're pretty bad. I'd give you a hundred to one against, if truth be told.'

'Why's that?'

''Cos this guy knows what he's doing and you don't. Simple as that.'

'Well, Arch, all I can say is that I hope you're wrong.'

The lift arrives and I step in, bid Archie goodbye and hit the button for the ground floor.

As I suspected, the ball of shit with the Action Man head on it has gone.

7

I press the button for the ground floor and the lift descends. Two floors down it stops and the doors open. I'm so preoccupied with what I've got to get done tonight that I almost forget I'm holding the elephant gun. I put it behind my back. A tall man in a long grey smock with a pointy hood pulled up over his head steps in and stands in front of me. The last thing I need at this moment in time are the unwanted attentions of a nutter, so as a pre-emptive measure I smile at him. The blank expression on his swarthy features changes not one bit, so I avert my eyes. The doors close and the lift descends once again. He's got a curious smell about him which, although powerful, is not altogether unpleasant.

Floor twelve. The lift stops and the doors open. There's another man dressed in exactly the same outfit, only his hood is pulled up so far over his head that his face is shrouded in shadow. All I can make out are his eyes staring at me. He too brings with him a strange smell that is different from the first but, again, curiously familiar. The doors close. I have the elephant gun and the Smith & Wesson but they're not much comfort. As the doors shut and the two respective odours are confined within the lift they blend together into an overpowering odour of spices.

On the ninth floor, the doors open once again and now I know what to expect. Sure enough, in steps another tall man in a long smock with a pointy hood. And so it goes on. With each new arrival the smell intensifies and they're so close now I can feel their combined breath on my face. I become groggy and my head lolls back and slams against the wall of the lift. Their hands are upon me, lifting me up, passing me through the ceiling to other hands that reach down and pull me out.

There's a moonlit sky above me and, below, the leather-and-mahogany interior of a 1950s sports car. The engine's running. I let out the clutch, depress the accelerator and I'm off. Up into fourth and the road swings out over the sea far below. Another bend and I head inland. The car holds the road with such ease that I feel I need to test it to the limit. Despite the bends and dips of the mountainous terrain, I push the pedal to the floor. The engine roars and the words come to my lips, one after the other, maintaining a uniform rhythm, becoming louder until I'm shriek-ing, 'Die, die, die, die, die.' Saliva streaks across my windswept face, my throat becomes hoarse and sore but the words continue one after the other, each one trying to outdo the other in its volume and intensity of emotion.

Tears fill my eyes. I can hardly see the road. The tyres scream against the asphalt. Each word rises out of me with the pain of a punch in the solar plexus. My hands flop into my lap. Up ahead there's a tight bend. I'll never make it. The tyres relinquish their hold on the road surface and the car swaps its forward momentum for a sideways roll. My aching jaw clamps shut with the finality of a machine-gun that's run out of bullets and there's just the whine of the engine as the wheels spin against nothing more resistant than air.

The car bounces down the road, twisting over and over. By the time it comes to rest the side of my head is caved in and my shattered jaw hangs open. Gouts of warm blood pump from a gash in my neck. The dashboard has been pushed down against my legs, almost severing them, and the steering wheel has splintered so that one of its spokes has gutted me from groin to breastbone, sending further plumes of blood to spout and splatter against the instrument panel. My left arm lies on the passenger seat next to me, severed at the shoulder. The fingers of my right hand are twisted at bizarre angles to one another, resembling some sort of sea anemone.

I flop from the wreckage of the car onto the ground. I look up and see that I'm lying on the driveway of a large white house. I make for the steps that lead up to the front door. As I pull myself along the ground, I can feel gravel working its way into the gaping wound in my stomach. It's a relief to reach the cold marble of the steps. At the top of them, I push the door open and crawl inside. A long flight of stairs with intricate wrought-iron banister rails leads up to a landing on which stand a man and a woman in the midst of a fierce argument. The man brandishes a knife and the woman screams as he plunges it into her chest. She turns around, flings her arms wide apart and topples forward, cartwheeling down the stairs. She hits the marble floor with a sickening thud and stays motionless, framed within a pool of blood. The man dashes after her and kneels down and cradles her in his arms. He utters some words but they are too softly spoken for me to make out what they are. He eases her back onto the floor and stands up and turns around to face me. He wipes away a tear from his cheek and strides towards me.

I try to speak but my throat is crushed and my mouth fills with blood that spills down my chin. The man reaches down, pushes his hands into my gaping stomach and starts pulling out my intestines that make a wet slapping noise as he throws them onto the floor.

The lift doors open and I step outside. The intensity of the illusion leaves me feeling weak and nauseous. Even though Mar Kettle lives on the twenty-third floor, I think I might take the stairs in future.

Walking down Lisson Grove, I pass a junk shop. In the window, lying in an old tin bath, is a leather golf bag. It'll be just the job as a holster for the elephant gun. I go in and buy it. It fits perfectly. A couple of minutes later, I'm in the back of a cab on my way home to the *Griffin*.

As I approach it along the towpath, I see that the curtains are drawn. I could have sworn I left them open when I went out yesterday. As I step aboard, I place the golf bag quietly on the floor, pull the Smith & Wesson from my pocket and grip it in my sweaty fist. It's dark inside. There's no sound apart from a faint wheezing. I take the steps into the dark interior as quietly as possible. Now I can see where the wheezing's coming from: there's someone in my bed, fast asleep by the looks of things. I pull back the covers. It's my father.

'Dad?'

'All right, son?' he says as he opens his eyes and peers up at me.

'What are you doing here?'

'Joyce let me in. I popped round yesterday but you were out. She cooked me dinner and said you wouldn't mind if I bedded down for the night.'

'Of course I don't mind. But what was so important that you couldn't call me?'

He looks at me as though there're so many words bursting to get out that they've created a bottleneck in his throat and are jammed in on one another. And then it comes to me, the question that, what with the surprise of finding him here and all, I've completely overlooked for the first time in years and one that just might explain all of this.

'Any sign?'

'That's just it.'

179

'You've seen Bernie Mann?'

'I've done more than just see him. I've had a meeting with him.'

'What about?'

'My career, of course.'

'That'll be your singing career, I presume.'

'Well, what *other* career do I have?'

It appears that, through his incessant waiting for a slice of Bernie Mann's delusional showbiz cake, he's created some sort of fictitious wish-fulfilment.

'What happened?'

'Bernie came good on his promise, that's what happened. He said he'd make me a star and, by God, he meant it. It's ironic, really: after all those years of waiting, what does he do but walk into the pub and sit down slap bang next to me. There he was, as bright as day, looking like he'd just stepped off the stage at the Locarno. It's fate, I'm telling you. I knew he'd come back.'

'I don't suppose he remembered you, did he?'

'Of course he remembered me. He came back for me, told me that he always thought of me as the one that got away. Obviously we'll take things one step at a time and secure the UK market first before moving on to the States but he doesn't foresee any problems with the record company side of things, says he knows all the right people. As far as image is concerned, Bernie feels that we should aim for a slightly younger Sinatra or a considerably older Harry Connick Jr, one or the other.'

'This man, you're sure he *is* Bernie Mann?'

'Listen, son, please don't go thinking I've gone senile. I know Bernie Mann when I see him. Christ, I've been doing nothing but wait for him for the past ten years.'

The way I see it, there's three possibilities here. Two of them feasible and one somewhat less so.

1. The man in question is a confidence trickster and, having heard of Dad's strange obsession, has decided to capitalize on it in an attempt to extort money from him.
2. It's our resident psychic prankster and this is just another way of bugging me. But as of tonight that's all going to change.
3. It really is Bernie Mann and he's as mental as Dad.

'Listen, Dad, I'm not saying you're senile or anything, it's just I'm concerned you'll get your hopes built up and then maybe it won't work out and you'll be disappointed. I don't want to see you get hurt.'

'Do you think Elvis thought to himself, "Oh, I'd better not reach for the stars as I might get upset if it doesn't work out quite as I'd hoped"? No, he didn't. Do you think Ol' Blue Eyes thought, "Oh, I'd better call it a day" when he got his first bad review? No, he didn't.'

'But Dad, they were young men. You're— How old are you?'

'I'm sixty-eight.'

I'm about to suggest that perhaps he's a little old to be considering a new career, especially one as taxing as international pop stardom but I stop myself. Maybe I should let him get on with it. If he really thinks he's met Bernie Mann and he's going to make him a star, then why should I stand in his way? After all, I played along with his waiting for all these years, why shouldn't I go along with this? But, deep down, I have a sneaking feeling that this is more than just my father's mind taking a turn for the worse.

'Dad, while you get dressed, I'm just going to pop round and see Joyce.'

'Right you are, son.'

I'm a little concerned that I might not get the best of welcomes as it's a weekday daytime and she'll be busy at work on *Up the Boulevard*. But I needn't have worried, she's as cheery as ever and greets me through the hatch with a 'Hello, stranger.' She goes on, 'I was beginning to wonder what happened to you. One minute, you tell me you're going to take things easy and lie around the *Griffin* for a few days, the next you go and disappear. You don't still think you've killed someone, do you?'

'No, not really.'

'How's your dad?'

'I presume he's told you about Bernie Mann?'

'He did, but if it makes him happy.'

'I need to ask a favour.'

'Sure, go ahead.'

'If something should happen to me, I'd like to think that you'd watch out for him. I don't mean that you should look after him full-time or anything like that but, you know, just check up on him once in a while.'

'What do you mean? *If something should happen to me* – what exactly do you have in mind? Is there something you'd like to tell me?'

'Not really.'

'Listen to me, young man. Why are you talking like this? First of all you march in here and tell me you think you've killed someone, then you start going on about what will happen if you die. I think, as a close friend, I have a right to be concerned. Now, I'm not going to ask you what's going on. You obviously don't want to tell me or maybe you think I won't understand. But let me tell you a story before you go on your way.'

It seems to me that Joyce thinks I've lost the plot. Maybe she's right, maybe I have. Maybe I'm as barking mad as my father and what Joyce feels for me is akin to what I feel for him. When the tea's made, we sit together on the red velvet seats with cups and saucers in our laps and rich tea fingers to dunk in them. This is something of a tradition for us and it's at times like these that I can't imagine Joyce leading the charge in all that porn. Well, I can, because I've seen her in action but somehow I can't equate the middle-aged woman sitting next to me sipping tea with the one I saw on Luke's thirty-two-inch colour a couple of years back. It was a Saturday night. We'd been lounging around at his place, huddled around the bong and the video. I must have nodded off and when I came to there was Joyce – or, rather, there was Joyce from twenty years previously – satisfying three men simultaneously. Later on I discovered from the biro-scrawled title on the side of the tape that we were watching one of her last movies, *Rendered Crack* (1979). She's often enquired whether I've seen one of her films and up until recently I always denied it but a while ago I admitted that I had. It didn't seem to bother her, though. 'No regrets' is her motto.

Joyce starts her story: 'When I was growing up in the East End, there was this old woman who lived on our street in a derelict house that had been bombed out during the blitz. She was what you'd call a bag lady, I suppose. We called her Harpy, although her full name was Elspeth Harp. Anyway, we were fascinated by her and terrified of her, all at the same time. We used to hang around outside her house just so's we could watch her. To us kids she was the nearest we got to a witch like the ones we'd read about in our story books. Anyway, one day there we were, me and my mates, sitting on the wall opposite her house just doing nothing, talking and hoping that we might get a glimpse of her. When she finally made an appearance, we goaded each other into attempting conversation with her. But you know what kids are like, it wasn't so much conversation as shouting. It was my friend Debbie who set the ball rolling with something childish like, "Hey, Harpy are you a witch?" That sort of thing. Well, that set us all off and we ended up following her down the street hurling abuse. You know how cruel kids can be.

'By the time we drew level with my house, I was so intent on shouting at her that I didn't notice my dad watching me through the front window. Whatever else my dad was, he was a man of honour. He'd had a hard life and maybe that was what gave him his intense hatred of bullying. I think he must have been bullied as a child or something. Anyway, when he saw me, one of a gang of kids following this poor old woman down the street, shouting at her, he flipped. He wasn't a violent man, he never hit me and he made a point of telling me he never would but that didn't stop him from going totally ballistic. When eventually he calmed down he told me the old lady's story. Of course Harpy was not always the sad old woman that we knew, living in the bombed-out remains of her life. During the twenties Elspeth Harp had been something of a trendy young thing about town with aspirations to stardom as an actress in the West End. She'd managed to land herself a couple of small parts but nothing special until one year when she auditioned for the part of Ophelia in a production of *Hamlet* at the Royal Court. Although she was a total unknown, the director took a shine to her and offered her the part there and then, over and above some of the leading women in the London theatrical world of the time. She was, understandably, beside herself with joy. Now, although she was an attractive young woman with plenty of friends and a close family, she was, according to my father, extremely fragile psychologically speaking. Cruelty in any form was something that she couldn't cope with, whether it was to animals or to people. She spent much of her time collecting money for the poor and needy of whom there were many in the East End of the twenties. Her father despaired of the stray animals that she brought

185

home to the house to nurse. Nothing and no one was a lost cause to her.

'So, anyway, there Harpy is, outside the Royal Court Theatre. Her dreams have come true. She's to play Ophelia opposite some big-cheese actor. Fame and fortune await. She can hardly believe her luck. All she can think of is telling her parents the news. Now, her parents ran a tobacconist's in Bow. It was one of those proper old tobacconist's that sold different types of pipe tobacco and snuffs. Anyway, she couldn't wait to get there. It was a fair walk from the bus stop in Bow to the shop, there were a lot of people around and it was raining hard. She pushed her way through the crowds with her umbrella up, thinking of nothing but getting to the shop and telling her parents the news. By the time she arrived she was so full of nervous energy that she didn't even think to take the umbrella down, just ran into the shop and started telling them about how she's got the role of Ophelia at the Royal Court. At first they listened to what she had to say but then their attention shifted away from her and her news and focused on the front of the umbrella that she was still holding above her head. Their expressions of joy rapidly turned to expressions of horror. She followed their gaze to one of the struts on the umbrella – and guess what they saw impaled on the tip of it, dripping blood?'

Joyce has become more animated and intense than I've ever known her. She leans towards me, awaiting a reply. I have no idea what was impaled on the end of the umbrella strut dripping blood so I shake my head and, feeling that this maybe isn't enough to satisfy her question, mutter, 'Dunno.'

'Well, I'll tell you what it was. It was an eyeball, an eyeball freshly plucked from the eye socket of some hapless passer-by. Well, you can imagine the scene.' I don't think I can but now's not the time to say it. 'They're all deeply shocked. God knows what he thought he could achieve by doing this but her father took the eyeball off the umbrella strut and set off down the street with it as though he might find the unfortunate victim and offer to put it back from whence it came. Stranger still, he never found the person. What he would have done if he *had* found them is anyone's guess but you'd have thought that the injured party would have still been there, wouldn't you? It's not as if you'd just wander off home with one of your eyes ripped out of your face.' She stares at me again in anticipation of my response.

'No, you wouldn't, no.'

'But there you go, they'd just vanished into thin air, one eye lighter.' Joyce leans back and takes a big slurp of her tea. If this is the end of the story, then it's gone straight over my head. I cannot for the life of me think what relevance all this has to my plight but I'm sure that if I'm patient, all will be revealed.

'That was the turning point, you see,' she says. 'From that day on no one could do anything for Elspeth Harp. She was like a zombie. Initially her parents thought that it was something that she would snap out of. But the acting all went by the board. She couldn't learn her lines, couldn't find any enthusiasm for the part

187

and finally just stopped turning up for rehearsals. She stayed at home and became more and more withdrawn until it was all they could do to get her to come out of her bedroom. She was referred to specialists but all they did was confirm that she was suffering from trauma and that in time she would recover. But she never did. Whatever strange effect the eyeball incident had had on her mind, it was permanent.'

Now I feel is the time to take the bull by the horns and ask her what the hell she's talking about. 'Joyce,' I say, 'what is the point of all this?'

'Don't you see?'

'See what?'

'Oh, come on, there's a pattern there, can't you see it?'

'Joyce, I'm locked into a complex psychological duel with an elderly Moroccan, a duel that involves murder, magic, drugs, and out and out weirdness of every kind, and you seem to think that I'm having a nervous breakdown like this Harpy woman down your street. I'm sorry, but I don't share your diagnosis. Believe me, I appreciate your concern but your assumption is way off the mark. Granted, I need all the support I can get at the moment and that's why I'd like you to keep an eye on my dad if something should happen to me. I'm sure nothing will but if it should.'

She shakes her head and lets out a sigh of resignation. 'Of course I'll watch out for your dad. You just go and do whatever it is you feel you must. But I would ask you to remember one thing, whatever it is that you're up against, be it psychological or not: no one's going to think any less of you if you just walk away from it. It really is that easy.'

'I'll remember. Thanks, Joyce.'

I give her a hug and make my way back along the towpath. I can hear my dad singing his heart out. He stops as he hears me come aboard and fixes me with a big grin.

'Hear that, son? I've still got the old magic. You just wait and see, this is going to be the big time for me now.'

8

Immaculate in his three-piece suit and fedora, the old man walks onto the stage and receives a cheer from the crowd for his troubles. He flicks a switch that sets off an explosion of sound and light. Then he turns around and walks off the way he came. It's the same set as last time at The Scala but the experience is rendered all the more epic by the cavernous interior of the Brixton Academy. People crane their necks to catch a glimpse of musicians, or a DJ at least. But there's no one, just some faint spots of light within the dry ice and an occasional distorted insect image projected onto the backdrop. The music is a lovingly constructed hybrid of all the best bits from forty years of pop music, imitated, parodied, deconstructed, reconstructed and often just stolen wholesale. And the bass is low down and dirty and gets into your brain and shakes you up and down.

At the end of the set, when the old guy returns to

switch it all off, a huge cheer goes up from the newly converted Gurning Mandibles fans. This appears to startle him and, instead of walking off, he approaches the front of the stage where there is a solitary microphone. He opens his mouth as though to speak but all that comes out of it is a shrill clicking sound. He backs away, takes a bow and exits. The house lights come on and the spell is broken.

'Cool, huh?' says Luke nudging me in the ribs.

'Yup,' I reply, thankful for the opportunity to break the rhythm of my jaw which has been pummelling a piece of chewing gum for the past half-hour due to the onrush of E that Luke gave me on our arrival.

'Luke, there'll be plenty of gear knocking around tonight, won't there?'

'Does a bear shit in the woods?'

'I was just thinking about what Baz said yesterday about how to neutralize the effect of curses and the like. Just wanted to make sure that, should the need arise, we were well stocked.'

'Put it this way,' Luke says, fixing me with a mischievous grin, 'if we draw an analogy between drugs and football and you take your average band's after-show party as being equal to a Sunday afternoon knockabout in the park, then tonight's party's going to be like the fucking World Cup.'

I fetch a couple of beers from the bar. The crowd's getting edgy, there's that atmosphere you get at a really special gig, a gig that people will talk about for years to come. People are more than just excited to see a band, they're celebrating their attendance at an epoch-defining event. This is the best band of their generation at the height of their career. Usually only visible half a mile away at the end of a field playing to tens of thousands, here they are about to hit the stage in London's coolest venue.

By the time we're halfway through our beers, the roadies have done their stuff and the bars empty as people become fearful of missing even a second. Others load up on reefers and a blue cloud hangs in front of the stage. At any moment, they'll be here, Sean Lord on drums, Gary 'Lymphnode' McKenna on guitar, Malcey Watson on bass and Baz Marshall on vocals. At the end of every song played through the PA a hopeful cheer goes up. Three or four times I think that this must be it, only to be disappointed. Then it happens: the lights go out, their shadows appear on stage and the entire place erupts. A couple of kicks on the bass drum, a single chord on the guitar, four clicks of the drumsticks and they crash into 'Kickin' It Off', their second single. The lights go up and there they are above us, the most famous bunch of scallies in the business. But then it all stops, everything is freeze-framed and there's total silence.

'We meet again.' The voice comes from the balcony above. I turn around and look up to see a man in a white suit walking down the steps between the rows of seats, the only movement in the whole place.

'This is what I like to think of as the Time Stop. And a word of warning so that you do not add another head wound to your collection: be very careful when moving

193

around as you will find everything as hard as rock to the touch.'

I've already found this out when I turned around and brushed against Luke who stands there frozen, like he's been forged out of steel.

'You will not be able to move anything, so do not waste your time trying. You could take a sledge-hammer to the head of your friend there and not leave a blemish. But then, you would have to find a sledgehammer that was part of your time and not part of his. Do not be overly confused by all of this, just relax and be assured that I know exactly what I am doing. To give you the most simplified explanation that I can, this is all an exercise in cutting and pasting. I have cut you out of your time and pasted you into another parallel one in which just you and I exist. I like to meet people under these circumstances. It is so much easier to talk. No distractions and so wonderfully quiet, do you not agree?'

I don't answer.

'It also leaves me very much in control of the situation and, as you are no doubt aware by now, I do like to be in control. I am sorry about the competition this morning. In some strange way I am sure it meant a lot to you but you have to understand that I was unable to resist.'

He's reached the edge of the balcony and stands against the rail, looking down at me. I can see him clearly now and he looks younger and more handsome than I had expected. He's dressed all in white with a silk cravat in the neck of his shirt. He looks as though he should be mixing cocktails on a marble terrace overlooking the Mediterranean rather than rubbing shoulders with the great unwashed at Brixton Academy.

A guy behind me has jumped up, such is his excitement at the sight of Gobshite on stage, and he's suspended a good foot off the ground. It's a strange image to contemplate. I move behind him out of Nazar's line of vision, pull the golf bag from around my shoulder and slide out the elephant gun.

'You are probably somewhat confused as to my motives for coming here tonight and I must confess that I cannot find a fully satisfactory explanation for them myself. I would hazard a guess that it has something to do with my starvation of experience for so many years of my life. You must remember that a few days ago I was living in a prison in the Atlas Mountains and here I am at a pop concert in London with a man who wants to kill me and, indeed, is levelling the sights of his gun on me as I speak.'

He's right. I've got the barrel of the gun resting on the shoulder of a short guy with glasses who's taking a big slug of lager from a plastic beaker and I'm drawing a bead on Nazar's forehead.

'I find your behaviour insulting. Do you really believe that a man who can stop time itself will not be able to realize that he is about to be shot at?'

I begin to squeeze the trigger. But as I do so the silent gallery of figures all around me bursts into life once again.

'Here what the hell do you think you're doing?'

shouts the guy whose shoulder I'm resting the gun on. 'Go on, fuck off.'

I holster the elephant gun in the golf bag and find my way back to Luke.

'That pill hasn't had much effect on me,' I lie, shouting into his ear. 'Have you got another one?' He passes me a joint, reaches into his pocket and pulls out a polythene bag from which he extracts another E and presses it into my hand.

As 'Kickin' It Off' finishes in a triumphant snarl of feedback, Nazar trips the time switch again. Silence. I wait for him to speak but the silence remains unbroken. I scan the balcony but he's not there. Then I hear him clear his throat and I spin around to see him standing next to Baz on stage.

'Pop music is a very interesting phenomenon, don't you agree?' he says. 'It's all so religious on the one hand and so fascist on the other. You mark my words, it won't be long before some pin-up who holds the hearts and minds of millions will to turn to politics and discover that the same rules of attraction apply. A society will develop in which entertainers double up as politicians, where the line between politics and entertainment will become so blurred that it no longer exists.'

I go to draw the Smith & Wesson from my trouser pocket but it's totally immovable. I can't even walk because it's locked in place. The golf bag is the same, seemingly moulded into the very air itself.

'You remember what I said about cut and paste,' says Nazar smugly. 'Well, I decided to leave your guns frozen in time. It would appear that this is the only way that I can get your attention without you reverting back to your pointless and, may I say, rather irritating attempts at killing me.'

But what he has left me with is the half-smoked reefer. I start blasting on it, pulling down huge lung-fuls. The smoke burns against the back of my throat but I ignore the pain. I could do with something more psychoactive and fast-acting but, in the absence of anything else, this'll have to do.

'Why not join me on stage and see what it's like to stand in front of all these people? I'm sure that you can manoeuvre yourself around the guns. Come along and join me, it's really quite exhilarating.'

I crouch down while holding the material of my trouser pocket away from the Smith & Wesson and pull my arm from the strap on the golf bag. Thus freed from my constraints, I hoist myself up on the people around me and clamber towards the stage, using their heads and shoulders as stepping stones. The drugs make me shaky on my feet but their bodies are so solid that it's easy going. I figure if I can reach Nazar I might be able to overpower him and either make him stop this Time Stop shit or go back and get the guns and shoot him. Alternatively, I can strangle him there and then and just hope that as he dies his psychic pause button will switch itself off. I don't know where that'll leave me. I haven't even started to think about how he does all this but I should imagine that if I succeeded I might be left on stage with my hands around his neck, suddenly transported there in the eyes of three and a half thousand baying Gobshite fans. The police wouldn't have a problem with witnesses, that's for sure.

I'm nearly there. Just another few steps. Our eyes meet. He smiles at me, winks and disappears as Gobshite start their second number, 'She's Demented', the opening track on their first album, *What You Looking At?*

Being near the front, I'm thrown into the crush of bodies and have to fight my way back to Luke who stands there with the elephant gun in one hand and the Smith & Wesson in the other.

'I presume these belong to you,' he says.

I shoot him a goofy grin and take them from him.

By the end of the gig, after the near-hysteria that's aroused by Gobshite's final number, 'Never Die Young', perhaps their quintessential anthem, my double dose of MDMA sends shivers down my spine and makes my head feel like a balloon full of helium, as though at any minute it might break free of my shoulders and float away. Murder is not a prospect I relish in this state but if I'm going to finish this tonight then I have little choice.

The house lights go up and the crowd disperses. I follow Luke up to the backstage bar where a crowd of beautiful people, music-biz players, showbiz stars and pop-star wannabes have gathered to rub shoulders with the mighty Gobshite. There's the usual gang of regulars like the Feng Shui kid who's so adept at eastern mysticism that his flat on Park Lane is said to exist in at least four parallel dimensions. Luke's been there but, as you'd expect, his findings were inconclusive. There's 'Snowflake' Manetti who's snorted so much coke that it's not just the bridge of his nose that's rotted away but most of his face so that he wears a huge eye patch – more of a face patch really, reaching as it does from his forehead to his top lip. Rumour has it he's going to receive bone grafts from an alligator's jaw. The Sandwich Sisters are working the room, driving all the men crazy and drawing dagger stares from the women. At some later stage in the proceedings these stunningly beautiful twins will choose a man for the night and bestow upon him 'the sandwich,' an experience that's been known to reduce grown men to tears. Baz has been one such lucky recipient and tells me it's the nearest he's ever come to religion.

Bob Todd's here. No one knows who he is as he never speaks to anyone but it's said that he killed a man. That's all anyone knows about him and that notoriety is in itself enough to guarantee him a place on the guest list whenever Gobshite are in town. Luke and I once tried to make conversation with him and he told us to fuck off. The problem was that Luke started right on in with his mock cowboy voice: 'Hi, Bob, 's been said you once killed a man. That so?' I have a sneaking suspicion that someone's having us on about him killing someone. In fact, I think it could be Luke but, because he was so caned, he forgot that it was him who started the rumour in the first place and now believes it himself. Whatever, it's fun to say to people who've never seen him before, 'That's Bob Todd, rumour has it he killed a man.'

Right in the thick of things chatting away to 'Snow-flake' Manetti (a man who should know better), is Milo (I don't know his surname, no one does), a tiny Italian who bears an uncanny resemblance to Al Pacino and operates as a one-man pharmaceutical industry. Whether you want the latest designer thrill-pill from California or the psychoactive residue off the back of a Peruvian toad, Milo's your man. The good thing about having Milo at a party like this is that all his gear is absolutely free. He deals such huge quantities that dishing out a few thousand pounds' worth at a party like this is nothing more than sponsorship. After all, some companies would pay a fortune to have a star like Baz endorsing their products. Milo gets it for free.

Huddled deep in conversation in the corner are Buddy Fags and Maceo Malanga, the pop critics. They're both off their heads and deep in argument as always. They've spent years competing with each other to find the next big thing and when one of them has found it, the other makes sure that, once the hype has dried up, he's the first to rubbish it. As far as Gobshite are concerned, they both claim they were the first past the post although both their initial features came out in different magazines in the same week. Constantly trying to outdo each other, and fiercely critical of each other's writing style, they are drawn together at parties such as this where they can provide a united front to the assorted record company PRs trying to talk up their hot new signings. Subscribing as they do to that peculiarly British style of build-'em-up-and-knock-'em-down pop journalism,

everyone knows, none more so than the bands themselves, that however high they're blasted out of the
pop cannon, Fags and Malanga'll be there competing
to write the first hatchet job and subsequent obituary
when they fall.

Standing behind Malanga is Doogie Skylark who
looks as though he's just dropped in from Cardboard
City. His increasingly erratic programming ideas of
late have culminated in his most recent format which
is a *You've Been Framed*-style home video programme,
the only new twist being that the hapless victims of
these more serious domestic accidents really do end
up dead. He wants to call it *You've Been Killed*. He
thinks that maybe he'll have to pay more up front
to encourage the bereaved relatives to part with their
videotapes but it'll be worth it. Sadly, this project, like
the one before it, *Celebrity Bong*, is unlikely ever to see
the light of day.

Gobshite's manager Nuno Macready makes a rare
appearance in the bar with his wife, the supermodel
Anastasia Crisp. Nuno is a man so driven that he will
only employ people that he feels share his ambition
and reckons he can tell whether someone's a 'good
person' by staring into their eyes. He's had numerous
industrial tribunals conducted against him because of
this unusual interview technique but cares not one jot.
What he thinks he can see is anyone's guess. Nuno's
chatting with Mark Fearnley, the Labour MP who
likes to maintain his profile as a man of the people
by appearing at events such as this for a spot of
flesh-pressing but who also looks a little nervous

as the air is rich with dope smoke: it won't be long before he'll have to think of his career, make his excuses and leave.

Flipper, Gobshite's longest-serving roadie and unofficial mascot, stands at the bar chewing maniacally. It's said that he gets through twenty packs of chewing gum a day and has jaw muscles like biceps to prove it. He is presently the subject of a television documentary which is exploring his claim that he hasn't slept for the past five and a half years. The scientific research team who are working on the programme are investigating the possibility that there may be some ingredient in the drugs he takes that enables him to survive sleep deprivation unharmed. Whether this is true or not remains to be seen but he doesn't look well on it: he has a permanent thousand-yard stare and looks as though he's been dead about a fortnight.

And there's Titch Allcock walking through the door, the little bastard, looking almost identical to the way he did all those years ago at school. His clothes are more expensive and there are some wisps of grey in his sideburns but other than that he's just the same. As was always the way, I can hear him right on the other side of the room. He's with the Laughy Woman and I have to say that she looks a damned sight better than she does in her publicity shots that occasionally find their way into listings magazines when the sub-editors need to fill a gap. She's very much on duty and dolled up to the nines, hoping, no doubt, to do a spot of networking in an attempt to upgrade her career from her present role as a professional hyena. There's no sign of Nazar so, unable to resist it, I approach them and just as Titch tells the punchline to a joke at which the Laughy Woman readies herself for hysterics I lean towards him and say, 'Hi there.' Clearly more than a little affronted that I should have butted in at such an important moment, he maintains a supercilious smile on his face nonetheless, just in case I turn out to be someone important.

'Remember me?'

'Erm.' He doesn't want to commit himself to a negative answer in case this reflects badly on him. After all, I could be a TV executive with a possible Saturday evening *Noel's House Party* format on the boil.

'From school?'

I can almost hear the mental connections being made in his oversized head and I know that his memory bank has located me when the corners of his mouth dip although he battles to maintain a grin just in case I've turned into some big cheese and might still be worth schmoozing. He shakes my hand and introduces me to the Laughy Woman who says 'Hi' and fixes me with a this-could-be-your-lucky-night smile just to cover all eventualities.

'I'm a big fan of your show,' I tell them, 'especially that competition you do. What's it called?'

'Titch's Triffic Trips,' they tell me as one, beaming with self-satisfaction.

'That's right. You have some colourful characters on that. Not just your average run-of-the-mill Joe Public.'

'Have you listened to it this week?' enquires the Laughy Woman.

'Unfortunately I've been in LA all week so I haven't managed to tune in.'

'It's been rather amusing,' continues Titch, 'we had this guy on who claimed to be a magician. He was a little retarded, I think,' – big laugh from the Laughy Woman – 'but he managed to get all the way through to today's round and was just about to win a couple of tickets to tonight's show when a Moroccan tourist came on the line and beat him. Actually, the Moroccan should be along in a minute. I think he's gone to the bar. Interesting chap, it's his first time in London. He's just retired from forty years in the prison service over there. What he makes of a Gobshite gig is any-one's guess. So, mate, what do you do with yourself these days?'

'I run my own production company. You might have heard of us, we're called Slowmo TV. We've just been commissioned to make a pilot for a new satellite channel starting in the spring. If we get the go-ahead, the show will have a twenty-two week early Saturday evening slot mixing a game show format with some chat and celebrity gossip. We're still looking for the presenter and his assistant.'

Titch and the Laughy Woman are virtually dribbling with anticipation. But then I throw my head back and emit a forced laugh that even the queen of forced laughter herself would be proud of.

'I've just remembered what we used to call you at school.' The smile withers on Titch's face. 'Oh, kids can be so cruel, don't you think?'

'Er, yeah.'

In response to the Laughy Woman's look of confusion, I tell her, 'No Balls, as in Allcock and no balls.'

Her allegiances are torn. On the one hand she wants to ingratiate herself with me but on the other she doesn't want to offend Titch, the man who has given her her first step up the ladder of media stardom. As a compromise, she wrinkles up her nose and flashes me a big grin.

I'm about to start on about how we also used to mock poor young Titch about the enormity of his head when I'm tapped on the shoulder and there's Baz, devoid of his usual happy-go-lucky demeanour.

'You'd better come with me,' he whispers in my ear. 'It's Luke.' I tell Titch and the Laughy Woman that they'll have to excuse me and relish the look of awe on their faces as they see how thick I am with the star of the show. It goes some way towards making up for my humiliation at their hands this morning. Following the world-renowned front man through the crowd of revellers, I can tell that it must be something serious by the way that he hurries along ignoring the ubiquitous greetings and praise aimed at him. He leads me through a tight ring of security to the band's dressing room where the atmosphere is anything but cheerful. A couple of security men are having head wounds tended to. People sit around looking like they're stuck in a bad trip.

'Are you going to tell me what's going on here, Baz?' I ask him once we're seated on a big threadbare sofa and he's sparked up a reefer.

'You're never going to fucking believe this one, I'm telling you. I wouldn't believe it myself if I hadn't seen it with my own eyes. We've just come off stage and we're sitting around in here enjoying the buzz, having a smoke, when Lance over there,' he nods at one of the security men having his head bandaged, 'comes over and tells me that there's this old bloke outside who's desperate to meet me, says he's come all the way from Morocco. Though I normally wouldn't bother as he sounds like a bit of a fruitcake, I'm in a good mood so why not? Besides, I think, laughing to myself, I've smoked enough of his country's main export. So I go out and we have a chat. He seems like a decent old bloke so when he asks me if he can meet the rest of the lads, I bring him in. He starts chatting to Luke who's chopping up some lines over there and after a couple of minutes I forget he's even in here. It was then that it happened. Luke, or whoever or whatever Luke had become, stood up and started going completely fucking mental. It didn't even look like him. His face had changed, it was all pushed out and covered in fur. And the noise he was making! Christ, it sent shivers down my spine. When Lance and Perry tried to restrain him, that's when they got hurt. Straight after that, we got a radio message from downstairs to say that the guy on the door had got his face torn up as they went out.'

'They?'

'Oh yeah, I forgot to mention, the old bloke didn't seem bothered about Luke's behaviour in the slightest and followed him out. It was like he'd caused it all.'

'So what exactly are you saying, Baz?' I ask, dreading the answer.

'I'd say the old bloke has turned Luke into some sort of creature, like some sort of giant dog. Totally fucking mental, I know, but there you go.'

9

These are strange times. What do you do when your best friend's turned into the Jack Russell equivalent of a werewolf? The way I see it, I have six options:

1. Continue with my current course of action, kill Nazar and hope that this will cause Luke to turn back into himself.
2. Abandon my current course of action, apologize to Nazar for my recent behaviour and hope that he'll turn Luke back.
3. Shoot Luke through the heart with a silver bullet or the equivalent for Jack Russells. (Bronze? Wood? Concrete?)
4. Shoot myself.
5. Leave Luke the way he is, house-train him and keep him as a pet.
6. None of the above.

In my book, it's either 1 or 5 and for the moment I'll plump for number 1.

All eyes are on me. People want a reaction. But how do you react to news like this?

'I'm going after him.' That'll do. It's short, to the point and sounds like something someone in a movie might say. On the coffee table is Luke's drug bag that contains various wraps of cocaine, a big lump of hash and pills of various sizes and colours. I snatch it up and make for the door. I take the stairs out onto the street two at a time. There are still a few diehard fans ever hopeful of a glimpse of their heroes. A couple of them move forward expectantly when they see me and then check themselves when they realize I'm not famous.

Before I stuff Luke's drugs into my pocket, I stick my hand in the polythene bag and pick out an acid blotter that I stick on my tongue and swallow.

I sprint to the Tube. There's a wino slumped by the entrance, watching my approach. I ask him, 'Have you seen an old Moroccan guy in a white suit with a young scruffy guy who looks a bit like a dog?' He nods, says, 'They went that way,' and points into the ticket hall. I'm down the steps but I'm not athletic enough to vault the ticket barriers so, still running, I shoulder the golf bag, crouch down and hit the ground on my side with my arms out in front of me. Just as I'd hoped, the momentum takes me sliding along the tiled floor and through the rubber flaps with the LUGGAGE ONLY sign above them. At the top of the escalator, I sit on the black handrest and slide down it, jump off at the end and dash onto the platform. There's only one train in and the dot matrix information board tells me that it won't move for the next five minutes. I climb aboard.

It's full of Gobshite fans. The tail-end of the audience. The diehards. The ones who didn't want to leave. All glazed in sweat and pissed. I pull out the Smith & Wesson and stare along the rows of faces as I walk between them.

'It's Dirty Harry,' someone says and people laugh.

'I'm a hit man,' I say weakly.

'Course you are, mate,' says another and I press on through the adjoining door into the next carriage, ignoring the mirth coming my way. How little they know. In the next carriage, the story is the same but as I move further down the train the numbers decrease until I come to the last carriage.

Well, here goes. Whatever events destiny has chosen to throw my way behind that door will be met by yours truly head on. No more messing around. I haven't exactly gone about my duties recently with any degree of commitment – or competence, for that matter – but that's all about to change. This is where I get serious. Situations like this are all about how you behave. The person who comes out on top is the one who forces his will on the events as they unfold. Defeat is not an option. I've got to walk through that door as though I own the fucking place, like Nazar's got nothing more than a walk-on part in my movie. I'm the star, I'm the one with the gun. He's just some pissy Moroccan tourist with a crap suit.

I open the doors and walk through. Suddenly, I'm horizontal and my face is pressed into some fat bloke's stomach. It appears I've fallen over. I raise myself up on my arms and move my gaze from Baz Marshall's stretched face on a Gobshite T-shirt and move it up to a comatose face framed with Indie bowl-cut hair. Not only have I fallen over but I've managed to drop the Smith & Wesson and the golf bag.

I pick them up and scramble to my feet. I can see the white of Nazar's suit down the end of the carriage. As I approach him, I can see that he's laughing at me. I point the Smith & Wesson at him but this does nothing but make him laugh harder. I'm right upon him now – Luke is slumped at his side – and he makes no attempt to defend himself. So this must be it. All I've got to do is pull the trigger and he dies. Then I grab Luke and run for it. But I hesitate. If I shoot him now, I'm a murderer. The other ones who died, they could be justified as self-defence, just about. But this? The drugs have messed with my head. I can't think straight and what flashes of clear thought are making their way through are of the peace, love, killing-him-like-this-is-too-heavy variety. His laughter's not even malicious. It's benevolent, kind even. There's something almost paternal to it. I can't shoot him, not at the moment. I just wish he'd do something evil to help me pull the trigger.

I think I could have managed it if I hadn't fallen over but, psyched up as I was, that succeeded in knocking the stuffing out of me. I take a seat opposite Nazar, put the golf bag next to me and point the Smith & Wesson straight at him, the end of the barrel not six inches from his forehead. I chance a glance at Luke and the sight that confronts me makes me want to forget everything and just run for it here and now. His features have taken on a bizarre humanoid approximation of a Jack Russell's. His tongue hangs out of his mouth, panting, and his dark eyes, seemingly devoid of iris and pupil, stare at me, blank and unblinking.

'Quite a transformation, do you not think?' asks Nazar. 'But I must say that I find your behaviour a little rude. You are very lucky that I do not make some spontaneous rearrangement to your internal organs. Certainly, I have done worse than that for much lesser acts of discourtesy in the past. However, I must confess I find this entire situation particularly amusing so I will leave it for now. But please, put your gun away or at the very least, if you feel that you must point it at me, if you feel more secure by so doing, then please remove it from my face. It is quite useless to you, anyway. You could not shoot me even if you wanted to.'

I lower the gun but keep it pointed at him. With my other hand I reach into my pocket and take out Luke's bag of drugs. I pick out a couple of pills. I pop them both. Luke growls as I swallow them.

'Are you sure you should be taking non-prescription drugs like that, especially with such a nasty head wound?' Nazar enquires. I ignore the question and he continues, 'Aside from a little kif or majoun, I have never been partial to drugs myself. I find that they muddy the focus of the mind.'

The doors close. The train pulls out of the station and into the tunnel. The drugs already at work in my system have lent the scene in front of me a cartoon aspect but a cartoon that's unspeakably menacing. In addition to my dubious mental state, my heart appears to be trying to piledrive its way through my ribs and it's all I can do to stop myself from breaking into a fit of hyperventilation that I feel sure would be so intense if I succumbed to it that I'd end up flapping around on the floor of the carriage like a fish on a deck.

'I must say that with your gun and your continuing silence I find your behaviour most offensive. Is this not just a little melodramatic? I admit your friend here has developed certain canine characteristics but everything is relative. You must accept that I am in control. There is nothing that you can do to harm me in any way. To draw a gambling analogy, I hold all the cards. Now, put the gun down and relax. Your employer believes that I want to kill her, hence her placing a bounty of £100,000 on my head. But have you actually stopped to consider that perhaps she is wrong? What if I have come back after all these years to carry on where we left off in Tangier? What if I still love her? Have you thought about that? I have already told you that I could have left Morocco years ago. My release from prison was not a decision made by anyone other than me. Your logic confounds me. I have demonstrated that I have powers way beyond anything you could ever dream of and yet you think that with an old revolver and an elephant gun you can dispatch me. I could almost mistake your stupidity for bravery.'

It's my turn to speak but I can't for the life of me think of what to say, so I say the first thing that comes to mind.

'Fuck you.'

Luke lunges forward, teeth bared, snarling like some diabolical hound defending his master. Thankfully, Nazar manages to pull him back before his slathering jaws clamp around my face. His animal savagery scares the hell out of me and I holster the Smith & Wesson in my pocket and fight an intense desire to weep.

'That is much more civilized. I must say I find conversation a little strained with a gun pointed at me. Now, please, just settle back in your seat and enjoy the journey.' As he says this, the walls of the tunnel speeding past the window fall away to reveal a sun-baked desert.

'Where are we, Nazar?'

'According to the chart above your head, we are between Brixton and somewhere called Stockwell. Unfortunately, I cannot be more specific than that, I am afraid, other than to add that we are underground, of course.'

'Don't be clever. I meant, what's all this outside the window?'

'Oh, my apologies: this is the Sahara desert.'

'Well, what the fuck's it doing here?'

'I thought it might be more pleasing to the eye than the usual view. Also, it reminds me of home. Have you ever visited Morocco?'

'No, never.'

'It is such a beautiful country. So varied both socio-
logically and geographically. So very different from
London. Which is not to say that I find this city
anything other than fascinating, but it could never
be home.'

As the sunshine pours through the windows, Nazar
pulls out a pair of sunglasses from the top pocket of
his jacket and smiles at me as he puts them on. In
the distance, the only vertical lines breaking up the
monotony of yellow sand and blue sky are occasional
figures dressed in white or the black silhouettes of
palm trees. Even Luke is calmed by the change of
scenery and appears content to stare out of the window, panting. He glances at me occasionally but there
is no hint of recognition in his face. I'm alone on this
one. He's not going to snap out of it, that's for sure.

'If you're so in love with your precious Morocco,
why aren't you there now? Why come here, if not to
settle a score with the woman who deprived you of all
this for over half your life?'

'As you can see, it doesn't matter to me where I am. I
can enjoy my country's scenery anywhere in the world
and I can even – just as you can testify – allow others
to do the same.'

'It must be so much better to actually be there.'

'I can be here and there at the same time. It is all the
same to me.'

'Admit it, Nazar, you're an evil bastard. Always
have been and always will be.' I don't really know
what I can achieve by this line of attack. It's not as

if he's going to say 'All right, then, I'll come clean, I am an evil bastard, you're right. It's a fair cop. Go on, shoot me.' But then again, the way my brain's feeling, nothing, and I mean nothing, would surprise me.

Every time the train pulls into a station, the scenery breaks up and, sure enough, there are Stockwell, Vauxhall and Pimlico. But in between each station nothing except Sahara as far as the eye can see. And the further we go, the more unreal the scenery becomes, so that by the time we pull into Victoria, the blue sky and sand dunes are melting into each other and it's difficult to distinguish what is Nazar's magic losing its grip on me and what is my own brain spinning out of control under the deluge of chemicals. People get in and out of the carriage and while I wouldn't expect them to see what I can see I find it curious that they don't even show a passing interest in Nazar and Luke: the former a man in a suit of such brilliant whiteness that I can barely look at it for more than a couple of seconds without being dazzled and the latter, well, a record company executive/Jack Russell hybrid.

As we pull out of Victoria, Nazar has changed the scenery. We're surrounded by crowds of people, Moroccans I can only presume from their clothes, who are going about their business in a busy street market.

'So I take it this is Tangier?' I enquire.

'Correct. But it is not the Tangier of today. What you are seeing here is Tangier in 1956, the year that I was incarcerated. This city no longer exists. This is drawn purely from memory. I am just a nostalgic old fool, I suppose, but it is good to see it how it was. There was an energy to the place. It was a city where you could indulge every passion imaginable. I enjoyed its freedom. You could do whatever you wanted and no one gave a damn.'

'But you couldn't murder people.'

'Well, to some extent you are correct – although many people who came to Tangier in those days did so to escape justice in their native countries for crimes at least as bad as murder. So, in fact, there were probably many murderers on the streets of Tangier in those days who went unapprehended.'

'But not you.'

'Sadly, no.'

'And you're bitter about that, aren't you? There you were in a place that was the very embodiment of freedom where everyone did what the hell they pleased and no one gave a shit and suddenly you're not welcome at the party any more and all just because of the trivial matter of your wife's murder.'

'You seem to feel that you are qualified to discuss events that took place many years before you were even born. Let me assure you that you are not. Now, I do not wish to be presumptuous as regards your social arrangements for the remainder of the evening' – the train pulls into Oxford Circus – 'but should you wish to accompany me then I must change trains here onto what I believe is the Bakerloo Line.'

He takes Luke by the arm and leads him off the train. My attempts at antagonism having failed, I follow them. But, as is often the case when I have taken large amounts of E, far from being in a fit state to dance the night away, I can hardly walk in a straight line and find all movement somewhat ludicrous. I pull Luke's drug bag from my pocket, take out a wrap of cocaine, throw my head back and uptip the lot onto my tongue. It's strong stuff: after a couple of minutes my mouth feels like I'm about to have a tooth pulled and my ribcage trembles.

We walk through the pedestrian tunnels between platforms in a line. There's Nazar, more Omar Sharif than late-night London Tube traveller; Luke, the dog-man who is unsteady on his feet and looks as though he'd be happier on all fours, which I suppose he would be, all things considered; and me, stumbling along staring at the curved walls, watching them undulate as they squeeze us along with a strange peristalsis.

'I should imagine,' says Nazar, 'that in your present condition you would find colours particularly vivid. Is that so?' I manage to nod my head and he goes on, 'I find enclosed walls are a marvellous canvas upon which to work. Would you like to see some creations of mine? I really think you might enjoy them.'

'Nazar,' I blurt out, 'where the hell are we going?'

'You mean to tell me that you have followed me all this way and you do not know where we are going? Of course you know where we are going. We have a date with our destiny, you know that. But in the meantime, watch this.'

That's all I need: the bastard's started to show off.

The drab cream walls and grey tiles explode into dazzling day-glo colours as though we're walking through some giant tubular lava lamp that's bursting with such a rapid flow of oils that it's created a foaming surf of kaleidoscopic colour that dazzles me and sends my brain reeling.

There's a train in on the northbound Bakerloo platform. We climb on and sit down. I can feel the acid sending little shivers up the back of my neck as it starts to wreak its havoc. Not long now until it beds down with the Ecstasy and destroys all rational thought. I'm in for a bumpy ride, that's for sure. I've pushed the Class A's to the limit with Luke in the past but never with anything more pressing to do than just to lie back and let it happen. But now, I'm lost in space. I need to make investigations and establish exactly what is going on here. We pull out of the station into the canals of Venice, only there's something not quite right about the scenery.

'You've never been to Venice, have you, Nazar?'

'No. You?'

'I went as a kid, on a school trip. So what we're seeing here is what you think the canals of Venice look like.'

'Yes.'

'You're a fraud, aren't you?'

'Whatever makes you say that?'

'Because you are.'

'That is not a strong argument. How are you feeling, by the way? How are the drugs? I must say, you look a little pale.'

220

'I'm fine. But why don't we just cut the crap and get down to the facts? Now, who the hell are you?'

'You know who I am.'

'I thought I did, I thought I had it all taped, the plot, the characters, everything. But now I'm not so sure. What do you want with me? What do you want with Luke? We're no threat to you: if you wanted your revenge on Mar Kettle then you could have had it a long time ago. You're just fucking with us all.'

'The drugs have made you paranoid. Surely you can see that.' Nazar fixes me with a smug expression, his head slightly cocked to one side, his shining brown eyes twinkling with laughter. We're up above the clouds now and the bright sunshine of a high-altitude sky pours through the windows. Luke leans against Nazar's shoulder and takes a nap. Nazar pats him on the head and, lowering his voice, says, 'So you don't think I am who I say I am?'

'Nope.'

'I can be whoever you want me to be,' he says, leaning forward, his smile gone. 'I can be good or I can be bad. Which would you prefer?'

'I just want you to be real, that's all. I just want you to be you.' Nazar throws his head back and roars with laughter.

'Don't laugh at me, you bastard,' I say to him and notice that the three teenage girls sitting next to Nazar on the row of seats opposite are watching me and giggling.

'Why don't we try a few different versions of me so that you can decide which you prefer?' says Nazar, his voice calm and conciliatory once again. 'How does that sound?'

Without really thinking about what he's saying I nod.

'Very well, then. Let's try this for size. My name is not really Hassan Nazar. I work for the US military. I studied pharmacology at Harvard after the war and ended up on a top secret research facility in New Mexico, working on what became known as Project Third Eye. This was a highly classified programme developing a drug that would endow the user with telepathic powers. We were of the conviction that if the drug could be developed and synthesized effectively, it would become a determining factor in the balance of power during the Cold War. It's been a long, hard struggle but what you are experiencing now is the fruition of years of research and development. All this Nazar business is rubbish. You've been duped. This is all just an experiment.'

The musculature of his face has altered as though he's dropped a forced expression and it's relaxed into its true form. His voice has altered, too: he now speaks with an American accent. I don't know what to say or do. I can't work out whether it's him doing this or whether it's me via my drug-addled subconscious mind. I glance at the three girls next to him and they are still staring at me and whispering to each other. When I look back, Nazar's reverted back to his former self and he's smiling.

Since leaving Oxford Circus station five or so minutes ago, it occurs to me that we haven't reached

Regents Park station yet despite going at full pelt. Nazar answers my unspoken query as though reading my mind.

'As you have no doubt realized, I am playing around with time a little. I hope you do not mind but we were nearing our destination and I am so enjoying our little game. Just think of this as the underground version of circling the runway, if you like. Anyway, what next? Another version of me? How about this? I am in fact from another planet. My planet is considerably older than this one and its inhabitants have evolved much further than the human race. Telepathy and telekinesis are as easy and natural for me and my people as eating and drinking are for you.'

Nazar's body starts to shrink. His suit is absorbed into his skin which becomes pale and translucent. His head grows. His hair disappears and his eyes widen and blacken. The train moves in ever tighter circles until the carriage curls back on itself and becomes a ring spinning round and around in a circular tunnel. Luke has slumped down in his seat and although he gives every appearance of sleeping – his breathing's regular and his head is tipped to one side – his eyes are half open and stare at me down his snout. Maybe he's awake and only playing along with all of this? What am I saying? He's a dog and now Nazar's turned into the fucking Roswell Incident.

'We have been living among you since the 1950s. We disclose our presence to only a tiny selection of the population. You are very lucky to have been chosen. Congratulations.'

'Stop this, Nazar. I know it's you.'

'Of course it's me,' he says, snapping back to his true form. 'But you are such an easy subject to work upon that I cannot help myself. Now, if you are still unsure who you would like me to be, perhaps it might be easier for you to browse through a selection of possibilities? You could have a fat me if you wished' – he swells out so that his belly is touching my knees – 'or you could have a thin me' – his body contracts so that his chest is no thicker than a broomstick – 'or you could have evil me' – his face contorts into the face of the devil, complete with red skin and horns – 'or perhaps you might prefer good me' – his face reverts back to normal except he's contriving a pious smile and there's a halo above his head. 'But then, perhaps you might prefer a female version of me' – his features become feminine – 'conversely, you might want a more masculine me' – his shoulders broaden and muscles bulge within his suit – 'but perhaps you would prefer to browse through all the different possibilities before you make your choice. In which case, just stop me when you are ready,' and he flashes through all the different versions of himself over and over, faster and faster. My head is spinning. The acid's taken hold and I feel as though I might pass out. I can't even bring myself to look away from him. All his different versions of himself pulsate in front of me, borrowing from each other until he becomes a terrifying androgynous alien, part thin, part fat, with a devil's face and a halo. I feel a sob rising in my chest and all my terror and indecision is focused into a bellowing 'Stop!'

And he does. Completely. So much so that he and Luke have disappeared altogether and there're just two empty seats in front of me. Everyone's staring.

'Are you all right, mate?' enquires one of the three girls who were sitting next to them. But I can tell she's not really concerned, it's just that she's been dared by her mates to talk to me and they snigger.

'Where did they go to?'

'Who?'

'The two men who were sitting here. One was Moroccan and old. The other one looked a bit weird. They were sitting just there.' I point at the seat.

'Ain't no one sitting there, mate.'

'They were there a minute ago.'

'You keep talking to yourself. Have you taken anything or are you just mental?' Her friends are openly laughing at me now but the girl who's doing the talking has run out of bravado and appears a little embarrassed by the amount of attention that's being focused on her by the rest of the carriage. She leans back in her seat.

'They were fucking there.' I'm shouting. The man sitting next to me moves to the other end of the carriage. Other people avert their gaze lest I pick on them. Londoners are well versed in how to deal with nutters. But I'm no nutter. They were there. I can't help myself now. I must have reassurance. I stand up.

'Listen, there's nothing wrong with me. OK? There were two men sitting there a moment ago and now they've gone. Come on, who's going to have the guts to tell me where they've gone to?'

We pull into Regents Park station. When the doors open about three-quarters of my fellow passengers get out and walk along to other carriages. As the doors close, I try to quell the terror that has me in its grip and think rationally. There are about six or seven people remaining.

'Look, I'm sorry about that outburst back there but let's get something straight from the start. I'm not mad. I'm not a nutter. There's no reason to fear me. I've taken some drugs tonight, I'll admit, but that doesn't alter the fact that a couple of minutes ago there were two men sitting there and now there aren't. They didn't get off the train, they just disappeared. Is there no one here who can explain what happened to them? You see, it's really important because one of them is my friend and he's in great danger.'

The nearest of my fellow passengers, a young serious-looking guy, stands up, gently places his hand on my shoulder and says, 'Why don't you take a seat and calm down? There was no one there. You're just a little confused.'

'You don't fucking understand,' I tell him through gritted teeth 'I have to find them.' He backs away, shaking his head. The doors open at Baker Street and I dash out onto the platform and into the next carriage where many of the passengers who were trying to avoid me went at the last station. There's a man dressed in London Underground uniform sitting at the end of the carriage. He's probably a ticket inspector or a driver or guard from another train on his way home. The acid's screwed my vision up good and proper. His face comprises all the necessary components – eyes, nose, cheeks and mouth – but they're all swirling around as though being sucked into the epicentre of a whirlpool in the middle of his head.

'What the fuck is going on here?' I ask him.

'I'm sorry, what do you mean?'

'There's something wrong with this train. People are disappearing. You've got to do something.'

'What would you like me to do, squire?' he asks. He's a joker, I can tell. He's one of those Underground employees who think they're hilarious and enjoy the opportunity to get on the tannoy to try to make the passengers laugh with their funny accents or amusing explanations as to why the train's late.

'You've got to do something about it.'

'OK, then. Ladies and gentlemen,' he announces to the carriage. 'This passenger would like you to exercise extreme caution as people have apparently been disappearing on this train. So, if at any stage you should find yourself disappearing or see someone else who is in the process of disappearing, I would be most grateful if you would report it to a member of London Underground staff who will be happy to assist you.'

There's laughter all around me. I toy with the possibility of pulling the elephant gun out of the golf bag so as to add some gravity to the situation but I decide against it and plump for the Smith & Wesson instead. Before I can reach it, the train makes a sudden lunge of acceleration and I lose my balance and stumble backwards so that my arse slams into the floor of the carriage. More laughter.

The train picks up speed and dips downhill. I've lost control of my legs, they feel like two tubes of foam rubber, so I stay where I am as the train goes faster, screaming through the tunnel, its angle of trajectory increasing so that I feel I might slide forward along the carriage that stretches out before me like a swirling vortex of seats and lights and limbs and bodies and laughing faces. It's getting hotter, sweat bubbles up on my forehead, my tongue lolls around in my mouth which is devoid of moisture. The flesh on my head feels as though it has become detached from my skull, rotating and hovering above the bone, and each hair follicle tingles and pricks my skin as though receiving an electrical charge.

I rub my eyes in an attempt to clear the madness but all I succeed in doing is throwing swathes of brilliant colour across the increasingly bizarre scene unfolding before them. My sense of visual perspective has inverted so that the lines and planes of objects don't move away from me and diminish in clarity as normal but turn about face and charge back at me with vengeful purpose. They pulsate and breathe and demand my unwavering attention. And still the train bores into the earth, spinning like some demented drill bit burning through the rock going straight to hell.

Blackout.

10

Time has passed, although how much I couldn't tell you. I'm lying face down on a stone floor. There are footsteps nearby.

'Do you suppose he's a golfer?' I hear an old woman say.

'Well, it certainly looks like a golf bag,' replies an old man, most probably her husband. 'Only there don't appear to be any golf clubs in it. Mind you, there is *something* in there.'

'Do you think we should take a look?' she says.

'No, Doris, you can't go snooping through people's bags. It's, it's just not right.'

'Maybe he's a down-and-out.'

'Maybe, but he doesn't look like a down-and-out. He looks quite well dressed, although that's a nasty wound on his head.'

'It's been stitched.'

'But not very well by the looks of things.'

'Perhaps we should alert someone.'

'I'm not sure we should get involved.'

'Well, the least we could do is alert a member of staff. Trouble is there are never any around when you need them.'

'Hold on, there are two people coming along the platform.'

'Yes, but they don't look like Underground staff. In fact, I don't like the look of them at all.'

'No, I think you're right.'

'Perhaps we should just move on and leave him where he is. Maybe they're his friends.'

'Yes, maybe they are.'

'Terrible, though, leaving a man like that on the platform. He could roll off and go under a train.'

'Mmm, terrible. Come on.'

My hearing is almost back to normal, which is a start. It's a bit wobbly on the spatial awareness but then, you can't have everything. I've now got to concentrate on motor functions. Speech is relatively unimportant, sight somewhat more so, although thought processes won't be back to normal for hours. Days, probably.

''Ere, Merv,' says a young guy from the direction of a new set of footsteps. 'Check this one out. I think we've got ourselves a dozer. We could have ourselves a bit of a laugh with this one.'

'Shall I check his pockets?' says another, his voice young and stupid and up for anything.

'Don't be such a thieving toe-rag. You fucking disappoint me sometimes, Merv, you really do. You've just got no class.'

'What, then?'

'Well, first things first, I need a piss. Now, I don't want to piss on the floor, do I?'

'No, Steve, you don't.'

'So I'm left with no alternative but to relieve myself on something absorbent, namely our friend here.'

'Right you are, Steve. Oh, Steve?'

'What?'

'There's an old couple up the end of the platform watching us. Just thought you ought to know.'

'Well, we'll have some fun with them too in a minute. Now, where was I?'

I have a myriad of options all exploding out of my brain, each one a perfect crystal of clarity and form, each one subdividing into further options that subdivide again so that there are lifetimes of possibilities opening up before me. I ignore them all, reach into my pocket and fish out the Smith & Wesson. It feels good in my hand, cold and heavy, and it spurs me on to attempt the next stage of the manoeuvre. I roll onto my back, open my eyes and point the gun upwards.

'Piss on me, pal,' I say, relieved that my speech function appears to be back to normal, 'and you'll find a bullet where your dick used to be.' My vision isn't back to normal, though. It feels as though I'm looking through a liquid haze. Thankfully, I can make out two figures standing over me and I aim the gun in their general direction.

'Oh, look at him, Merv. Don't he look cute with his little toy gun?'

'You sure it is a toy gun, Steve?'

'Don't you think I'd know a real gun when I see it? Come on, let's do him.'

He's only about eighteen or nineteen, I can tell, and his youth combined with a few pints of lager and maybe a line of something cheap has made him think he's the tastiest geezer on the block. Whether he's going to carry out his threat of pissing on me or not I have no idea but one thing's for sure, I'm not going to hang around to find out. I press the end of the barrel against his leg and pull the trigger.

No sooner has the sound of the gunshot finished reverberating against the walls of the tunnel than he's started screaming, 'He's shot me, Merv, he's fucking shot me. I'm bleeding. For God's sake, do something, don't let him shoot me again, Merv. Fuck, it hurts. Do something, Merv.'

I'm up on my feet. I'm in serious trouble. Not only have I shot someone live on CCTV but I've done it in front of three witnesses, four if you include the victim, who have not only got a good look at me but actually stood over me and studied me in detail. I run before I can walk, literally, and end up falling over again. This is getting to be a habit. I stand up, take a couple of deep breaths and stagger towards the escalators. There's no one around but I can feel the static of radios and the hum of telephone lines as information about me is exchanged, processed and acted upon. Ways to entrap me, ways to disarm me, ways to render me safe. At the top of the escalators, I see a man in London Underground uniform running across the ticket hall, speaking into a walkie-talkie. I crawl under a ticket barrier and out through the station into the street. I've got to get out of here fast. There's a car approaching. It's an old black Merc. A chauffeur-driven limo, by the looks of it. I point the gun at it. It stops. I walk around to the driver's window. The chauffeur's ancient. He winds down the window and says, 'Can I help you?' and I almost wave him on. But sod it, I need immediate transport and this isn't exactly rush hour. I have to take what I can get.

'Get out of the car.'

'I'm sorry?'

'Get out of the car or I'll shoot you.'

I open the door and he's so frail I have to help him to his feet. It's like the blind leading the blind. I get in, slam the door, gun the engine and we're off. There's a couple in the back but I can't make out any more than their outlines in the rear-view mirror.

'What the bloody hell do you think you're playing at?' asks a plummy voice.

'I'm making a getaway.'

'Well, you can't, I won't allow it. Stop this car immediately.'

'Sorry, I can't do that. Who are you, by the way? Anyone famous?'

'I am Viscount Hawley and this is my wife, the Viscountess. And if you're thinking of kidnapping us, I shouldn't bother, we haven't had a pot to piss in for years, as you can probably tell from the state of the car. Now who in God's name are you?'

If I wanted to be corny, I'd tell them I was their worst nightmare. But then, I'm not really. I don't

mean them any harm at all but they're not to know
that.

'Well, folks, you're in luck. Fate has chosen to smile
on you because tonight, for one night only, you're
privileged to be chauffeured by London's premier
drug-crazed lunatic. So fasten your seat belts, settle
back and enjoy the ride.'

The interior of the car smells of perfume and leather
and cigar smoke. It's not a new smell, its components
have permeated the upholstery and matured throughout the lifetime of the car. All car interiors have their
own olfactory signature that reflects the lifestyle of
their owners and this one hints at old wealth, of
Knightsbridge, Bond Street, the ballet, Ascot and a
stinking great mansion in the country. The Beamer
smelt of marijuana and hinted at high speeds and
dark excesses.

'Where are you taking us?' asks the Viscountess.

'I'm not taking you anywhere. I've borrowed your
car and you just happened to be in it.'

'So why don't you let us go?'

'You're my insurance, I'm afraid. You see, recently I
have become subject to an alarming new trend in law
enforcement in which the police have started shooting
at me and if I'm at the wheel of a car with other people
in it then the chances are that they won't. It's a stroke
of luck that you happen to be who you say you are.
Once they find that out, they're even less likely to shoot
at me.'

The Viscount's right about the car. Even in my state,
with my reflexes and reactions jackknifed somewhere

along the roaring autobahns of my central nervous system, I can still tell that it's in a shocking state, brake pads like sponge cake and a gearbox action like stirring turds in a toilet.

Doesn't matter much, though, as we're fast approaching Mar Kettle's tower block. I plan to ditch the car and continue on foot but a police car turns out of a side road up ahead and accelerates towards me. They're bloody quick, these bastards, I'll give them that. But, thinking about it, this is probably the worst place in England to be attempting all this. Paddington Green's not half a mile away and that's where they keep the anti-terrorist brigade, the heavy mob. They'll be tooled up to the nines. I hang a right and head east and as I do a siren starts to wail.

The days of the nar-nar police siren are long gone and I, for one, am sorry to see them go. I know everything's got to move on, what with technology and psychology and all that, but the American-style waily siren just doesn't work here. For starters, for anyone of my generation or older, when you hear a waily siren, you're more likely to think of a seventies American TV cop show like *Kojak* or *Beretta* than the boys in blue on their way to tackle crime. That's the trouble, the US waily siren makes a big announcement. It makes a statement that some Bob or Keith in an Austin Maestro just can't live up to.

With all efforts to reach Mar Kettle's place quickly and anonymously now in ruins, I stand on the accelerator to see if I can get some life out of this sluggish old jalopy. Street lights and road signs swim around my peripheral vision as the sirens wail in my ears. Although there is undoubtedly much glory to be had in going down in a hail of bullets à la Butch and Sundance or Bonnie and Clyde, it's not for me. I have to extricate myself from this situation as quickly and effectively as possible. I've shaken them off before, I can do it again. I hang a right on Park Road and head south but before I commit myself to the multi-lane one-way sweep of Baker Street, I take a left through a No Entry sign and end up on the Outer Circle of Regents Park. I've got about a hundred yards on the police car. As I'm trying to wring every last molecule of acceleration from the old Merc's engine, an idea comes to me. What I need to do is disappear. I need to get off the road. I look at the hedge to my right behind which lie the dark shadows of the trees in the park. I check in the rear-view mirror. There are no vehicles behind and up ahead I can make out some headlights but they're a good way off.

'OK, folks,' I tell my passengers, 'we may experience a little turbulence at this point in time.' And I swing the Merc across the road, up onto the pavement and straight through the hedge. There's some sort of fencing behind the hedge through which we plough but thankfully it isn't iron railings or anything too solid and we make it through onto the grass relatively unshaken. I take a left and pull up by a tree. My logic, twisted as it no doubt is, is that hopefully the gap in the hedge won't be so obvious that it will draw attention from a speeding squad car and may buy me a few minutes to make alternative travel arrangements.

'What the hell do you think you're playing at?' shouts the Viscount. 'You could have killed us all.'

'I figure they might not notice the gap in the hedge.'

'You're completely mad. Of course they'll bloody notice it. It's about six feet wide and you've flattened about twenty feet of fencing.'

'Listen, mate. Just shut up, they might not notice.'

'They'll definitely notice,' the Viscountess adds in a told-you-so tone of voice.

'If you'll pardon my French, madam,' I tell her, 'just shut the fuck up.'

We sit in silence while the sirens wail. The leather upholstery creaks as the Viscount and Viscountess turn in their seats to stare expectantly at my impromptu attempt at topiary. I watch it too in the rear-view mirror but they're right, of course, the police tailing us are bound to notice it – and they do. A moment later, a couple of jam sandwiches come hurtling through and make straight for me. I gun the engine, slam the Merc into first and make off. One car goes one side of me and one the other in an attempt, no doubt, to close in around my front and draw me to a halt in a pincer movement.

'Come on, you bastard,' I implore the car through gritted teeth. But it's useless, I just can't achieve the necessary speed, so I swing out to the right and veer towards the lake. For the car on my right, it's either drop back or get wet and as it brakes I swing back to the left to give the driver of the car on that side the option to either change course or wrap his front end around a tree. This manoeuvre buys me a few seconds but with more cars pouring through the hole in the hedge this is no time for complacency. The flashing blue lights cast on the trees and shrubbery ahead of me send my already fucked-up vision into some sort of colour spasm so that it feels as though I'm driving into a storm of fireworks. If I'm not careful, I'll be the one rammed into a tree. Cutting my losses I head back towards the hedge and as the Viscount shouts, 'Oh my God, not again,' I crash through it back onto the road. This time I'm not so lucky. The fence poles there are of an altogether more robust variety and we are thrown forward in our seats.

In the past eighteen hours or so I've been clubbed, beaten, shot at and stitched up; I've fallen over twice, passed out once and now, to cap it all, I've become intimately acquainted with a Mercedes windscreen which is not one of the more forgiving surfaces to find one's forehead rebounding off. To cap it all, I've got the might of the Metropolitan Police bearing down on me.

Tyres screaming, I take a left at the mosque on Hanover Gate and then a right through a red onto Park Road, somehow missing the bone-crushing bumper bar of an articulated lorry, its air brakes howling in a frenzy of deceleration. The police car behind me isn't so lucky. There's a metallic crunch that means that my most immediate pursuer is now out of the game.

'You're a damned nuisance, aren't you?' says the Viscount as I swing left off Park Road and head back towards Lisson Grove. 'You've upset me, you've upset my wife, you're putting at risk the lives of police officers and members of the general public. You can't hope to escape from all this. Look, I've got friends in the judiciary. I could put in a good word for you, I could help you make a deal with the authorities. Pull over before someone gets hurt.'

'We're nearly there,' I tell him. 'Just sit tight and this'll all be over before you know it.'

Things are looking up. As I swing onto Lisson Grove, there's not a blue light in sight. I glance in the rear-view mirror and it takes a moment to register that what's reflected in it is not the road behind me, which by rights it should be, but the top of the Viscount's head as he makes towards me. Before I can do anything to stop him, he's leant over into the front and pulled on the handbrake. To make matters worse, he proceeds to pull the steering wheel out of my grasp which sends the Merc careening onto the pavement and slap bang into a lamp post. My foot was flat to the floor when the Viscount started his heroics and, despite the best efforts of the Merc's brake pads, we were still moving at a good lick, certainly fast enough to volley me into the windscreen once again. My head is beginning to resemble a war zone both inside and out. If I manage to survive all of this without brain damage, it'll be a bloody miracle.

There's no more than fifty yards between me and Mar Kettle's tower block but the sirens are close by. I'm going to have to run for it. If my legs will cooperate, that is. The golf bag has come to rest on top of the Viscount who is wedged, puffing and red-faced, between the front passenger seat and the dashboard.

I grab hold of it, throw open the door and step out. My first few paces are OK but then, in an endeavour to pick up speed, I bring my knees up too high and it's all I can do to remain upright. I try again. The sirens are getting louder. Brakes, doors opening. I've achieved some sort of rhythm but it's erratic and although I'm expending a good deal of energy very little of it appears to be concerned with forward momentum. Now someone's shouting at me through a loud hailer. Something about 'Give yourself up.' But it's too late to turn back. I've come too far. My destiny is inextricably linked to Mar Kettle and that old Moroccan bastard. I pull the Smith & Wesson from my pocket and without even looking around I point it behind me and fire off a shot.

I've reached the patch of grass at the foot of the tower block but this is no ordinary tower block. My acid goggles conjure up an ancient monolith lunging from the earth, hurling its ghastly secrets at the moon. There's another gunshot for which I'm not responsible. And now I get the feeling that I've always been here, running across this scraggy patch of grass with a million eyes staring out at me from the darkness. The rest of my life is just a preamble, a plinth for this terrible grail to rest upon. I'm still alive and still running so they'd better sack the marksman. I reach the lift and spank the call button.

There must be at least a hundred people who live here. There's no way they'd wake them all up in the middle of the night to ask them if they were harbouring a mystery gunman with a peculiar running style, now would they? The doors open. I climb in and press the button for the twenty-third floor. The doors close. It's hot in here and the smell of spices is so intense that my eyes smart and tears stream down my face as my lungs heave in huge gasps in an attempt to filter some oxygen from the polluted air.

There's no one to meet me when I step out and the security door stands wide open. It feels cold after the heat in the lift and the smell of spices fades to be replaced by a musty smell not unlike the interior of a church. If this is a trap, it's a whole lot different from last time. All the lights are on, for a start. I approach the room where I am usually brought by Archie for my meetings with Mar Kettle. Cautiously, I push the door open and step inside. It's deserted but everything's as it should be and in its place even down to Mar Kettle's tiger-tooth cigarette holder on the table next to the chaise longue. The glass-eyed stares of the stuffed creatures mounted along the walls follow me around the room and out of the door. I try the next room along the corridor, which turns out to be Mar Kettle's bedroom. Pride of place is given to a huge four-poster bed with stuffed snakes coiled around the four posts. The one nearest to me is a huge, elaborately marked serpent that has its jaws bent back at 180 degrees to one another in order to accommodate a young bok that it is in the process of swallowing. It's a masterful piece of taxidermy, two animals in one. All the ticks and wobbles of my peripheral vision encroach upon it so it glows and trembles as though subject to one of Nazar's time stops: at any moment it will burst back into real time and continue munching on its hapless prey.

Opposite the bed, against the wall, is an ivory dressing table that's crammed with jars and bottles of perfume. Above it is a mirror surrounded by light bulbs like those used in actors' dressing rooms. I take a look at myself in it. The face that's peering back at me has the general appearance of mine, the features are the same, but aside from the bruises and the crude stitching on the side of my head that's leaked a thin trail of blood there's one major difference. It's my expression – which is one of abject terror. It's unnerving because, although I'm scared and I know I'm scared – I'm shit-scared, for God's sake – I didn't quite realize how much it showed. And it just makes me feel worse. There's no way I can face anyone looking like this, least of all the man who's playing villain to my hero.

'You're the man,' I growl at my reflection in a mid-Atlantic drawl, 'and no one fucks with the man.' It doesn't make me feel much better but I say it again anyway and sneer and hold my chin up and try to make myself look as menacing and fearsome as possible. It's pathetic.

The next room along the corridor is the bathroom. Its only feature of note is half a dolphin mounted above the bath as though leaping out of the blood-red tiles. Almost opposite the bathroom is some sort of study with backlit mahogany shelves lining the walls, shelves that house specimen jars of various sizes. Each jar contains a freak of nature suspended in formaldehyde. In among the two-headed billy goats, legless foals and headless puppies are animals born with organs outside their bodies. Spleens, livers, kidneys, intestines, brains, feathery flanges of red gunk and in one jar what must count as the leading light of the genre, a cat born almost totally inside out. Jesus, I could swear I saw it twitch. The only specimen that appears at first glance to be free of deformity is the one that arouses in me the most revulsion. It's a pigmy of some sort, preserved so well and with such an expression of surprise on its face that it looks as though someone's just popped him in the jar only moments before.

The corridor doubles back on itself and in the apex of the hairpin bend there's an alcove that contains two stuffed wolves in the act of copulation, the male rearing up, locked for all time in mid-thrust with a startled look I fear he must have worn when shot. It's unbearable to look at stuffed animals when your brain is humming with hallucinogens. It's as though some trace of a sentient being still remains within the stretched carcass, locked in some unimaginable agony.

I turn away and continue down the other stretch of corridor at the end of which there are some ornately carved double doors reaching from floor to ceiling. No sooner have my eyes settled on them than they are flung open and there's Nazar, his arms outstretched towards me, dazzling white light pouring from his suit. He shoots into and out of focus. One moment he's standing so close I could touch him, the next the corridor's half a mile long. His presence permeates the space between us. He's all around me, in the walls,

243

in the floor, in the very air itself, invading my lungs as I breathe. And he's smiling again. That welcoming benevolent smile. And I walk towards him like I'm drawn down the line of a laser beam.

'Ah, my friend,' he booms, 'I hoped you would make it. I did not want to start without you.'

'Where the hell did you go to?'

'When?'

'On the Tube, you disappeared.'

'Disappeared? I am not sure I know what you mean.'

'Yeah, right.' I can't be bothered to argue. 'Now what is it that you don't want to start without me?'

'All will be revealed in due course. Please, come in.'

This must be Mar Kettle's dining room and the jewel in the crown of her bestial interior design. Her man Ernesto Kuroyan really pulled out the stops for this one. An ivory table, at which elephants' skulls are modified into seats and upholstered with a fine white fur whose former occupants I would hazard to have been baby seals, runs the length of the room. Suspended above the table, bleached white and inlaid with tiny light bulbs, is a whale's skeleton, complete with harpoon and rope protruding from an eye socket.

Archie is seated at one end of the table and Mar Kettle at the other, both unconscious, eyes shut tight.

'Where's Luke?' I ask.

'Please be assured,' says Nazar, 'your friend is in the best of health and is at present enjoying a rest under the table.' I crouch down and take a look. Sure enough, there he is, curled up fast asleep.

244

'Please take a seat,' Nazar says. 'Can I take your bag?'

'No, I think I'll keep it with me.'

I walk around the catatonic form of Archie and take an elephant-skull seat opposite Nazar who sits next to Mar Kettle. I put the golf bag on the seat next to me and watch him as he stares into the old woman's face as though tracing every line and crease. Gently, almost tenderly, he picks up her hand from the table and presses it to his cheek. She opens her eyes.

'You,' she says, a single syllable endowed with a rich cocktail of horror and fear.

'Yes,' he says. 'Me.'

They stare at each other in silence, each one waiting for the other to speak. I slip my hand in my pocket and grab hold of the Smith & Wesson.

Mar Kettle speaks first: 'You're going to kill me, aren't you?' she says.

'No,' he replies, 'I am not here to kill you. Nothing could be further from the truth. You judge me by events that took place a lifetime ago.'

I pull the Smith & Wesson from my pocket and rest it on my knee.

'Firstly, let me apologize for rendering you unconscious. You appear to have been labouring under the misapprehension that I wish to do you harm so I thought it might be better this way. My recent actions have caused you a great deal of distress and this is most regrettable. I hoped that perhaps by coming to London and not visiting you immediately, you would get used to the idea of me being here and realize that my intentions are peaceful. I now know I should have sent you a letter to explain my actions but I thought that, in view of our last correspondence after the trial when I was somewhat less than conciliatory, this might have alarmed you further. It is easy to see the errors of one's ways with the benefit of hindsight. I am a man of impulse, a man who lets passion hold sway over reason. If only this were not true then perhaps our respective lives might have been very different.'

There are tears in his eyes. If this is an act, it's a bloody good one. He gazes at her with such intensity that there's no way he can focus on what I'm up to. I have to try a shot if for no other reason than to see whether I can. It's almost like I need to know that I can't. Once I've tried and failed, then I can resign all responsibility as a hit man. I will have carried out Mar Kettle's orders to the best of my abilities. If I do kill him, then it's meant to be, it's destiny – and I'm a hundred grand better off.

I wait for him to speak and, as he does so, I pull out the Smith & Wesson, point it at his head and pull the trigger. Nothing happens. The trigger won't budge. I'm done for this time. Trying to kill a man is bad enough but trying to kill a man during a love scene is unforgivable. He turns to look at me and, for the first time in the few hours I've known him, I can see an expression of anger on his face. He says nothing but I can hear Luke making his way towards me under the table as though operated by remote control and before I can even formulate an apology (how do you apologize to a man who only moments before you tried to kill?) he buries his teeth in my leg.

I slide off the chair and come to rest on top of Luke. Best friend or not, I have to extricate my leg from his jaws so I punch him on the side of the head. This does little except make him more angry. I try to prise his mouth open and, thankfully, despite Luke's physical appearance, Nazar's attempts at canine facsimile have not included strong jaws and, as I begin to feel them opening under the pressure, an idea comes to me. Perhaps now is the time to administer some medicine to him. Baz's contention regarding the neutralizing of psychic weaponry by narcotics does not necessarily ring true with me – I can't tell to be honest, I'm too far gone – but with Luke in the state he's in, anything's worth a try. I reach into my pocket, pull out the bag of drugs, split the polythene and, pulling on his bottom jaw with one hand and his upper one with the other, I succeed in opening his mouth far enough to push the contents of the bag – namely a wrap of cocaine, a lump of hash, a couple of acid blotters and various pills – down his throat. He chokes and splutters but down they go.

Nazar has also omitted to equip Luke with teeth sharp enough to puncture my jeans. Lucky for me, I suppose, or I could be turning into an oversized ankle-biter myself.

'Please take your seat,' says Nazar. 'I can assure you that your friend will not trouble you again unless you give him cause.' Luke backs off and I pull myself back onto the chair. As a show of surrender I lay the Smith & Wesson on the table.

'You really are a most tiresome young man,' Nazar says. 'I thought you realized that any attempts on your part to harm me would be entirely futile and yet you persist with your murderous endeavours. It is most distracting. I have waited over forty years for this moment and all you do is annoy me. You leave me no option other than to treat you like the child that you are and take your toy away from you.' He stares at the gun which glows red and melts onto the table as though it were chocolate. It's a bit Marvel Comics but not a bad trick.

Mar Kettle attempts a juggling act with her facial expressions: one minute she tries to convey to Nazar an appearance of calm benevolence in an attempt, no doubt, at placation and for the few moments when he looks away from her she shoots me venomous stares.

'Can I offer you something to drink?' she asks him. 'A Martini, perhaps?'

'A Martini would be lovely, thank you. It will remind me of the old days.'

'Perhaps we could drink it out on the balcony. It's a pleasant night, after all, and it will be dawn soon. It's so charming, I find, to watch the sun come up over the rooftops of London. Archie? Archie?' she calls to her faithful butler. He wakes with a start. 'It's quite all right, Archie,' she says in a tone of voice that conveys the exact opposite. 'Everything's all under control. We were wondering if you might like to mix us all a Martini.' She says the words slowly, as though willing him to decode the hidden subtext – like, 'For Christ's sake, do something.'

Archie, dressed tastefully in navy plaid skirt and matching silk blouse, rouses himself from his enforced slumber and, frowning with confusion, makes for the door.

'Please follow me,' says Mar Kettle. She pushes herself to her feet, walks to a French window set into the wall behind me and opens the glass doors to reveal a wide stone balcony giving out onto the night sky of London. There's an ornately carved balustrade that looks bizarrely out of place next to the grey tower-block concrete. The dining room's grotesque elephant motif is continued with the poor beasts' hollowed-out feet serving as plant pots which are home for some decaying, long-dead plants.

I don't know whether Mar Kettle's invitation was meant to include me but I follow them out anyway.

'So,' she says, adopting a tone of voice that's a vain attempt at relaxed chit-chat. 'You look very well.'

'I feel very well.'

'How long has it been?'

'Forty-three years.'

'Is it really that long?'

'I fear it is.'

There's an embarrassed silence and then Nazar chuckles. 'I must confess I find this whole situation somewhat absurd. Forty-three years ago you chose to betray me; forty-three years later you hire someone to kill me and even as we speak, at this very moment, your servant is putting poison in my drink. Despite all this, you attempt to engage me in conversation. I must say, I find your English pleasantries most strange.'

Mar attempts a smile but her lips tremble so much it's more of a grimace. She's cornered. She knows she needs to do some fast talking. She swallows hard and, conscious no doubt that these are perhaps the most important lines she will ever speak, says, 'I must admit to having been terrified by the news of your release from prison. And fear, as I am sure you are well aware, motivates us in peculiar ways. So, if you want a confession from me, then yes, I have tried to have you killed. Lucky for you, I suppose, that I chose to employ a moron to do the job. I can't expect you to think anything other than the very worst of me. But what I would ask you to bear in mind when deciding my fate is that I am an old woman fiercely jealous and protective of her last few years on this earth. I realize that what I did all those years ago was a little unfair.'

This comment causes Nazar to raise his eyebrows, an act that betrays what I can only presume to be incredulity at Mar's massive use of understatement. 'But I was heading for a nervous breakdown. I was confused and, as you know, I was frightened,' she continues. 'I didn't mean for you to kill your wife. I didn't even want you to tell her about us. It wasn't meant to be like that. It was just meant to be a little bit of fun. I realize that your feelings for me were stronger than mine for you but you went too far, way too far. I didn't even know you. I mean, I don't know you now although, God knows, it feels as though I do after all these years of thinking about you and worrying about what might happen. You threatened me. Remember the letter? I've lived half my life in the shadow of what happened in Tangier. There's nothing I wouldn't give to go back and change it all.'

I can tell she feels she's said too much and needs some reassurance from Nazar that he acknowledges her plight. But he says nothing, just leans towards her, maintaining his unblinking eye contact, and kisses her full on the lips. She couldn't look more shocked if he'd shot her.

He says, 'That is the first and only time I have ever or will ever kiss an old woman in a – how should I put it? – a romantic way. I just wanted to see what it felt like. I can see that you are confused but please, do not be. Just think of it as the first of many.'

This is all too much for Mar and, giving free reign to her true feelings, she shrieks, 'What do you want with me? If you have come to exact your revenge then be done with it. I will not be party to some tortuous game of cat and mouse.'

'Please accept my most heartfelt apologies,' Nazar says, turning away to look out at the lights of London below. 'I am jumping ahead of myself. It is most wrong. I have so many feelings that are bursting to escape.' He stands with his back to us. Mar Kettle looks at me and, drawing on all her abilities of silent enunciation, mouths to me, 'Push him over.' My obvious indecision irks her and leads her into even more desperate acts of facial gymnastics: 'PUSH HIM OVER,' as though shouting her silent order.

How the hell did I get involved in all this? Why must I be the deciding factor in a chain of events that started over forty years ago? Do I push him over? Can I push him over? Do I have any options? Well, yes:

1. I push him over.
2. I don't push him over.

That simple. Mar's face becomes flushed and the tendons on her neck strain harder against her flesh as each moment passes and her order goes disobeyed. I think if I don't try to push him off the balcony, she might die before my very eyes.

'All right, I'll have a go,' I mouth back at her and step back a pace in order to give myself some room to build up speed. Charging forward, arms outstretched before me, I realize there's something seriously wrong when my hands don't make contact with the white material of Nazar's suit which I'm aiming at but seem to pass straight through it as he sidesteps me or just plain disappears – I couldn't tell you which, to be honest – but then that's not the most burning issue on my mind at this particular moment. I'm far more concerned that there's just an old wooden railing between me and the concrete paving slabs three hundred feet below. My stomach slams into it and the momentum of my upper body makes me pivot around it and now I'm over, arms flailing, reaching out, craving something, anything for my fingers to close around and hold firm.

But there's nothing, just cool night air and, despite

every muscle in my body, every particle and every cell attempting to defy gravity and achieve some upward lift, I fall. Then, from nowhere, a hand. But it's not a hand that's searching out mine to offer salvation: it's a hand that holds mine just long enough to prevent me falling, then lets go, then catches and lets go over and over, as though playing with me, juggling with me. Nazar's laughing.

'This is a good game, is it not?' he asks as his fingers slip through mine and I contemplate the abyss once more.

'You love a good game, no? You enjoyed the game on the radio, so why not this?' I can't speak, every thought in my head is concerned with clinging on and staying alive. I've got both my hands around his wrist now but with his other hand he prises my fingers free and I'm falling again. He offers an open hand to my grasping fingers and, as they slip along it, he says, 'In those old movies I used to watch when I was a boy, they often had scenes where a character was hanging over a cliff or off a high building, holding another's hand. Now I am lucky enough to act out such a scene for real.'

I must have taken a deep breath when I found myself on the wrong side of the balcony rail and now it comes out as a horrified gasp as Nazar lets go of my hand for the last time.

11

Of all the ways I could have died during this whole sorry saga, somehow I never thought of falling. Mangled in the wreckage of a car, yes, riddled with bullets, for sure, but not falling. In the movies, which are all I have to draw on, never having actually seen anyone fall to their death in real life, there are two types of falling death. The first type utilizes the dummy. One minute, you're watching an actor or actress going over the edge of a cliff or building and then it cuts to a similarly dressed dummy that falls either stiff-limbed or floppy, depending on its construction, sometimes maintaining just one posture or occasionally cartwheeling if the person doing the dropping has put an unfortunate spin on it. It is rarely used nowadays, due to improvements in special effects. The second type of movie fall is the flailing-arm, shouty, stuntman fall where the rationale is that if you're going to go to all the trouble and expense of having a person jump from a great height then you might as well make the most of it.

My falling death follows neither pattern. I am in a seated position. If I was acting this out and there was a film crew and cameras and a big inflatable crash mat beneath me, I'd be sacked for under-acting. As it is, I'm just hanging around, waiting for the big concrete 'thank you and goodnight'. But it doesn't come. I've fallen the requisite distance but there's no body-bursting splat, just an ongoing descent. Perhaps it's already happened and it was so quick that I missed it. The scenery's changed, though. The blurred outline of the tower block has gone and it's like I'm just falling through space. I'm no longer even conscious of which direction I'm falling or even if I am falling any more. There's a white object approaching. As soon as I can make out that it's a man in a white suit, I know who it is. He stops just in front of me, in the exact same seated position as myself. It's like we're sitting in opposite armchairs.

'What's going on, Nazar?'

'Have you ever considered that none of this is actually happening?'

'What do you mean?'

'I will put it another way. Have you considered that you are going mad and that me and this whole story are nothing more than overblown hallucinations brought about as part of the disintegration of your mind? Do you often find yourself falling through space like this?'

'It's you. I know it's you and you know it's you. This is just another way of messing with my head.'

'But just suppose that, as you say, your head is being messed with but it is not me who is messing with it but you.'

'Then what the hell are you doing here?'

'I am not here. You are creating me. You are making me up as you go along. Just as you are with all of this, just as you are when you suddenly find yourself back on the balcony having been pulled to safety by my own fair hand.'

'Go on, then, pull me to safety.'

'No, you do it.'

'It was your idea.'

'No, it was yours. My ideas are your ideas. Everything about me is of your creating. I am part of you. Now, let us return to the balcony.'

And we do. Nazar is helping me to my feet. Mar Kettle is trying to ingratiate herself with him, telling him how she can't understand how clumsy I was to have fallen over the railing and how lucky I am to have been saved so miraculously. Archie returns with the drinks and hands us one each.

'Your name is Archie, is it not?' asks Nazar.

'Yeah, that's right.'

'Well, Archie, explain something to me. Why have you poured us all a drink and not one for yourself?'

'I don't want one. I don't like Martini.'

'Come now, Martini is such a refreshing drink.'

'Look, I'm the butler. I just fetch and carry, all right?'

'Please, have mine.'

'No.'

'But I insist.'

Archie pulls up the front of his blouse to reveal his Smith & Wesson stuffed into the top of his skirt. He pulls it out and points it at Nazar. He hesitates and, as he does so, Mar Kettle shouts, 'Shoot him, for God's sake.' He squeezes the trigger and, as I could have told him if only he'd asked me, nothing happens.

Nazar stares at Archie and Archie begins to struggle with the gun as though it's taken on a life of its own. He drops to his knees, clasping it with both hands. His left hand battles with his right as it turns the gun back towards him. It's a pitiful sight, a man fighting himself. As it approaches his mouth, he tries to turn his face away but this does no good. The gun changes direction within his hands and continues until pressed against his lips. A shove and it's into his mouth. His eyes roll in terror as his head is pushed against the floor.

'For the love of God, don't kill him,' shrieks Mar Kettle.

'I have no intention of doing so,' says Nazar as though indulging in some amusing prank. 'I am acting purely in self-defence and as a safeguard against any further attempts to shoot me I will leave the gun where it is for the time being.' Archie scrambles to his feet and stands there, trying to pull the gun out of his mouth.

'Please desist,' Nazar tells him. 'Any attempts to remove it will result in a single shot being fired. It would be difficult to miss from there, I think you will agree. Now, having admired the view, perhaps we should all return inside and relax at the table.' We follow him through into the dining room.

'I cannot blame you for your hostility towards me,' Nazar says to Mar Kettle once we are all seated at the table once more, Archie cutting a somewhat ludicrous figure pointing his revolver into his own mouth. 'You are still under the illusion that I wish to do you harm whilst, in reality, nothing could be further from the truth. I am here to bestow upon you a great gift. A gift that will, I am sure, convince you of my sincerity.' He takes hold of her hand again, raises it to his lips, kisses it and says, 'My English rose, soon you will be mine once more.' It's a terrible line but what do you expect from a man in a white suit?

It's only when he lets go of Mar Kettle's hand and it remains suspended in mid-air that I realize he's stopped time once more.

'I just thought I might take a few moments out,' he says, 'to gauge your reaction now that our roles have reversed.'

'What do you mean?'

'Well, I am supposed to be the villain of the piece and you are supposed to be the hero, as though this were some sort of morality play. Good must always conquer evil. That is correct, is it not? But I think you will agree that in the light of recent events, and especially now that my true intentions are revealed, we are hopelessly miscast. I ask you, does a hero murder three innocent people?'

'They weren't innocent,' I tell him, irked by his confidence and composure. 'And anyway, I thought you were supposed to be just a figment of my imagination.'

'Whatever makes you say that?'

'Just now, when we were falling through space together, you said that I was going mad and that you were just a hallucination thrown up by my fucked-up mind.'

'Falling through space together? Hallucinations? I am very sorry but I have no idea what you are talking about. Now, where was I? Oh yes, our role reversals. Now, when I killed my wife it was in a moment of madness. A crime of passion, I think they call it. So, let me ask you, who do you think is the villain of the piece?'

'Get to the point.'

'The point is, my dear friend, there will be no riding off into the sunset for you at the end of all this. As for me, well, without being smug, I have paid my debt to society, albeit a very different society from yours. I can see the error of my ways. The horror of what I did to my dear departed wife weighs heavily on my shoulders to this day. But I have been true to my beliefs and now, despite your attempts to the contrary' – he switches time back on – 'I have returned to claim my bride.' At this, Mar Kettle looks up and there's a change in her expression: her furrowed brow relaxes and a look of relief passes across her face as though she realizes that, against all the odds, salvation might be at hand.

'Did you say "bride"?' she enquires, with an upturn at the corner of her mouth that signals the beginnings of a coquettish smile.

'You do not think I spent all those years in prison

for you without wanting something in return.'

'I knew there had to be something,' she says, leaning forward, eager to hear what the 'something' is.

'You were once a beautiful woman. I do not mean to be rude by suggesting that you are anything other than beautiful now, but we must face up to the fact that you are an old woman just as I am an old man. This is not the best time of life to be carrying out a romance. The spirit is willing but the flesh is weak. How much better it would be if we could return to how we once were, if we could grant ourselves a second chance.'

Nazar's abrupt silence invites a response from the old woman.

'Yes, yes, of course,' she says.

'Well, we can.'

'What? Don't be ridiculous.'

'Allow me to explain. I am what is known in Morocco as a djeemadjalloon, which means, quite literally, a mind demon. I was endowed with psychic powers from birth but only ever used them casually. It was not until I was faced with a life sentence that I decided to develop them further. Through years of practice and with the help of an accomplished teacher, they flourished to the point where I am now capable of making modifications to the very fabric of time itself. I started off with rats. I found I could take a fully grown rat back to a baby rat and in one instance, back to an embryo. Having come that far, I was eager to test my abilities on a human. My cellmate of the time took to his bunk one night a notorious forty-year-old bandit and awoke the following morning a six-week-old baby.

The prison authorities realized there was some magic and trickery at work. But they could not keep a baby in prison, so one of the warders whose wife was unable to bear children adopted him. Not only had I effected the bandit's escape but I had also given him another forty years of life. You will be pleased to hear that I have now mastered the process.'

'You mean to tell me that you are able to make me young again.'

'That is exactly what I am telling you, yes.'

'I don't believe it.'

'Then perhaps you will allow me to demonstrate.'

'When?'

'As the expression goes, there is no time like the present.'

'What will you do to me?'

'To us, you mean. I will not let you travel on your own. Together, we will return to the exact age we were when we first met. But, as I am sure you will appreciate, I have to protect myself, particularly in view of your recent behaviour. Should something happen to me after the process has been completed – for example, you may decide to double-cross me again – then, in the event of my death, you will immediately revert back to your present state. Just call this a little built-in safety mechanism if you like, although I am sure that my worries are unfounded. Shall we begin?'

'What do I have to do?'

'Just hold me and I will do the rest.' Nazar turns towards Archie and me and says, 'Just in case you were planning something stupid, I have rendered the pair of you immobile for the next few minutes while this delicate process takes its course.'

It's a strange feeling. It's as though I'm encased in invisible plaster from head to toe. The only parts of my body that he has allowed me any freedom of movement with are my eyes and eyelids. Other than that and the ability to breathe, nothing.

Nazar takes Mar Kettle by the arm and leads her into the middle of the room as though he is about to dance with her. He stares deeply into her eyes and then gently pulls her towards him. Points of light that burn with the brightness of oxyacetylene torches appear on their bodies. It's as though their insides have metamorphosed into white-hot molten steel that is burning through their outer casings of flesh. But there's no evidence of pain or discomfort. They stand stock-still, making not the slightest movement. I can feel the intensity of the heat from where I'm sitting and my sweat glands go into overdrive. As the holes in their bodies grow in size, the searing white light behind them falls away to reveal a darkness like a starless night sky.

Within a couple of minutes, there's nothing left of them, just a holographic pool of blackness like they've been cut out of the fabric of present time and space and dropped through a gateway into another dimension. In a sober state and free of hallucinogens I might find this all rather strange and disturbing. As it is, with my mind twisted into parabolas of narcosis, it's just about par for the course.

I struggle with my paralysis, testing it to its limits until I manage a tremble. Whilst this isn't much good for securing my escape, at least it means that it's possible to loosen the invisible shackles Nazar's put me in, even if it's only to the most minute degree.

Within the black hole left by Mar Kettle's and Nazar's absent bodies, a storm starts to rage. There are flashes of light, claps of thunder and a howling wind that blows warm against my face. Intermittent flashes of light increase in regularity to achieve a stroboscopic rhythm that locks into some undiscovered lobe of my brain and communicates with me on a long-lost primeval wavelength. There are people in every flash. Millions of them, billions. It's as though in each cataclysmic burst of light I catch a glimpse of a vast tapestry on which the history of humanity unfolds in all its insect tragedy.

The darkness lightens, almost imperceptibly at first, but increases in intensity until the white-hot light burns brightly once again. Whereas before it erased all trace of Nazar's and Mar Kettle's respective physical forms, now it offers up small sections of clothing and flesh that build up on each other like a giant three-dimensional jigsaw puzzle until they are whole once more. Other than a distinct reduction in Mar Kettle's bulk, at first glance it's difficult to see much change in the two figures holding onto one another. It is only when they pull apart that their respective metamorphoses become apparent. Due to a dramatic weight loss, her dress hangs off her like a tent. It's easy to see why the young Nazar must have found her so attractive. She has shown me photographs of herself at this stage of her life and I always found her somewhat plain in them, but the camera didn't do her justice. She has an allure and presence that can only be fully appreciated in three dimensions. For Nazar, on the other hand, there is less of a change. The regression to his thirties has sharpened his features, darkened his otherwise grey hair, tightened his skin and stripped him of excess fat.

She is the first to speak: 'Has it worked?' But the very tone of her voice answers her question. Gone is the croaky rattle in the back of her throat, gone is the breathless wheezing brought on by a lifetime's tobacco abuse. As Nazar stares at his handiwork, a broad grin spreads across his face.

'Oh yes,' he says inspecting her, 'you have finally returned to me. This is truly a great moment.'

'And you,' she tells him, 'you look the same as you did all those years ago. If anything, you are more handsome. Oh Hassan, come, let's look at ourselves in the mirror.'

They rush from the room like two star-crossed lovers and moments later I hear giggling and whooping from Mar Kettle's bedroom as they study their new-found youth. A couple of minutes later, as is inevitable, I suppose, it all goes quiet apart from the occasional creaking bedspring.

I glance at Archie sitting holding the gun in his mouth. He's as locked solid as I am and looks as frustrated as I feel. Perhaps, if I concentrate on the chemical explosions in my head, I can loosen Nazar's hold. I shut my eyes and peer at the bizarre world unfolding behind them in glorious Technicolor. If there's one aspect of the hallucinogenic drug experience that I find a pain in the arse it's a period of long silent introspection. But needs must and if I'm to wrap myself up in my own cocoon of narcotic invincibility to Nazar's psychic arsenal then, instead of trying to sidestep the profundity of the drug experience, I need to collide with it head on. I shut my eyes and dive into my stream of consciousness that is not so much a stream as a churning torrent. Instead of pulling out of steep dives at the last moment for fear of some mental crash-and-burn, I ride them to the very core of my psyche and back again with a loop-the-loop over the awestruck crowd who shriek and applaud. I can move my arm. It's a start.

I manage to reach the zipper on the golf bag and pull it open. The bedsprings reach a squeaking crescendo and then go quiet. I haven't got long. Got to move fast but any attempt to pull the gun out of the bag with one hand is out of the question. I need my other hand to hold the bag and that entails not only swinging around my left arm but leaning across with my entire upper body. Nazar's grip on me is too strong. I make a last-ditch attempt to rein in the cartoon apocalypse going on inside my head but it's useless. I open my eyes just in time to see the pair of them walk back into the room, washed and dressed. Mar Kettle has managed to dig out an old dress and looks a picture of fifties feminine chic.

'Here they are, your two faithful servants just as we

left them,' Nazar says, his arm around her shoulders. 'Would you like to tell them our news? I suppose, by rights, they should be the first to know.'

'OK, darling.' 'Darling'? They've been reunited for less than an hour and already it's 'darling'. 'This might come as something of a shock to you all in light of recent events but Hassan and I are to return to Tangier at the first possible opportunity where we will begin preparations for our wedding.'

'Forgive me,' says Nazar. 'I would release you both from your bondage to allow you to congratulate us but we are in a hurry. Unfortunately, it will be impossible to invite you to the wedding as it will be a quiet ceremony and numbers will be kept to a minimum. Rest assured that all your respective states of being, including our half-canine friend's here, will be lifted once we are gone and you will be able to resume your lives as before.'

'Archie,' calls Mar Kettle to her hapless butler, 'there's some money for you in the usual place. Make sure you keep in touch. I will forward details to you of what is to be done with my London properties. Maybe you could join us for a holiday some time.' She looks at Nazar for his approval and he smiles and nods. 'And as for you,' she says, turning to me, 'no hard feelings. I'm sorry that I won't be able to pay you. But then, the circumstances of our business arrangements have changed rather drastically, as you can see. I hope what's-his-name, your friend, has not found his ordeal too traumatic.'

I've never heard her speak like this before. But

I've never known her like this before, either. She's young and beautiful, although if truth be told there's something unreal about her – as though she's just stepped out of some low-budget Sunday-night period drama. There's nothing unreal about her happiness, though. Her unexpected good fortune hasn't had a chance to sink in yet. An hour ago she was a lonely, paranoid old woman. Now she's had a death sentence lifted, had her youth restored, been given an offer of marriage and got laid.

'Bye, then,' she says awkwardly. Archie's lips tremble around the gun barrel. There are tears in his eyes. I suppose he really does care for her. He makes a sound, faint and sorrowful. Nazar takes Mar Kettle by the arm and they walk away.

In a way Nazar's right. If they leave like this then I am the villain. Three men dead and for what? Just so's the newly appointed hero can not only walk off into the sunset but also get the girl.

They reach the door and he stands back to let her go ahead. He remains motionless but as she passes him he yanks her arm back which spins her around to face him. He lets out a short cackle of such gleeful malevolence that I know he's been lying all along. I knew it couldn't end like this. If he'd just wanted to come and whisk her away and marry her, he could have done it when he first arrived. With his powers, he could have done it whenever he pleased. There would have been no point in playing with us as he has. All the love business and promise of marriage was just setting her up for the sucker punch.

'You are just so wonderfully gullible,' he says to her. 'But now we are even and your dreams will be shattered just as mine were all those years ago.'

'What do you mean?' Mar Kettle pleads, a razor of fear slashing her face.

'As I am sure you remember only too well, I once vowed revenge on you. Much as I would like to renege on the pact I made with myself, I am a man of honour and as such I cannot.'

'Come now, Hassan, don't be ridiculous.' The words come out of her mouth, tripping over themselves in their attempt to maintain a tone of upbeat happiness as though by acting as if nothing has changed, nothing *will* change.

He smiles and shakes his head.

'But you don't want revenge,' she pleads, 'you said so yourself just now. You love me. We are to be married.'

'I lied.'

'You can't do this. Doesn't what we've just done mean anything to you?'

'We did the same thing before but it did not seem to mean much to you.'

'But you'd killed your wife. We've been through this. It's all in the past. Let's just forget about it and get on with our lives.'

'We *will* get on with our lives. It is just that your life will be a little more – how can I put this? – progressive than mine. Let me demonstrate something to you. As you have already seen, moving someone back through time is a difficult and sometimes dangerous activity but moving them forward at high speed can be done as easily as this.'

Nazar puts his hands either side of Mar Kettle's head and squeezes. She lets out a wail of despair which changes as it goes so that it correlates in tone and strength to the ageing process visible in her face. Wrinkles fan out from her eyes and around her mouth, flesh loosens, loses its tone and definition, folds of skin droop down around her jowls, her hair recedes and thins and the wail deepens in pitch, becomes more desperate until it's nothing more than a gurgle. Her body fills out to stretch the fabric of her dress, becomes more pear-shaped as gravity wreaks its accelerated havoc and then shrivels away to nothing as the death rattle sounds in her throat and her eyes shut. Nazar chuckles to himself all the while as he watches the colour drain from her face until it collapses into her skull and disappears altogether, leaving him holding just a skeleton in a dress.

'And that,' he says, letting her bones drop to the carpet like a bag of sticks, 'is the end of that.' He approaches the table and grins at me.

'You must admit,' he says to me, 'I had you fooled, did I not? I had you all believing that I was a decent, honourable man. But, you see, the truth is that I am anything but. With a straight choice between good and evil, I would choose evil every time. It is just so much more fun. Take her, for example.' He points at the skeleton on the carpet. 'There she was, young and beautiful once more, thrilled with her new life. And then, just as I gave with one hand, I took away with the other. Did you see the look on her face when I told her? It was a picture. And what makes everything all the more fun in these cases, I find, is if you tell your victim what you are going to do to them before you do it. Fear is a fascinating emotion. It is wonderful for focusing the mind. I feel so much better now. I'd quite like to bring her back to life so that I could kill her all over again. But now I have you two to play with.

'Have you ever given serious thought to the manner of your death?' Nazar asks me. 'Being a young man, I should imagine not. I myself have mused upon this subject at great length. For many people it is a matter of great importance that they die in a particular way. For others, it matters not one jot that they die a death of the utmost ignominy. I would suggest, however, that for most men, given the choice, they would opt for a death that came about through the execution of a glorious deed, such as saving someone's life. You, for example, may have tried to justify your murderous exploits with the misguided notion that you were trying to save someone's life. Margaret Kettle's over there.' He points at her sorry carcass. 'And that if the worst came to the worst and you should die, then your death would have been in some way honourable and not without purpose. But, sadly, you are not an honourable man. You kill people for money, or at least you try. You are a prostitute who trades in death. Therefore it pleases me to inform you that your death will be utterly pointless. It will serve no purpose other than to make me happy. Not for you the respect and admiration of your peers. Not for you the mourning of friends and family. Just a death that is as slow and painful for you as it is exciting and pleasurable for me. How does that make you feel?'

'Fucking marvellous, Nazar. Now let's get on with it, you twisted freak.'

'Your insults amuse me: watch me laugh as you writhe in agony. Now, how shall I kill you? Will it be quick or will it be slow? Just one shot from a revolver,' he looks at Archie as he says this, 'and you could be dispatched in a split second. You would hardly know that it had happened. Burning to death, on the other hand, would be slower and a deal more painful. It is one of those deaths that terrify people. I suppose their fear is justified when you consider the pain you feel when you burn even so much as a finger. Life is all about experience. I want to have as many experiences as I can, especially after so long in prison. I've seen people die in many ways but I have never seen anyone burn and I must confess to being somewhat curious. I have heard it said that the first parts of the body to succumb to the heat are the eyeballs, which burst at a certain temperature. Can you imagine anything more painful? Then again, suffocation might be good. I like a slow suffocation brought on through intermittent lung paralysis. I could probably keep you gagging and choking for hours on end, maybe even days. If truth be told, we have a number of possibilities. There's electrocution which can be particularly amusing to watch and then there're the more traditional methods such as disembowelment or being torn limb from limb. You could even be crucified, if you so wished.'

A cold bead of sweat breaks free of its surface tension on the back of my neck and trickles down my spine. Tears stream down Archie's face. Nazar turns to him.

'Are you weeping for yourself or for your erstwhile employer? Either way, I admire a man who can show his emotions. I hope very much that during your imminent destruction you will be equally demonstrative. Perhaps you would like me to remove the revolver from your mouth to allow you more vocal range.' He finds this amusing and giggles as Archie, now free of his invisible constraints – as, too, am I – pulls the gun from his mouth, turns it around and pulls the trigger.

'You are so boringly predictable,' Nazar says.

'You fucking bastard,' Archie retorts.

'"You fucking bastard",' mimics Nazar and roars with laughter. 'Come, my friends, let us not be abusive to one another, we are to take part in a great game. I could not play it without you.'

Archie lunges out of his chair, fists flying. Nazar sidesteps him and he falls to the floor, choking and holding his neck.

'You can teach a dog to stop doing something if you beat it hard enough. But not a transvestite, it appears.' Archie makes little gasping sounds as he struggles for breath. His wig has slipped and his skirt has ridden up over his brawny thighs. If it weren't for the terrible nature of his predicament, he would cut a comic figure. Nazar pulls up an elephant-skull chair opposite me and sits down.

'And what about you?' he asks. 'Any plans for the future?'

'What future? You said you were going to kill us.'

'OK, your short-term future then. The next five minutes, perhaps. No sudden conversion to Christianity? No sudden revelations as to the nature of life and the universe?'

'Get on with it, Nazar, just finish whatever it is that you've come here to do.'

'There is no rush. I thought we might have a chat, get to know one another before I consign you to oblivion.'

Archie's face has turned blue and his eyes bulge from his forehead as he struggles for breath.

'For God's sake, stop choking him.'

'I will not kill him. Not yet. I want to have some fun with the pair of you. You especially.'

'Are you such a sadistic bastard?'

'As a matter of fact, I am.'

'Well, just leave him alone.'

'All right, if it bothers you so much. We have plenty of time.'

Archie gasps in lungfuls of air through his newly dilated wind pipe.

'Satisfied now?' enquires Nazar.

'And what are you going to do with Luke?' I ask him.

'Luke?'

'My friend currently doing an impersonation of a dog.'

'Oh, you mean my muqabba jamal. He is a most

prized possession. I will keep him with me. You see, he is probably the first of his kind for hundreds of years. "Muqabba jamal" means "dog man" in Moroccan. Ancient texts handed down through the indigenous populations of north Africa tell of a technique of fusing the soul of a dog with that of a man. Modern-day Moroccans think that talk of muqabba jamals is superstition but ancient texts that outline the procedures for creating one are still in existence and to a djeemadjalloon like myself they are not unduly taxing. The most important thing is to find two compatible entities, namely the dog and the man. I must admit to being a little disappointed with my two subjects in this case but compatibility is very rare. As a first attempt it is not too bad, although it is a little unfortunate-looking, I grant you. In answer to your question, I shall be taking him with me on my impending travels around Europe. It will be nice to have some company.' Nazar stops, and for the first time I see a frown crease his brow. There's something wrong. He stands up and walks to the end of the table. He bends down and peers at Luke.

'What have you given him?' His voice is even and measured as though in an attempt to mask the rage trembling within.

'You should know, you're the telepathic one.'

Nazar pulls Luke into the chair at the head of the table and takes a seat opposite him. Luke's face has changed. It's still distorted, twisted into an expression that is half canine grimace and half idiot leer, but his features have relaxed and become more human.

'It seems you're not so marvellous after all,' I say, conscious that each word I utter could be my last.

'What did you give him?'

'When in human form, Luke supports the more alternative sectors of the pharmaceutical industry. I was merely giving him a top-up. Something the matter, Nazar?'

He doesn't reply, just stares at Luke as though willing him to do something. Nothing happens.

'He's right, you know, man,' says Luke in a voice like a Mancunian Yogi Bear, 'I just love the drugs. I'm the drug hero. I've fucked myself on every drug known to man, stared Mr O'Blivion full in the face, banged up some gear with him and walked away. Shit, man, I can tell a good drug story. Fill a hundred glossies. Way things are going, I'll have a job for life. When I'm old I'll hit the chicken-and-chips-in-a-basket circuit, tell some favourite old drug reminiscences – like the time I was so far gone I shit my pants and that other time I turned into a bleeding Jack Russell terrier. How we laughed. The kids'll love it, man.'

'What is he talking about?' asks Nazar. 'What is a "drug hero"?'

'Relax, Nazar, nothing to worry a djeemadjalloon.' But it clearly is. Looks like Baz was right all along. My problem was I hadn't taken enough of the medicine. But Luke being presently outside the range of Nazar's psychic powers doesn't mean we're out of danger. He's always been endowed with the ability to snatch defeat from the jaws of victory right at the last minute. Besides, he seems to be more intent on expressing his opinions on the subject of his impending celebrity rather than saving us and getting the hell out of here.

'Of course, to capitalize fully on the potential market,' Luke continues, 'I'll have to give it all up. Everyone loves a reformed drug abuser and none more so than the reformed drug abusers themselves. I'll sit there being interviewed with a glass of sparkling mineral water – not even a no-tar Silk Cut – and I'll wax lyrical about the old days. I'll be cleaned up, dried out and mining a rich seam of PR gold with a sanctimoniousness that'll make you puke. Even the oldies'll think I'm great, setting a good example to the children.'

'Shut up,' shouts Nazar. Then, as though shocked by the ferocity of his outburst, he says in a more measured tone, 'Please, stop.'

Luke turns his attention to Archie's Smith & Wesson on the table, picks it up and waves it around. Nazar flinches and now I know for sure that Luke's beyond his grip. Trouble is, he's beyond mine too. Nazar stares at him with a look of intense concentration, trying to win back lost ground. Nothing, not even a flicker of recognition.

I rack my brains for ways of capitalizing on Luke's immunity to Nazar but if I try anything I'll most probably end up like Archie who is still regaining his breath in a semi-conscious state on the carpet or, worse still, I'll go the way of Mar Kettle. If only Luke'd just drill a couple of holes in him then we could get the hell out of here. I have only one option and that is, do nothing and see what happens.

'And then there's celebrity suicide,' says Luke, peer-ing down the barrel of the gun. 'Always an option, although not always a pleasant one. Not so good if, for example, you're an ageing game show host but great for shifting units in the live-fast-die-young market. Plenty of round-the-clock vigils, wailing fans and copycat suicides to maintain the column inches. Then there's tribute albums, greatest-hits packages, T-shirts, badges, CD-ROMs – the possibilities are end-less.'

'Perhaps you should try it,' suggests Nazar.

'Do you think I should?' asks Luke.

'Very much so,' says Nazar, a smile forming on his lips. 'I think it's a great idea.'

'Thank you, that's very kind,' says Luke, as though taken aback that someone should agree with him so vociferously. 'Where's best, do you think? In the heart? In the forehead? Maybe the mouth?'

'Yes, I think the mouth would be the best option,' says Nazar. He's regained his composure now and it's all he can do to stop himself from laughing.

'I suppose it's as good a place as any,' says Luke, 'and it'll provide a striking image when the pictures appear on the Internet. Anyway, here goes.'

I'm paralysed by indecision. The way I see it, I have nine options:

1. Hurl myself across the table and try to pull the gun from Luke before Nazar can render me immobile.
2. Tell Nazar: 'If you let him die, you'll never be free. You'll spend the rest of your life looking over your

shoulder. Wherever you go, whatever you do, I'll be right there behind you until one day, when you're off your guard, you'll turn around and see me smile as I pull the trigger.'

3. Tell Luke not to shoot himself, explain to him that he is half man, half dog and that both halves are subject to a dose of narcotics of such vastness that, should he desist with his suicide bid, it's unlikely he'll be straight for a fortnight.

4. Tell Nazar: 'He dies, you die.'

5. Ask Nazar how he could live with himself if he took away Luke's daughter's daddy. Luke has no daughter, but hey.

6. Concentrate really hard and try to communicate with Luke on a telepathic/subconscious level and tell him not to shoot himself.

7. Throw something at Luke, maybe the melted remains of my Smith & Wesson, and hope to knock *his* Smith & Wesson out of his hand.

8. In the hope that Nazar has some feeling for his countrymen, tell him that Luke has recently adopted some Moroccan orphans who will be parentless without him.

9. Do nothing and hope that the gun is either out of bullets or faulty.

Desperation sets in. None of my nine options are viable but then, just as Luke puts the barrel in his mouth, takes it out to say, 'Huh, tastes a bit funny,' and puts it back in again, option number ten comes galloping out of the mist. There's no time to evaluate its merits. I put it into action immediately and say, 'Don't forget, Luke, that's you sitting over there.' I point at Nazar. The smile freezes on his face as Luke pulls the gun from his mouth, says, 'Oh, so I am,' points the gun at Nazar's head and fires off a shot. A small black mark appears on the Moroccan's forehead but any hope that he may be dead is extinguished when I glance at Luke and see that he's locked solid in time. When I look back at Nazar, he's smiling.

'That was very close,' he says, pulling the bullet from his forehead where it has made a small indentation in the skin. 'Another few thousandths of a second and this would now be lodged in my brain. Once again, you underestimate me and once again I have to show you who is in control.' He flicks away the bullet and it clatters across the table.

'Well, as we appear to be indulging in a little target practice, I think you will agree that it is now my turn.' He stares at the golf bag on the chair next to me and it flies across to him as though thrown by an invisible force. He pulls out the elephant gun and holds it up to admire it.

'This is a splendid weapon. Crude but highly effective. There is no animal alive that could take a shot from this and live. Shall we see what it does to your friend's head?'

'Luke means nothing to you. There's no point killing him. It's me you want. Leave him alone.'

'Come now, I took you for a good sport. It is nothing to do with whether you are important or whether I have anything to prove. It is about having fun, and blowing your friend's head off with an elephant gun will be *so* much fun. I should imagine the head will disintegrate on impact, something like a water melon would, and provide, I hope, an interesting collage on the wall behind. What do you think?'

'Fuck you.'

'Your English pleasantries are most charming. To make it a little more interesting for you, instead of blowing his head off in real time, I will do it in slow motion so that you can watch a gradual explosion of face and skull. You will love it. You have seen it in films, I am sure. Now you can see it done for real, live if you like.'

'I thought you wanted to keep him. I thought you said he was the first dog-man for hundreds of years.'

'Unfortunately, you spoilt all that with your silly drugs.'

Nazar takes aim and, with a smug, self-satisfied smile creased across his lips, pulls the trigger. Everything slips into quarter-time and the elephant gun explodes. The noise is deafening and prolonged due to the time speed we're at. Nazar's in trouble. Guns, even elephant guns are not supposed to explode. *House* an explosion, sure, but not *be* an explosion. As the flash subsides I can see through the smoke that his lower jaw is gone, as is a chunk of his neck. The gun has broken in two and the barrel curls back over his head while the butt is flung out to the side of him with his severed hand still attached. A slurry of blood and scraps of flesh splatter from the massive wounds.

Time stops. The realization of what has happened

has reached Nazar's brain and he's attempting a counter-measure. The sensation of being paused in time is like the moment when a train pulls to a stop and, although it's stationary, everything leans forward for a moment before settling back at rest. Then time inches forward and shards of flame burst out all over his body. He's trying to cut himself out of time but it's too late and already his lower jaw and the flesh from his neck that looks like something from a butcher's slab have hit the wall behind him.

Not content with the first shot of his flawed suicide bid, Luke fires off a second and, as Nazar's head whiplashes back from the initial explosion, it hits him straight between the eyes.

Everything slips into normal time. Nazar rises to his feet, blood streaming down the front of his white suit. A third bullet from Luke's Smith & Wesson hits him in the chest and he swells up to almost twice his size, his body nothing more than a sheet of white light from which flames drip and spurt like burning gasoline. Time shudders and snags as he makes his last-ditch attempt to prevent it from carrying him towards the inevitable. His face – or what's left of it – mutates into what I can only presume is the face of the true djeemadjalloon, a twisted terrible visage contorted in agony. He topples over backwards and, as he does so, arcs of flame shoot from his wrists and ankles as though from some diabolical stigmata. By the time he hits the carpet, his entire body is ablaze and throwing flames around the room.

I rush to Luke, pull the gun from his hand and

drag him towards the door. He still mumbles some nonsense about marketing his own suicide but I'm not listening. Roused into consciousness by the heat and the explosions going on all around him, Archie joins us in our mad scramble for the door.

We race into the corridor as Nazar emits a final disembodied howl and a sheet of flame follows us from the room, igniting everything in its path. We reach the security door and dive out onto the landing where I punch the button for the lift.

Relieved as I am to have made it this far, I am now presented with two further problems. Firstly, Archie turns around, tells me that he's forgotten something and disappears back into the inferno. Secondly, Luke drops to his hands and knees and starts howling the place down. It's as though a red-hot poker's been stuck up his arse.

'Luke, there's no time for this,' I tell him. 'Even if there's only one minute fraction of your mashed-up brain that still functions, for God's sake use it. We've got to get out of here fast.'

The fire rages behind the security door. I fear Archie's a goner. Luke's screams have become more desperate, as though at any moment he will either pass out or die. He rolls onto his side, tears streaming down his face, his eyes shot through with primal fear. He struggles with his flies, tears them open, pulls his jeans down, then his boxers, and finally resumes his position on his knees with his arse in the air, his skinny white buttocks trembling with exertion.

He lets out a mighty roar of pain and then the

strangest thing happens: the Jack Russell pops its head out of the cleft of his arse. It too appears to be in a great deal of discomfort and howls as it struggles to be free of Luke's bursting ringpiece. I have no prior experience to call on to deal with this. Does anyone? What do you do when a dog starts crawling out of your friend's arse?

'Push!' I shout as the lift approaches, working its way up the row of numbers. 17, 18, 19: the Jack Russell has his front legs out and heaves the rest of his body after them. 21, 22, 23: the doors open, the Jack Russell jumps free, rushes into the lift and I follow on after it, dragging Luke by the scruff of the neck.

I keep my finger on the door-open button and shout 'Archie' at the top of my lungs. It looks hopeless. A geyser of flame roars through the doorway onto the landing. Even if I was brave enough to go in there, I'd be burnt to a crisp in seconds. The flames scorch my face and I try a final 'Archie', more as a farewell than anything, and take my finger off the button. The doors start to close and as I press myself against the back of the lift a surge of flame erupts from the doorway. As though propelled by its force and trajectory, Archie sprints out, carried aloft within a tunnel of fire, a canvas bag tucked under his arm, legs pumping like a phantom rugby player dashing for the line. His wig's gone, his skirt's up around his waist, his tights are shredded and from top to toe he's covered in soot. The flames deliver him up through the doors in a cloud of smoke and he comes to rest on top of Luke who adds one more groan to his ongoing litany of them.

The lift descends. Thankfully, the stench of spices from earlier has dissipated and been replaced by the usual aroma of urine. There's not even a turd figurine for me to muse over. Luke and Archie scramble to their feet and I can now get a better look at Luke and see that mercifully his bowels have offered up the last vestiges of Nazar's were-trickery in the form of the Jack Russell itself which appears unfazed by its recent experiences – namely dying, living as one of the undead and being anally resurrected.

'Where did the dog come from?' Archie enquires when he's caught his breath.

'Luke's arse,' I tell him. As a sign, perhaps, of how absurd this whole tale has become, he nods his head and accepts it without another word.

'Man,' says Luke, 'I'm completely off my face. What's happening?'

'You can't remember?'

'I can remember the gig. Fucking great gig, yeah?'

'Yeah.'

'Hey, my arse is sore. What the hell's been going on?'

'I'll explain everything later.'

As the lift reaches the ground floor, the fire alarm goes off. Instead of being freaked out by the sight of the dog, which I would have expected after his recent experiences, Luke gives it an affectionate pat on the head, picks it up, tucks it under his arm and leads us out into the dawn. On the patch of grass outside, we stop and look up at the flames pouring out of the blackened remains of the twenty-third floor which has become nothing more than an elevated crematorium for the worldly remains of Mar Kettle and Hassan Nazar. Damned together in life and damned together in death.

'OK, gents,' says Archie as the first few residents of the tower block appear at the bottom of the stairs. 'I think I'd better get going, so I suppose you'd better have what's due to you.' He reaches into the canvas grip, pulls out a plastic shopping bag and passes it to me.

'Hundred grand, wasn't it?'

'Er, yeah, I suppose so.' I take the bag, open it and peer inside. It's crammed full of banknotes.

'I'll miss the old bird,' he says. 'She was good to me. She was going to buy me a pair of tits. None of your rubbish, neither. Best Harley Street job. Guess I can get 'em done out of this lot, though. There's about three times what I gave you in here but I figure I deserve it after all them years.'

'Course you do, Arch,' I tell him.

'There's a load more in the bank but I don't suppose any of us can get our hands on that.'

'No, I suppose not.'

For a moment, Archie appears confused as to what to do next. But the approaching sirens focus his mind. He shakes my hand and then Luke's and says, 'Maybe catch up with you again one day and you can explain what the hell was going on up there.'

'Yeah, maybe. Take care, Arch.'

A smoke-blackened monster of a man, he strides off through the growing throng of pyjama-clad tower-block inhabitants. Most carry a few belongings they've chosen to save from the flames. Some have TVs or videos and others just this and that, a clock perhaps, a favourite picture or a piece of china. Funny what people count as precious. Me, I just stand here next to Luke with my shopping bag full of cash. The effects of the drugs have subsided a little. Luke, I should imagine, is still wired to the gunwales but he can handle it. After all, that's his job.

Through a loud hailer a fireman tells everyone to move away from the tower block. There's virtually nothing left now of the twenty-third floor, just burning embers like the tip of a giant cigarette.

'Hey, don't I know you two?' growls a short fat policeman striding through the crowd. 'You're the two jokers who were sticking that body in the boot of your car the other night, aren't you?'

'I haven't got a clue what you're talking about,' says Luke, turning away from him.

'Yes, you have. Up in Hampstead. I was off duty, walking the dog, and you two were carrying a body across the road. You resisted arrest.'

'Listen, officer,' says Luke, turning back to face him, 'I can assure you that not only have I never been to Hampstead in my life but I have certainly never put a body in the boot of a car there as I am not prone to murder, abduction, kidnap, slavery or any other activity that would involve the transportation of bodies, dead or otherwise.'

'What have you got to say for yourself?' asks the policeman, turning to me.

'There's no point asking him anything,' says Luke,

suddenly angry. 'Can't you see that he's deaf and dumb?'

Without thinking, I nod, but the policeman doesn't seem to notice.

'Now, if you've quite finished,' continues Luke, 'my dog here is most alarmed by the fire and I would appreciate it if you would let us go about our business without having to answer your spurious questions.' He spins around on his heels, takes me by the arm and we walk off. Under his breath, he mutters, 'Keep walking and don't look back.' For once, I do what he says.

12

I'm doing 200 down the Côte d'Azur. K.p.h. that is, of course. I haven't got a clue what the French Laughy Woman is talking about as I don't speak the language but, boy, can she laugh. The French Riviera's answer to Titch Allock – Rien de Ballons, I like to think of him as – has a hell of a time reining her in. As for the new Beamer, well, what can I say about the new Beamer? A more perfect marriage of man and machine I have yet to encounter. Same spec as last time but convertible, with white upholstery. A little cheesy, I grant you, but what the hell? This is the south of France, after all. It's a right-hand drive, which isn't ideal on these roads, but I only planned to stay for a couple of months until the heat died down.

Besides, I've got to get back: it's not every day that your dad does a gig at Ronnie Scott's. It's his official debut. He's done a couple of warm-ups in pubs. One of them was in his local, the Hope & Glory, to an audience made up of his drinking buddies, and apparently he went down a storm. The thing that I never reckoned on throughout all this was his singing ability. As a kid I heard him sing at home all the time. But you just don't think that your dad's crooning in the shower is going to set the world alight, do you? Bernie Mann was right about one thing, he does have a great singing voice. I can't testify to it myself, due to my self-imposed exile, but Luke, who went along to the Hope & Glory gig, tells me it's a cracker and Dad's got an excellent lounge-lizard stage persona to boot. And Luke knows his music.

The old man's not right for Wow Man Smell My Finger Records, of course, but the all-new dried-out, cleaned-up, teetotal Bernie Mann has managed to strike a deal with an easy-listening label by the name of Languid Records who want to put out a mail-order album of big-band classics with Dad on vocals. They're not looking to worry Michael Jackson, that's for sure, but it's a start. Not bad going when you consider that eight weeks ago he was thought of as something of a nutter and now he's performing at Ronnie Scott's with a full backing band and a record contract in the bag. Because of his age, Languid have decided to market him as though he were an established artist from yesteryear who's making a comeback. People will, apparently, feel sure that he's someone they should know about and that's half the battle won. Luke's convinced that, with the right choice of ironic cover version in the run-up to Christmas, Dad could have a novelty top ten hit on his hands. What makes me feel so guilty about all this is that there I was, his only son, and I was just as convinced as everyone else that he was insane. Still, I'll make it up to him. I'll be his number one fan.

As for Luke, he's just the same as always. He can't remember much about that night. He gets the occasional flashback but it's all shrouded in a drug haze. Not unlike most nights for him, really. The funny thing is that once the Jack Russell had disembarked from his arse it wouldn't leave him alone. It followed him everywhere, so he ended up adopting it and now it's become something of a mascot around the Wow Man offices. Whatever weird psychic spell Nazar wrought between man and dog, it appears to have left them inseparable. And whereas other pets come and go, Luke's most likely got a pet for life, seeing as it's already died once and been resurrected.

Gobshite have started their world tour with the usual flurry of media activity. As always, it only takes a couple of choice quotes from Baz to send the tabloids into a feeding frenzy. This time it was a reference to his teenage years when he was something of a drugstore cowboy around the Salford area, breaking into chemists and liberating their more psychoactive goods. Inhabitants of the moral high ground have had a field day. The police are said to be investigating but with a number one album, *Gonna Put One Through You*, a sold-out tour and the adulation of millions, Baz could easily be mistaken for a man who doesn't give a shit.

Joyce, too, is creating some media ripples now that her memoirs, *Up The Boulevard*, have won a six-figure advance from a major publishing house. All those years of work have finally paid off for her and it looks as though her old films will now find a new audience, once she's canonized as a cult star by the readers of the bloke mags. She won't let fame change her, though, that's for sure. She says she'll stay on the *Porcupine*, although she might give it a lick of paint. I tried to tell her on the phone what had happened with Nazar but, as always, she thought I'd lost it and started telling me one of her indecipherable parables. This one was about some guy who was walking down the street one day and someone threw a turnip at him from a passing car. Thankfully, the turnip missed him but it gave him quite a shock. A few months later, he was walking down the same stretch of pavement when another turnip was thrown from another passing car (or perhaps it was the same car, she didn't specify) and this time it hit him on the head and killed him stone dead. What bearing the story had on my plight is anyone's guess so I've decided to give up trying to make her understand what happened with Nazar and just assure her that I'm rested and feeling much better now, thank you very much.

What I'm especially looking forward to about Dad's gig is that they'll all be there – Joyce, Luke, even Baz, which should ensure some heavyweight media exposure. But the one person who won't be there, the one person who knows almost as much as I do about what happened that night at Mar Kettle's, is Archie. I wonder if he's got his tits done yet?

It's difficult for me to focus on the events of that

night with Nazar with any degree of clarity. Partly it's due to the drugs I took in my attempt to render myself immune to his wizardry and partly it's due to the nature of the events themselves. Whether good did finally conquer evil is anyone's guess. I don't feel particularly good but then, I don't feel particularly evil either. My job was to kill Nazar and he wound up dead, so on the one hand I was partially successful. But seeing as I was meant to kill him so that he wouldn't kill Mar Kettle, then, on the other, I failed dismally. I'm just glad to be alive.

It was Nazar's desire for revenge that killed him in the end, I suppose, just as it was my desire for revenge due to the Titch's Triffic Trips debacle that was the extra ingredient I needed to make me go all out for him. Revenge is a stupid motivation, when you think about it. It's like putting a curse on someone, a curse that can just as easily rebound on its perpetrator, and in Nazar's case that's exactly what happened. It quite literally blew up in his face.

And poor old Mar Kettle was damned by a decision she made over forty years ago. There she was one afternoon, thinking to herself what fun it would be to create a little mischief to enliven her otherwise boring existence. Little did she know that the object of her seduction would not only haunt her for the rest of her life but come back and exact his terrible revenge.

There's a synchronicity at work here but what part I play in it is beyond me. I killed two men and was instrumental in the killing of a third. Were they meant to die too? What strange twists of destiny tied them into all this? Maybe they were just extras, just caught in the line of fire. After all, this isn't one of those American action adventures where guns blaze, bombs explode, bodies hurtle through the air and no one ever gets hurt. Their deaths make me think that perhaps I'm wrong to talk of destiny and events being linked by threads through time. Maybe there's a moral vacuousness to all this and any attempt to search for patterns and connections is just wishful thinking, nothing more than a desire to impose some sort of reason on a set of random events. I don't know.

Whatever forces were at work and whatever significance I am meant to derive from their outcome, the events of those few days have had a profound effect on me. After we made it out of the tower block that morning, I hit an adrenalin rush so pure and strong that I had to go and hire myself a Beamer so I could drive through the streets of London shouting at the passers-by. Nothing new there but, for some reason that I can't fathom, I chose to change my usual subject matter and started on about how everyone was going to live forever. Funny, that.

So what'll I do now? I was thinking, these past few weeks, that I might write this all down, see if I can earn some celebrity for myself. Everyone else seems to be doing OK. Even the old viscount managed a couple of articles, so I'm told, which tell of his encounter with a maniac. So maybe I'll start tomorrow.

Hitman

There's open road ahead as far as the eye can see and, as the French Laughy Woman starts laughing her head off once more, I settle back in the seat, adjust my sunglasses and floor it.